UNTIL
we
TOUCH

Also available from Susan Mallery and Harlequin HQN

SUSAN MALLERY

UNTIL *we* TOUCH

ISBN 978-1-62953-089-5

UNTIL WE TOUCH

This edition published by arrangement with Harlequin Books S.A.

® and TM are trademarks of Harlequin Enterprises Limited or its corporate affiliates. Trademarks indicated with ® are registered in the United States Patent and Trademark Office, the Canadian Intellectual Property Office and in other countries.

Printed in U.S.A.

To 2013 Fool's Gold Co-Head Cheerleader Jayme.
Meeting you last summer was a highlight
of my year. You embody the spirit
of Fool's Gold—you're sweet, you're fun, and
you have a lot of heart. Thank you for everything!
This story is especially for you.

Being the "mom" of an adorable, spoiled little dog, I know the joy that pets can bring to our lives. Animal welfare is a cause I have long supported. For me that means giving to Seattle Humane. At their 2013 Tuxes and Tails fundraiser, I offered "Your pet in a romance novel."

In this book you will meet a wonderful cat named Dyna. She's a beautiful Ragdoll with incredible eyes and a loving, gentle disposition. Her family was one of two auction winners, and this is her story.

One of the things that makes writing special is interacting in different ways with people. Some I talk to for research. Some are readers who want to talk characters and story lines, and some are fabulous pet parents. Dyna's family is devoted to her. I loved hearing all the stories about her life. What a sweetie! She's such a beautiful cat that she inspired a series of humorous conversations between my heroine and her new cat. Larissa, my human heroine, is a little nervous about measuring up to Dyna's beauty. :)

My thanks to Dyna's family, to Dyna herself and to the wonderful people at Seattle Humane (www.seattlehumane.org). Because every pet deserves a loving family.

CHAPTER ONE

"You know why I'm here."

Mrs. Nancy Owens made the statement with a firm voice and an unyielding stare. All of which were impressive.

Unfortunately for Jack McGarry, he didn't have a clue as to what she was talking about.

He knew a lot of things. He knew the L.A. Stallions wouldn't get to the Super Bowl this year, that his right shoulder ached when it was going to rain, that there was a saucy merlot waiting in his kitchen and that while every part of his being wanted to bolt right now rather than have this conversation, he couldn't. Because Mrs. Owens was Larissa's mother and even if she wasn't, she was old enough to be *his* mother and he'd been raised better.

"Ma'am?"

Mrs. Owens sighed. "I'm talking about my daughter."

Right. But the woman had three. "Larissa?"

"Of course Larissa. Who else? You moved your business to this godforsaken town and my daughter moved with you and now she's here."

An excellent recap, he thought, struggling to find the point.

"You don't like Fool's Gold," he said, stating what was probably the obvious.

"I neither like nor dislike the town." Her tone implied he was an idiot. "That's not the point. Larissa is *here.*"

He knew that, what with signing her paycheck—figuratively rather than literally—and seeing her every day. But Mrs. Owens already knew that, too.

"She is here...with you." Mrs. Owens sighed heavily. "She loves her job."

Okay, fine. He was willing to admit it. He was just an average guy. Maybe a little taller, with a used-to-be-better throwing arm and a strong desire to win, but at his heart, he was pretty much like every other beer-drinking, truck-driving man in America. Ignoring, of course, the merlot in his refrigerator and the Mercedes in his garage.

Nancy Owens, an attractive woman in her early fifties, smacked her hands palm down on the table and groaned. "Do I have to spell it out for you?"

"Apparently so, ma'am."

"Larissa is twenty-eight years old, you moron. I want her to get married and give me grandchildren. That is never going to happen while she's working for you. Especially not after moving here. I want you to fire her. That way she'll move back to Los Angeles, find someone decent to marry and settle down."

"Why can't she do that here?"

Mrs. Owens sighed the sigh of those blessed with intelligence and insight most could only aspire to.

"Because, Mr. McGarry, I'm reasonably confident my daughter is in love with you."

LARISSA OWENS STARED at the blue-eyed cat standing in the center of her small apartment. Dyna was an eight-year-old Ragdoll, with big, beautiful eyes, a sweet face and a thick coat. She had white fur on her chest and front paws and bits of gray on her face. She was the cat equivalent of a supermodel. It was kind of intimidating.

Larissa's instinct was always to rescue. Cats, dogs, butterflies, people. It didn't matter which. She knew her friends would claim she jumped in without thinking, but she wasn't willing to admit that. At least not without prompting. So when she'd heard about a cat in need of a home, she'd offered to take her in. She just hadn't thought she would be so gorgeous.

"You're a little overwhelming," Larissa admitted as she crossed to the small kitchen and put water into a bowl. "Should I dress better now that we're roommates?"

Dyna glanced at her, as if taking in the yoga pants and T-shirt that were Larissa's work wardrobe, then continued to explore the small apartment. She sniffed the sofa, checked out corners, studied the full-size mattress in the bedroom and totally ignored the small bathroom.

"Yeah, I know," Larissa said, putting the water on

a place mat by the back door and then trailing after her. "The bathroom is really tiny."

There wasn't a counter—just a pedestal sink, a toilet and a stall shower.

Okay, so the apartment wasn't grand. Larissa didn't need much. Besides, the place was clean and the rent was cheap. That left her with more of her paycheck to give to her causes. Because there was always a cause.

"The windowsills are wide and you'll get a lot of light," Larissa told the cat. "The morning sun is really nice."

The small apartment came with one unexpected feature—a laundry room. She'd tucked Dyna's litter box next to the dryer. The cat perused the facilities, then jumped lightly onto the kitchen counter and walked to the sink. She glanced at Larissa, her gaze expectant.

Larissa knew this was why she'd always resisted actually adopting an animal before. She'd told herself it was her lifestyle—that she was so focused on saving them all that she couldn't be with just one. But in her heart, she'd been afraid she simply didn't have it in her. Now, as she stared into big blue eyes, she knew she'd been right.

"What?" she asked softly. "If you just tell me what you want, I'll do it."

Dyna looked at the faucet and back at her.

"From the tap?" Larissa asked, then turned on the cold water.

The cat leaned in and delicately lapped at the

water. Larissa grinned in triumph. Maybe she could conquer this pet thing after all.

She waited until Dyna was done, then picked her up. The cat relaxed in her arms, gazing at her for a second, before letting her eyes slowly close. From deep inside, came a soft, rumbling purr.

"I like you, too," Larissa told her new roommate. "This is going to be great."

She settled Dyna on the sofa, then glanced at the clock. "I hate to bring you home and run," she said, "but I have to get to work. It's only for a couple of hours and then I'll be home." She grabbed her battered handbag and headed for the front door. "Think about what you want to watch on TV tonight. You get to pick."

With that, she closed the door and raced down the stairs to the ground level of her apartment building, then out onto the street.

She'd only been in Fool's Gold a few months, but she loved everything about the town. It was big enough to be thriving, and small enough that everybody knew her name. Or at least enough people to make her feel as if she belonged. She had a great job, friends and she was a comfortable 425 miles from her family.

Not that she didn't love her parents, her stepparents, her sisters, their spouses and kids, but sometimes she felt a little overwhelmed by so much family. She hadn't been sure about leaving Los Angeles, but now she knew it had been the right thing to do. Her mother's two-day visit, while enjoyable, had been an intense campaign to get her to move back home.

"Not happening," Larissa told herself cheerfully.

Ten minutes later she walked into the offices of Score, the PR firm where she worked. The foyer was huge, with high ceilings and plenty of life-size pictures on the wall. There was a photo of the four principles of the firm, but the rest of the wall space was devoted to all things Jack, Kenny and Sam.

The three guys had been NFL stars. Sam had been a winning kicker, Kenny a record-breaking receiver and Jack was the brilliant and gifted quarterback.

There were pictures of them in action on game day and others of them at various star-studded events. They were smart, successful, good-looking guys, who didn't mind exploiting themselves for the betterment of their company. Taryn, their lone female partner, kept them in line—something of a challenge, considering the egos she was dealing with. Larissa was Jack's personal assistant. She was also the guys' private masseuse.

She enjoyed both aspects of her job. Jack was easy to work for and not overly demanding. Best of all, he supported her causes and let her manage all his charitable giving. As for being the company masseuse—each of the men had played a rough sport professionally. They all had injuries and ongoing pain. She knew where they hurt and why and when she got it right, she made them feel better.

Now she headed directly for her office. She had phone calls to return. There would be a Pro-am golf tournament in Fool's Gold in a few weeks. She had to coordinate Jack's schedule with the publicity folks from the tournament. Later she would go over requests from a charity that helped families with a member in need of an organ donation—the cause Jack supported the most. Sometimes he was asked to reach out to a family personally. Other times he provided direct funding for the family to stay near a child in the hospital. He'd done PSAs and been in several print and internet campaigns. Larissa was his point of contact. She could gauge how much he was willing to do at any given time and when it was better for him to simply write a check.

Her other duties were of a more personal nature. He was between girlfriends, so there were no gifts to buy or flowers to send. Because, in that respect, Jack was a fairly typical guy. He liked women and they liked him back. Which meant there was a steady stream of them through his life. Lucky for him, his parents lived on the other side of the world. So he didn't have a mother demanding that he settle down and produce grandchildren.

She'd barely taken her seat when Jack walked into her office.

"You're late," he told her, sitting across from her and stretching out his long legs. His words sounded more like a statement than a complaint.

"I told you I would be. I had to see my mother off and then go pick up Dyna."

One dark eyebrow rose. "Dyna?"

"My new cat." She rested her elbows on her desk. "I told you about her, remember?"

"No."

Which was so like Jack. "That's because you weren't listening."

"Very possibly."

"She's a rescue."

"What else would she be?"

She waited for him to say more or tell her why he was here. There was only silence. The kind of silence that she understood as clearly as words.

She'd first been hired in 2010 when Jack had left the L.A. Stallions and joined Score. He'd been a silent partner since the firm's inception and Larissa would love to know how Taryn had reacted to Jack changing from the guy who had fronted her the cash to an actual working member of the team. She would guess there had been fireworks. Or maybe not. Jack and Taryn had a past.

Larissa had graduated from college with plans to work for a nonprofit. Paying jobs in her chosen field had been impossible to find and she'd quickly learned she couldn't support herself on volunteer work. So she'd gone looking for another job.

She wasn't the type of person who enjoyed faceless corporations and had settled into waitressing while putting herself through massage school. Then a friend had told her about a job as a personal assistant at a PR firm. That had sounded like a better paying option than her shifts at the diner.

Her interview had been with Taryn. It had lasted

two hours and had ended with words that Larissa had never forgotten.

"Jack is a good-looking guy with beautiful eyes and a great ass. But make no mistake. He's not interested in more than a couple of nights with any given woman. If you fall for him, you're an idiot. Still interested?"

Larissa had been intrigued. Then she'd met Jack and she'd been forced to admit Taryn hadn't been lying about Jack's appeal. She'd taken one look at his studly manliness and had felt the shivers clear down to her toes. But instead of flirting with her, the former quarterback had rubbed his shoulder and sworn.

She'd recognized the pain and reacted instinctively. She'd dug her fingers into the scarred and tense muscles, all the while explaining that she was only a few weeks away from graduating from massage school. She'd gotten a job offer thirty seconds later.

In the past four years Larissa had become a part of the Score family. By the end of the second week, she'd ceased to see Jack as anything but her boss. Six months later, they were a good team and close friends. She regularly chided him about his choices in women, made sure he used ice and anti-inflammatories when his shoulder acted up and offered a daily massage to any of "the boys" and Taryn. She loved her job and she loved that they'd moved to Fool's Gold. She had a new kitty waiting at home. Life was very, very good.

She returned her attention to Jack and waited. Because that was the kind of silence in the room. The one that said he had something to tell her.

"You seeing anyone?"

The question surprised her. "You mean like a man?"

He shrugged. "You never said you dated women, but sure. Either sex will do."

"I'm not dating right now. I haven't met anyone in town and besides, I'm too busy."

"But it would be a guy?"

Amusement danced in his dark eyes.

Jack was one of those men blessed by the gods. Tall, handsome, athletic, charming. He pretty much had it all. What very few people knew was that there were demons he carried around with him. He blamed himself for something that wasn't his fault. A trait Larissa could relate to, because she did it to herself all the time.

"Yes, it would be a guy."

"Good to know." He continued to study her. "Your mother is worried about you."

Larissa slumped back in her seat. "Tell me she didn't talk to you. Tell me!"

"She talked to me."

"Crap. I knew it. She stopped by, didn't she? I knew there was something going on." Her mother was nothing if not determined. "Let me guess. She wanted to know if I was seeing anyone. I hope you told her you didn't know. Or did you tell her I was? Because that would seriously help."

"She didn't ask me if you were seeing anyone."

"Oh." She straightened. "What did she ask?"

"She wants me to fire you so you'll move back to

Los Angeles, fall in love, get married and give her grandchildren."

Larissa felt heat flare on her cheeks. Humiliation made it hard to think, let alone come up with something reasonably intelligent to say.

"She already has two married daughters," she muttered. "Why can't she leave me alone?"

"She loves you."

"She has a funny way of showing it. Are you going to fire me?"

Jack raised both brows this time.

She drew in a breath. "I'll take that as a no. I'm sorry. I'll do my best to keep her away from here. The good news is Muriel is due in three months and the new baby will be a distraction." In the meantime Larissa would figure out a way to convince her mother that she'd moved to Borneo.

"Anything else?" she asked.

"Yeah, there is. Your mother said you're never going to settle down and get married because you're secretly in love with me."

JACK HADN'T KNOWN how Larissa was going to react, but he'd guessed it would be a show. She didn't disappoint. Her face went from red to white and back to red. Her mouth opened and closed. With her jaw tightly clenched, she muttered something like "I'm going to kill her," but he couldn't be sure.

Nancy Owens's words had hit him like a linebacker. Larissa in love with him? Impossible. For one thing, she knew him better than anyone except

Taryn and to know him was to understand he was all flash and no substance. For another, he needed her. Love meant a relationship and having a relationship meant she would eventually leave. No. There was no way Larissa could be in love with him.

But he'd been unable to shake the words and had realized he had to get the truth from the only person who actually knew.

Larissa drew in a breath. "I don't love you. We're friends. I like working for you, and the charity work is terrific, and I know you have my back, but I'm not in love with you."

Relief eased the tension in Jack's always aching right shoulder. He kept his expression neutral.

"You sure?" he asked.

"Yes. Positive."

He shook his head. "I don't know. I'm pretty hot. I could understand you having a thing for me. You've seen me naked. Now that I think about it, your reaction is inevitable." He sighed. "You love me. Admit it."

Larissa's mouth twitched. "Jack, you're not all that."

"But I am. Remember that fan who had my face tattooed on her breast? And the one who begged me to father her child? And the woman in Pittsburgh who wanted me to lick her—"

Larissa rested her arms on the desk and dropped her head to her arms. "Stop. You have to stop."

"Stronger women than you have been unable to resist my charms."

"In your dreams."

"No. Apparently in yours."

She looked at him then, her blue eyes wide, her mouth smiling. "I give."

"In the end, they all do."

The smile faded. "I'm sorry about my mother. She shouldn't have said that. I swear I am not, nor will I ever be, in love with you. I love my job and you're a big part of that. But we're friends, right? That's better. Besides, you have terrible taste in your 'let's end this now' gifts."

"Which is why I let you buy them." He hesitated a second. "We're good?"

"The best." Her smile returned.

The last of his worry faded. This was the Larissa he knew. All funny and earnest. Hair pulled back in a ponytail and not a speck of makeup on her face. She wore yoga pants and T-shirts and always had some cause to discuss with him. She believed the world was worth saving and he didn't mind if she used his money to try. They made a good team. He didn't want to have to do without her and having her love him... Well, that would have changed everything.

JO'S BAR WAS the kind of place you'd only find in a quirky small town. From the outside, it looked perfectly normal, but the second you stepped inside, you knew that this was a bar unlike any other.

For one thing, it was well lit. There were no dark shadows, no questionable stains on the floor. The colors were girl-friendly mauve and yellow, the windows were uncovered and the big TVs were always tuned to the Style Network or *Project Runway.*

Larissa walked inside. She saw the countdown sign that pointed out the number of days until the new season of *Dallas Cowboy Cheerleaders: Making the Team* started and grinned. Yup, life was different here and she liked it.

She glanced around and saw her friends in a booth by the windows. They looked up and waved her over.

When she'd first decided to leave Los Angeles for Fool's Gold, she'd been nervous about starting over. What if she didn't fit in? What if she couldn't make friends? But those fears had been groundless, she thought as she waved back and crossed to the big table.

"I saved you a seat," Isabel said, patting the empty space beside her. "You're just in time to join the debate about whether we're going to order nachos for the table and have margaritas and pretend we don't have to get back to work or if we're going to be good and order regular lunches and drink iced tea."

Larissa settled in the chair. She glanced at Taryn and grinned. "My vote depends on my boss. If she's drinking, I'm all in."

Because right now, a drink sounded great.

What had her mother been thinking? The same question had circled in her brain for much of the morning. Talk about humiliating and inappropriate. As soon as she'd calmed down and could talk about it rationally, she was going to have a very long chat with her mother.

She was lucky that Jack had handled the situation
with his usual easy charm, but jeez. What if he'd
thought her mother was telling the truth? She didn't
want to think about it.

Love Jack? She had flaws but being an idiot wasn't
one of them. Besides, they were a great team. She
would never mess with that.

"You okay?" Taryn asked quietly.

"Yeah. Great."

Because faking it was much easier than telling
the truth.

Taryn, ever stylish in a designer suit that probably
cost more than half a year's rent on Larissa's apartment, tossed her menu onto the table. "What the hell.
Let's be wild."

Dellina, a local party planner and Sam's fiancée,
tossed her menu down, as well. "I don't have any client meetings this afternoon."

Isabel laughed. "I have a store to run. I'd better
be careful or I'll accidentally put the new merchan-
dise on sale."

"I love being bad," Taryn announced. "I just love
it."

"You've always been bad," Dellina told her.
"You're the type. I can tell about these things."

Larissa leaned back in the booth and prepared
to listen. She enjoyed being around these women.
They were smart, successful and yet so very different. Taryn was one of the partners at Score. While
all four partners were equal owners, the three guys
would admit that Taryn was just a little more equal

than the rest of them. She was good at keeping her "boys" in line.

Larissa had always admired her. Taryn dressed in beautiful clothes, walked around in five-inch heels and had a handbag collection that belonged in a museum. Better than that, Taryn was a good friend.

Dellina handled events of all kinds in town. Birthday parties, weddings. A couple of months ago she'd planned and managed a big weekend event for Score's biggest clients. She was also recently engaged to Sam.

Isabel owned Paper Moon. On one side, a clothing store, on the other, wedding gowns. All three women were professionally dressed in suits or dresses. Larissa glanced down at her yoga pants. Maybe in her next life she would inherit the fashion gene, she thought wistfully. Until then, she was going to dress for comfort and practicality.

Jo, the owner of the bar, came over and took their order. Taryn ordered nachos for the table and a pitcher of margaritas. Jo raised her eyebrows.

"Not planning to work this afternoon?" she asked.

"We're going to see how it goes," Taryn told her.

"I've heard that before."

"She doesn't think we're behaving responsibly," Dellina murmured when Jo had left.

"Then my work here is done," Taryn said. "So what's new with everyone?"

"I'm busy with fall clothes." Isabel smiled. "You have to come in and see what's new. There are some beautiful things." She turned to Taryn. "There's a suede jacket you'll love."

"I'll come see it when we're done here."

Dellina shook her head. "No way I'm stopping by," she told her friend. "You tempt me with gorgeous clothes."

Isabel laughed. "That's the point."

"I'm saving my pennies."

"For a wedding?" Larissa asked, her gaze settling on Dellina's shiny new engagement ring.

"No. I'm going to be moving into an office. Sam's house is great and he's mentioned that I can set up my office there, but I think it's time I joined the real world and had an actual office." She wrinkled her nose. "I'm kind of getting to the point where I need to hire an assistant. That means more space."

"Wow! Good for you." Isabel leaned over and hugged her friend. "That's a big step. Congratulations."

"Yes, congratulations," Larissa said, pleased her friend was doing so well.

"You're a tycoon," Taryn teased. "Impressive."

"I'm no tycoon, but I'm doing well. So what's going on with everyone else?"

Taryn mentioned a new account Score had just signed, then all eyes turned to Larissa. She froze, painfully aware that her life wasn't like theirs. She didn't own her own business. In fact, there was a sameness to her days that was kind of sad. The newest thing in her life was her mother's talk with Jack and there was no way she was mentioning that.

"I adopted a cat," she said instead. "A lady died. She was ninety-three. Her kids couldn't take in her cat, so I did. Her name is Dyna. She's a Ragdoll cat. Really beautiful."

She pulled out her phone and showed them a couple of pictures.

Dellina's eyes widened when she saw the photograph. "She's stunning." Her mouth twitched. "Taryn, if she were human, she'd give you a run for your money in the fashion department."

"I'm more impressed you committed to an animal," Taryn told Larissa.

Isabel frowned. "I don't get it. Larissa is always jumping into causes. That cat rescue last month was fantastic."

Larissa squirmed in her seat. "Taryn means that I tend to give in big gestures. Saving forty cats, not adopting one."

Jo appeared with a very large pitcher of margaritas and four glasses. She poured and said the nachos would be out shortly.

Isabel raised her glass. "To the women I adore. Thank you for getting drunk with me. One day very soon Ford and I are going to be getting pregnant and then I'll be on a drinking hiatus."

"Anytime," Larissa said. She was going to add something else when Taryn slapped her hands down on the table.

"Okay," her friend said. "Here goes. I'm getting married."

Larissa looked at both Isabel and Dellina. They seemed equally confused by the statement.

"You're engaged," Larissa pointed out gently. "You have a really big ring. We all noticed."

"Yes, but I've decided on a wedding. Angel and I are going to have a real wedding."

Larissa nodded slowly. "That will be nice."

"I'm happy to help you plan it," Dellina added, sounding equally cautious.

"I have some gorgeous dresses I want you to come see," Isabel told her. "Designer stuff that will make you look like a sexy fairy princess. Or a slutty one, depending on what you want."

Taryn squeezed her eyes shut, then opened them. "Really? You think it's okay?"

Then Larissa got it. Taryn and Angel weren't young kids. They'd both been married before. Taryn wanted the fabulous dress and traditional service, but she wasn't sure she deserved it. Because everybody had their weak spots. Some were just better at hiding them than others.

She reached across the table and touched her friend's hand. "You should have the biggest wedding ever. In a dress so beautiful, it will make us cry."

Taryn's mouth quivered. She squeezed Larissa's fingers then shook off the emotion and reached for her margarita. "Thanks."

Dellina reached for her bag and pulled out an appointment book. "I'll call you in a couple of days and we'll talk."

Isabel turned to Larissa. "I nearly forgot. Your mom was in yesterday. She bought a dress and a handbag. She's my new favorite person. Did you two have a nice visit?"

Larissa grabbed her margarita and took a big gulp.

"Uh-oh," Taryn murmured. "That's not good. I thought the visit went fine. That's what you said this morning."

If only, Larissa thought. "That was before I found out what my mom did."

Her three friends stared at her. "And that would be?" Isabel prodded.

These women loved her, Larissa reminded herself. They wouldn't laugh and point. Or if they did, it would be when she wasn't in the room, which was almost the same thing.

"My mom went to see Jack. She asked him to fire me so I'd move back to L.A. and get married and give her grandchildren."

Dellina frowned. "Okay, that's not great, but it's not horrible, either."

"There's more," Larissa admitted. "She said the reason I had to leave Fool's Gold was that I was secretly in love with Jack."

She paused, waiting for the hysterical laughter. Or any laughter. Instead, the three women exchanged a look.

Larissa felt herself start to blush. "I'm not in love with Jack," she insisted. "I'm not. I work for him. He's great. But there's nothing between us."

"If you say so," Isabel said knowingly.

"If Felicia were with us, she would say that the

boss-secretary romance is a classic archetype," Dellina said.

"I'm not his secretary."

"Close enough," Taryn told her, then picked up her drink. "If you say you're not in love with him, then I believe you."

Just then, Jo appeared with the nachos and the subject got dropped. Larissa reached for a chip, but found that she wasn't the least bit hungry all of a sudden.

This was all her mother's fault, she thought grimly. She'd opened a can of worms. Larissa was going to have to find every last one of them and put them back where they belonged.

CHAPTER TWO

BEING CALLED IN to see Mayor Marsha was a bit like playing against a rival team, without knowing anything about them, Jack thought as he headed up the stairs toward the good mayor's office. There was always the potential for something unlikely to happen—and not in a happy way.

Mayor Marsha was California's longest-serving mayor. Not only did she get intimately involved with the residents of her town, she seemed to know everything and no one knew how. Jack tended to be wary of people like that. He preferred life to be blurry. Honesty could be uncomfortable. Like his talk with Larissa's mom. He could have gone his whole life without hearing those words.

Larissa had reassured him, which he appreciated, but being relieved and forgetting were two different things.

He paused outside the mayor's office. A pretty redhead smiled up at him. "Hi, Jack. You can go on in."

Jack nodded, thinking he should know the receptionist. He was sure he'd met her before. She was friends with Taryn and Larissa, he thought as he entered the mayor's office.

Mayor Marsha was in her sixties, with white hair and a habit of wearing pearls. Now that he thought of it, he wasn't sure he'd seen the woman wearing anything but a suit.

What concerned him more than her appearance, however, was her habit of getting other people to commit to things they didn't want to do. No way he was going to be guilted into something, he told himself. He was a tough ex-jock. She was no match for him.

"Jack," she said warmly as she stood. "Thank you so much for coming by to see me."

"Ma'am." He crossed to her desk and shook her hand.

She motioned to the seating arrangement in the corner. "Let's get more comfortable."

As they crossed the floor, he remembered something about her having been gone for a couple of weeks. "How was your vacation?" he asked.

"Very relaxing." She settled on one of the chairs.

He took the sofa and realized immediately he was now sitting below her. Clever, he thought, respecting her power play. He was right to be wary.

"I went to New Zealand," she continued. "Beautiful country. Did you know a lot of our skiers go there to train in the summer? Of course, it's during their winter."

Jack did his best to look interested as he waited for the mayor to get to the point. He hadn't been summoned to talk about skiing.

Her gaze settled on his face. "I've followed your philanthropic work with some interest."

Jack felt himself tense. He consciously relaxed and waited for her to continue.

"With the organ transplants," she added.

Because that was his cause, he thought. Being a star with the NFL came with plenty of perks and some obligations. One was the expectation that he would take on a cause. Finding his had been easy and over his career he'd often spoken out about the importance of organ donation and transplants.

"I'm happy to help where I can," he said easily, knowing it was true. Larissa handled the logistics and he showed up every now and then. She was able to serve a cause, which she loved, and he got to pretend he was involved. A situation that worked for both of them.

"The family connection must make it even more meaningful," the mayor said.

Jack had known that was coming so he was able to nod. "Of course."

"You lost a brother," the mayor said. "Is that correct?"

"Yes."

"A twin?"

"Yes."

An identical twin, Jack added silently. Only somewhere in utero, Lucas's heart hadn't formed right. Cells had misstepped or stopped dividing or something. The doctors had never been able to explain it well enough for him to understand. Or maybe they just didn't know, he thought grimly. So one brother had been born perfectly healthy and the other... hadn't.

Jack didn't want to go there. He didn't want to remember what it was like to grow up always worrying about his twin. He didn't want to feel the guilt that came with being the one who never got sick, never felt weak, never wondered if he was going to make it to his fifth birthday or his tenth.

Jack knew where this was going now. Mayor Marsha wanted his help. Or more specifically, the money his presence would bring. She knew a family who needed help paying for surgery or finding temporary housing while their child went through a grueling but lifesaving surgery.

Easy as pie, he thought. Or in his case, as easy as telling Larissa what needed to be done.

"Who's the family?" he asked.

The older woman smiled. "Oh, I don't need your help with a transplant patient, Jack. It's something else entirely. Are you aware that we have a four-year college here in town?"

The change in topic surprised him. "Uh, sure. UC Fool's Gold."

"Cal U Fool's Gold, actually, but yes. They have an excellent academic reputation and they're doing some work with UC Davis to expand the enology department."

"The what?"

"The study of wine. Our vineyards are doing very well here and we're starting to be known as a small but prestigious region. We're petitioning the Alcohol and Tobacco Tax and Trade Bureau to make Fool's Gold an AVA." She paused. "American Viticulture Area. For example, the Napa Valley is an AVA here in California. There's also Red Mountain in Washington State. We want a Fool's Gold AVA."

"Okay," Jack said slowly. "I don't know anything about growing wine or AVAs." Although he did enjoy a nice merlot.

"Of course you don't," Mayor Marsha told him. "I invited you here to discuss football."

Jack's head hurt from the lightning fast change in topics. The old girl sure knew how to keep a guy confused.

"You want help with your fantasy team?" he asked cautiously.

The mayor laughed. "No, but thank you for that offer. My problem is more real world than that. Cal U Fool's Gold needs a new football coach. Well, more than that. The school needs a whole program."

Coaching? A program? "Not my area of expertise. The athletic director handles that sort of thing, in conjunction with the chancellor and the president of the college. There are also headhunters who specialize in finding coaches."

"All of which is being explored. However, there is a citizen advisory position on the search committee. That's where you come in, Jack. I want you to be our citizen adviser. You're an experienced player, you know what makes a good coach and knowing you're helping will inspire the group. You are uniquely qualified for this. You've made Fool's Gold your home. I hope you'll be willing to give back to the community that has taken you in and made you feel welcome."

He grinned. "You're not even subtle with the guilt," he said.

"I don't see any point. We both know you're going to agree. Sooner rather than later suits me best, but if you need to be persuaded, I can do that, too."

"Somehow I know that would involve Taryn."

"She is only one of many options I have at my disposal."

"I appreciate the honesty."

She smiled, but didn't speak.

Jack shook his head and knew there was no point in avoiding the inevitable. "I'm sure you have better things to do with your day than manipulate me. Sure, I'll serve on your committee. Give them my contact information."

Mayor Marsha rose and held out her hand. "I already have. Thank you, Jack. I appreciate your volunteering."

He shook hands with her. "You're a scary broad, you know that, right?"

Her smile turned mischievous. "I count on it."

LARISSA DIDN'T LIKE feeling unsettled. It wasn't her way. When there was a problem, she dived in headfirst. If something needed saving—she was there. But as far as she knew, no mammals, birds or reptiles needed her help. Not that she was allowed to help reptiles anymore. There had been an unfortunate incident a couple of months ago involving venomous snakes and Taryn's fiancé, Angel. Larissa still felt really bad about that.

She walked around in her too-large office. It was attached to Jack's. She had a computer where she managed his calendar and some file cabinets that were mostly empty. She wasn't really a filer. She preferred to pile and when the piles got too tall, she shoved them into a cabinet. Maybe a messy system, but it worked for her.

This office was something she accepted but didn't really like. *Her* tiny kingdom was the massage room at the other end of the building. There the space was exactly how she wanted it. From the color of the walls to the sound system to the massage table she'd had customized to fit her specifications. The linens were soft yet absorbent. She special ordered oils with an increased capacity to reduce inflammation and deaden pain while keeping the guys from smelling like flowers. For Taryn, she had a collection of organic oils. She had music playlists customized to each of her clients and had personally chosen all the robes and towels used in the massage room, showers and saunas.

In that place, she was comfortable. Calm. In control. But in the rest of her life, well, it was always a crapshoot.

Larissa shut off her computer and walked down the hall to Taryn's office. Her friend was on the phone, but waved her in. Larissa crossed the thickly carpeted floor. The plushness was required because Taryn had a habit of kicking off her shoes the second she got to work. She spent most of her day barefoot—something Larissa had never understood. Why buy shoes that were too uncomfortable to wear? But then she didn't get any part of Taryn's wardrobe.

Today her boss had on a black-and-white color-block sleeveless dress. There was a jacket slung over the visitor chair and some lethal-looking shoes by the desk. The shoes were also black and white. Some kind of fur, with wide stripes and a scary four- or five-inch geometric, sculpted heel.

While Taryn wrapped up her call, Larissa kicked off her own comfy flats and carefully stepped into Taryn's ridiculous shoes. The additional five inches made her totter precariously and she had to hang on to the desk to stay upright. Once she was fairly confident of her balance, she shrugged into the jacket and then carefully made her way to the closed doors behind Taryn's desk.

"Sure, Jerry," Taryn said, her voice thick with suppressed laughter. "I'm all over that. Does Tuesday work for you?"

Larissa pulled open the right-hand door and studied herself in the wide full-length mirror.

The jacket was too small. Taryn might be taller, but she was a good size thinner. But even with it pulling across the shoulders and not coming close to closing, she could see how the cut defined her upper body and made her waist disappear.

The shoes might technically match her black yoga pants, but they looked ridiculous with the casual style. And they were impossible to walk in. Still, they were sexy, she thought wistfully. Sexy and sophisticated.

"I swear to God, you're going to kill yourself one of these days," Taryn said, coming up behind her. "You know you can't walk in high heels."

Larissa carefully turned to check out the shoes from more than one angle. "I know, but you always look so stylish. I look like I shop at a resale store."

"Because you do."

"My clothes are new," Larissa said, trying not to sound defensive. Which was hard, because she felt defensive. "New-ish. They were when I bought them."

"Uh-huh," Taryn said, sounding unconvinced. "We have this conversation every few months. You say you want to dress better, I offer to help. You promise to set up a shopping date with me and never do."

Larissa stepped out of the shoes and handed the jacket to her friend. "I know. I'm not really the make-over type. I like to keep things simple." She studied her face in the mirror. It was clean and her skin was nice. Her hair was a good color. Medium blond and the only color she used was for highlights, which she got done maybe every six or eight months.

"Mascara wouldn't kill you," Taryn informed her. "I'm not saying you have to dress like me. You could still be comfortable but more pulled together."

"Are you saying that as my friend or my boss?"

Taryn rolled her eyes. "You work for Jack. He's the one you have to make happy. I'm simply pointing out that about once a month you come in here, try on something of mine and then talk about making a change. That has to mean something."

Larissa was pretty sure it did, but that wasn't why she was here.

"I need to talk to you," she said instead.

Taryn immediately pointed to the sofa in her office. "Sure. What's up?"

Larissa sat in a corner of the comfy couch and tucked her legs under her. She angled toward her friend. "It's about what happened yesterday. With my mom and Jack and what she said."

She waited, hoping Taryn would jump in with a laugh and an "Of course no one believes you're in love with Jack. How ridiculous."

But Taryn was silent.

Larissa drew in a breath. "I don't love him. We're friends. We work well together. I like him—he's a likable guy. It's just my mom wants me married and I guess I want that, too. Eventually."

Because from the outside, marriage seemed really great, but from the inside—at least what she'd observed with her parents—it sucked.

She supposed that assessment was harsh. After her parents had gotten divorced, they'd both been much happier people. Everyone agreed. Her parents liked to joke that they never should have gotten married. And they wouldn't have. If there hadn't been an unexpected pregnancy. Namely her.

"I could just as easily find the right guy here in Fool's Gold as in Los Angeles. Probably more easily. It's hard to date in Los Angeles. There are a lot of unrealistic expectations what with the movie business so close." She pressed her lips together. "Why aren't you saying anything?"

"Because you're doing fine without me," Taryn told her.

"Do you think I'm in love with Jack?"

"I think you have an interesting and symbiotic relationship."

"That's not an answer."

"Maybe, but it's the truth. Jack wants to make a difference in the world, without getting too involved. You want to save the world, but you lack resources. You have heart and Jack has money. Together you make a great team."

"Exactly," Larissa said quickly. "We're a team. Not a couple. We're friends. There's love between friends, but it's different. It's not romantic. Like when I needed a temporary place for those three fighting dogs to stay. Jack let me use his house."

Taryn's mouth twitched. "You mean you put the dogs in Jack's house before telling him and they wouldn't let him inside his own home so he had to stay at a hotel for a week but he didn't get mad at you?"

"You don't have to put it like that," Larissa told her. "But, yes, that would be an example of us working as a team." Although she wasn't completely sure Jack would agree with her example.

"Jack's a good guy," Taryn said. "He goes along with what you want because it allows him to be connected without getting involved. You like that Jack is always there in the background to rescue you if you need it. You get to take risks without actually putting yourself out there."

Larissa winced. "I am not so excited about the total honesty part of this conversation." She wanted to disagree with her friend's assessment, but didn't think she could.

Taryn touched her arm. "I love you, but I can't help with this. What you have going on with Jack is complicated. You're both getting something out of it, but the relationship also keeps each of you from looking for more. You know Jack's a bad bet, so you are careful not to take things too far. Which is smart. But I wonder if what your mom meant is that you're just committed enough that you're not interested in looking for someone else."

Larissa sprang to her feet, crossed to the door, then stopped and turned back.

"I'm not hiding from falling in love."

Taryn raised her eyebrows.

Larissa frowned. "Not completely. I just… I'm not in love with Jack."

"Prove it. Go fall in love with someone else."

"Not everyone wants to get married."

"What does that have to do with being in a relationship? Don't you want more than friendship? Don't you want passion and sex and romance and knowing there's someone you can call at two in the morning and he'll be there, no matter what?"

Larissa nodded because it was the answer Taryn expected. The truth was more complicated. Yes, she wanted passion and sex and romance. But if she needed to call someone at two in the morning, she knew all four Score owners would be at her side in a heartbeat, with Jack leading the way. Was that what Taryn was trying to say? That the reason Larissa hadn't found *the one* was because she didn't need to?

She doubted the truth was that simple.

HUNAN PALACE WAS conveniently located in Larissa's neighborhood. The vegetables were fresh, the sauces delicious and Jack had to admit they had the best egg rolls he'd ever tasted. As he wasn't the kind of guy who cooked and Larissa was too busy saving the world to provide a meal, their regular Tuesday-night dinner meant takeout. They met at her place. He brought the food. She provided the beer or wine. It was nice. Easy.

As he crossed the street, he nodded at the people he knew, or at least recognized. Fool's Gold was that kind of town. You were expected to get involved. Hell, even Sam was teaching finance classes for small businesses a couple of times a month. Kenny would be sucked into something before long, Jack thought. Which meant being asked to help find a new coach wasn't much of a surprise. Plus, it was the kind of thing he would enjoy. Even though he couldn't still play, the love of the game had never gone away.

He reached Larissa's apartment building. She had an upstairs unit in a place without an elevator—which was just like her. He happened to know she could afford something much nicer and larger, but that wasn't her way. She wanted her money to go toward her causes. His money, too, he thought with a grin. But what the hell. He had enough.

He knocked once, then opened the door. Larissa wasn't one for locks.

"It's me," he called and he stepped into her small one-bedroom apartment.

Larissa looked up from the book she'd been reading. "Hi. Meet Dyna."

He glanced down and saw a cat hurrying toward him. She had long hair and almost-human blue eyes.

"You really got a cat."

"I told you I did."

"I know, but I thought you were kidding."

Dyna wound her way around his legs in a tight figure eight, depositing light-colored cat hair on his suit pants with every step.

"Nice," he murmured, making a mental note to change into jeans before visiting again, even if that meant keeping an extra pair at the office.

Larissa stood and crossed to him. "Don't whine. Isn't she beautiful?"

She picked up the cat, who immediately relaxed in her arms.

Dyna's fur was a creamy white in the front of her body, darkening to a taupe-beige, then darkening even more until it was a deep brown on her tail.

"She's great," Jack said.

"She intimidates me a little," Larissa admitted. "I've never had a cat this gorgeous before."

"Your eyes are the same color. That's a little weird."

Larissa laughed and set down the cat. "Afraid we have an otherworldly connection? That together we can move objects and read minds?"

"It's never good when a woman can read my mind," he said honestly. "By whatever means."

She took the bag of food from him and led the way into her small kitchen.

The eat-in table was already set with two place mats, plates and flatware. A vase filled with a few carnations sat in the center. The pink petals were turning brown on the edges, he noted. Probably because Larissa had bought them at 70 percent off at the grocery store. You wouldn't want to waste money on something like flowers at full price. What if there was a mad squirrel in need of therapy?

She picked up a bottle of merlot. "Wine or beer?"

He considered the question. "Beer."

She carefully put the bottle back into the rack on her counter. It was one he'd brought over, along with the inventory of a few of his favorite merlots. While he trusted Larissa to buy beer, he was not willing to drink the cheap wine she favored.

She pulled two bottles of beer from the refrigerator, then nudged the door closed with a bump of her hip. He set down the bag of food and crossed to the drawer to pull out the opener. While he was there, he also grabbed a few serving spoons for their dinner.

He turned in the small kitchen and handed her the opener. She walked back to the table.

The windows were open and a nice breeze drifted through the kitchen. Dyna had settled on the back of the sofa to watch them from a safe and regal distance. Larissa opened both bottles, then unpacked the containers of food. She turned to him and smiled.

"You got the crispy shrimp," she said happily. "Thank you."

"You like it."

"You don't."

"Yeah, whatever. Eat the rest for lunch."

"Real men don't eat shrimp?" she asked.

"I love shrimp. Just put it in a butter sauce and drop it over pasta. Is that too much to ask?"

She sat down and motioned for him to do the same. Jack started to move toward the table, or at least he planned to, but suddenly he found it difficult to move.

From this angle he could see Larissa's bare shoulder. She'd replaced her usual work T-shirt with a tank top. One of those cottony, billowy ones with little ruffles around the arm and neckline. The soft fabric dipped low enough for him to be aware of feminine curves.

He shook his head. So Larissa had breasts. She was a woman—it wasn't unexpected. Only he wasn't sure he'd ever noticed them before. Or how long her legs were in her shorts. She had great legs. Tanned and toned.

No, he corrected himself. Lanky. She was lanky. His gaze drifted to her bare feet. She'd painted her toes a dark purple and added little pink dots. Who did that?

"What?" she asked. "You okay?"

"Ah, fine."

He sat across from her and reached for one of the containers. It was the damned crispy shrimp and he quickly passed it over to her.

"How'd you get her?" he asked, motioning to the cat.

"Mayor Marsha mentioned she knew an older lady who had passed away. Her family couldn't keep Dyna—everyone's allergic. So I took her." Larissa lowered her voice. "I think she's starting to like me. When I pet her, she purrs."

Jack wanted to point out that liking or not liking wasn't the issue. Larissa was Dyna's meal ticket and the cat was smart enough to know that. But the words sounded harsh, even in his head, so instead he said, "What's not to like?" and then wondered why he felt weird saying that.

Something was wrong. Or different. Or both. And he didn't like it. He was comfortable around Larissa. He understood her. They were friends. So what was off tonight?

"Speaking of Mayor Marsha, what did she want with you?"

Jack told her about the need for a new coach and a football program, and how he was going to be on the committee.

"That will be fun for you," Larissa told him. "College kids are great. So much enthusiasm. And you have a good eye. You'll be able to see who has real talent."

"Don't get carried away. I'm not mentoring anybody or paying for their mother's goiter surgery."

Her blue eyes twinkled with amusement. "You sure about that?"

He sighed. "I won't tempt fate by fighting with you on that. Besides, you know what I mean. I'm helping with a committee, not getting involved."

"You like getting involved."

He picked up his beer. "No. *You* like getting involved and dragging me with you. There's a difference."

"You're an excellent role model."

Only in her eyes, he thought as he took a drink. He knew the truth. In his heart, he was about as selfish as the average Joe, only with more resources.

Larissa chattered on about her various causes and he half listened. This was what he liked, he thought. Just being with his friend. Their relationship was uncomplicated, although apparently a mystery to the outside world. Why else would Mrs. Owens have made such a bonehead statement? Larissa in love with him? Impossible.

Jack relaxed back in his chair and watched Larissa's hands move as she talked. Her face was expressive. He supposed on a purely impersonal basis he could admit she was pretty. Her skin was smooth and soft-looking. She never wore makeup, as far as he could tell, which was a change from the other women in his life. The long hair was nice, especially when she wore it down. At work it was always back in a ponytail. He remembered a client spotting her and asking if it was bring-your-daughter-to-work day. Because she could look kind of young.

He grabbed another egg roll and bit into the crispy shell. Yeah, he was a lucky man, he thought. Good friends, good food and very few problems.

"Mary's not doing well," Larissa said with a sigh.

"Who's Mary?"

Larissa's mouth twisted down. "She's the little girl who got the liver transplant last year. She's been running a fever on and off for a few weeks now. Her parents are worried and the doctors are running tests."

Jack nodded as if he knew what Larissa was talking about, but in truth, he didn't. Mary was just one more kid his money had helped.

"I've been checking in with her family regularly," she added. "I sent her an American Girl doll book. *Kit Saves the Day.*"

Okay, now he was lost. "Who is Kit?"

"Kit Kittredge. She's one of the American Girl dolls. I showed you them before."

"Was I paying attention?"

"Probably not." Some of the sadness left her eyes. "You never were into dolls."

He winked. "Not unless they were anatomically correct. What other causes should I prepare for?"

"There's going to be a chiweenie rescue."

"A what?"

"Chiweenies. They're a Chihuahua-dachshund mix."

"Someone has a sense of humor," he murmured. "And this is my problem how?"

"A breeder is being investigated. There's concern

it's not a good situation. That she has more of a puppy mill than a healthy program."

Jack could figure out the rest of it pretty easily. If it was a puppy mill or a hoarding situation, then there would be an intervention and Larissa would get involved. Which meant somehow he would end up involved, as well.

"Don't bring any to my house," he told her, but without a lot of energy. Telling her no didn't help and for the most part, he didn't really mind whatever she dragged into his life. It always made for interesting conversation.

"I don't always get you involved," she protested.

"What about the butterflies?"

She wiggled in her seat. "That was a special situation."

Yeah. One that required him to not make noise or turn on lights for several days. Of course, butterflies in a cage had been a lot easier to take than the fighting dogs that wouldn't let him in his own house.

"You're never boring," he told her. "I'll give you that."

Later, when they were done eating and he'd helped her clean up, he gave her a brief hug goodbye and left. Once on the sidewalk, he breathed in the cool night air and started back for his place.

Yup, he had it all, he told himself. His Score co-workers were his family, Larissa was his best friend and, when he got the itch, there were plenty of women to be had. Best of all, he could go back to his quiet, empty house whenever he wanted. He was a blessed man. Most days it was very good to be Jack McGarry.

CHAPTER THREE

SCORE STAFF MEETINGS were generally short and to the point. Because of that, no one tried to get out of them. Larissa sat at one end of the big conference table and took notes on the items that affected her or Jack. She also had a short presentation prepared for when Kenny called on her.

The areas of expertise were delineated by ability. Jack and Kenny brought in new clients, Sam took care of the money and Taryn handled the existing clients, while keeping her "boys" in line.

The day-to-day management was mostly shared between Sam and Taryn, but Kenny had an active role in most of the hiring and he ran the staff meetings.

Larissa listened to him now and idly wondered how many people would be surprised to know the former receiver had a degree in English. A degree he'd earned the hard way—by going to class and writing papers. As a star football player, there had been easier options for him, but he hadn't taken them. He'd earned his B+ average by studying and doing well on his tests. Kenny joked that his first year of college, his teammates had been forever stealing whatever he'd been reading on the bus or plane, convinced there had to be secret porn hidden in the pages of his book. They couldn't understand that a guy who could play like Kenny might also like to read.

Taryn shifted in her seat. Larissa smiled, thinking how her boss sort of reminded her of Dyna. Sure the coloring was different, but they were both beautiful females, confident of their place in the world. Dyna had adapted well to the small apartment and had spent the past two nights sleeping on the bed. Progress, Larissa thought happily. This morning Dyna had awakened her with happy purrs and snuggles.

Like the cat, Taryn had mellowed when she'd found security in her personal life, i.e., when she'd fallen in love with Angel. The sharp edges that kept the world at bay had softened a little. Larissa supposed it wasn't a surprise. Everyone was different when he or she fell in love. Or so she'd observed. It wasn't as if she'd ever felt the emotion herself.

Someday, she promised herself wistfully. If she was lucky.

"Larissa's going to report on the golf tournament," Kenny said.

She drew herself back to the meeting and glanced at her notes. "The charity event is a fund-raiser. Raoul Moreno's foundation runs it and you three are on the schedule to play." She went through a few more details.

"Think what we could have done with the Stallions if we'd had Moreno," Sam mused.

Larissa looked at Taryn and rolled her eyes. Taryn nodded in agreement. They went down this same path every time they talked about the tournament. The humor of the comment was that Jack had been the Stallions quarterback while Kenny and Sam had been with the team and they'd done just fine. Including a Super Bowl win. But they liked to joke that if they'd had Raoul Moreno, a quarterback for the Dallas Cowboys, everything would have been better.

Kenny leaned back in his chair and sighed. "That would have been great."

"You don't deserve as good as you got," Jack told him. "You're lucky I was willing to play with you at all."

He kept talking, but Larissa wasn't listening. Her part of the staff meeting was over. She had a massage in twenty minutes and there was prep work to do.

She collected her notes and stood. Taryn looked at her.

"Run while you can," her friend murmured.

Larissa grinned and did just that.

After dropping off her notes in her office, she walked toward the locker rooms. Her space was between the two, down a short hallway. Once inside, she clicked on the lights and turned up the thermostat.

When she wasn't working, the room adjusted to the ambient temperature of the building, but when she was with a client, she liked the air to be warm. Less comfortable for her but better for the massage.

Her ritual was always the same and she found that soothing. First she warmed up the room; then she turned on the music. Jack was up first today, so she chose his MP3 file and pushed the start button.

She started the countertop machine that heated the thermal packs. When she took them out for use, they would be about 160 degrees.

She cleaned the massage table when she was done for the day so that when she began her work, she only had to put the heating pad in place, cover it with a thick padding, then tuck in the linens on top. She did that next, securing the sheet.

For Jack, she used moist heat on his shoulder. That was where he hurt all the time. He had a lot of general aches and pains, but his shoulder was where she concentrated her work. Kenny had injuries all over. He'd been hit the most and there wasn't a part of him that didn't cause him pain every now and then. Sam, as the kicker, had the fewest injuries.

Larissa found it interesting to work on them. They were athletes, yet so different from each other. Especially Taryn. She was smaller. Muscled, but compared with the guys, she was puny. Her massages were always later in the day. If all three guys needed Larissa in one morning, her hands, arms and shoulders were tired for hours. By contrast, massaging Taryn was practically a vacation. There weren't any thick ropes of muscles to manipulate. No scarred cartilage to break down, no stiffness to ease.

Larissa crossed to her cabinet and pulled out the bottle of oil she used on Jack. Everything was personalized. That was the advantage of only having four massage clients, she thought. And the point of them having her on staff. She knew what they liked. She and Taryn talked about girl stuff. Sam never spoke at all. Kenny was friendly enough. He would mention a book he was reading or a movie he'd seen.

But with Jack it was ninety minutes of hanging out. They discussed everything from current events to restaurant reviews to the various causes he was supporting through her.

She glanced at the big clock on the wall and saw it was nearly time. She turned down the lights, then checked the temperature of the heating pad on the table.

Perfect, she thought, feeling the warmth through the soft sheet. She folded the top sheet back, and then pulled open a drawer and picked up her brush. She smoothed her long hair, then pulled it back into a ponytail. She pushed the drawer shut as Jack walked into her massage room.

"Hey," he said by way of greeting.

"Hey, yourself."

Jack wore a white terry-cloth robe, as he always did, along with shower shoes. Everyone came to her like that. She politely turned her back so he could hang the robe on the hook and slip onto the table.

In a spa setting, she would step out of the room. After all, during a massage, her clients were naked. But the first time she'd tried that with the guys here, they'd told her not to bother. As Kenny had put it, "None of us have anything you haven't seen before." There was also the fact that she was frequently called into the sauna to rub aching muscles and they were all naked there. It was weird, but she'd gotten used to it.

During her massage training there had been plenty

of instruction on how to handle the awkward "you're naked and I'm touching you" part of what she did. There were specific laws and codes of ethics that had to be followed. Not that her guys ever pushed the boundaries. They weren't like that.

None of them wanted to be covered at all when they were facedown. Larissa had fought that battle and lost the first year. When they turned over, she draped a towel across the, ah, private areas. Taryn didn't even want to bother with that. As for the natural male reaction to a woman touching his body... Kenny sometimes got an erection, but he laughed about it. His humor made her completely comfortable with the situation. Sam rarely got hard. The man had a will of iron. And Jack, well, he seemed to fall in the Sam camp.

Now she waited until she heard Jack slide onto the massage table.

"Why do you always put out that stupid sheet?" he asked.

"Because it's my job."

She turned and saw the top sheet had been kicked to the floor, just like always. The regularity of the event made her smile.

She picked up the sheet and tossed it in her dirty linens bin, then collected the moist heat pack. She worked quickly to slide it into its cover, then wrapped the ribbed warmth around Jack's right shoulder. There it would loosen the muscles and scarring while she worked on the rest of his back.

She began the massage by touching his upper

arms, then moving across his back. She felt for any new tension, any areas of tenderness. Her touch was sure as she lightly kneaded familiar muscles. She worked her way down to the small of his back before retracing her steps.

"Taryn's keeping a stash of bridal magazines in her office," she said conversationally. "But when I asked her if she and Angel had set a date, she wouldn't say. I think she's weirded out about what to do."

As she spoke, she dug into his left shoulder. While it was nowhere near as beat-up as the right, he'd suffered plenty of hits on that side.

"Taryn can't figure out if she wants a big wedding or to run off," Jack said, his voice slightly muffled.

"I know. A couple of days ago she announced she's having a big wedding. Yesterday she said they were going to elope. I hope she decides on having a wedding. She would totally rock a great designer dress. It would be like theater."

"You'd have to dress up, too," he pointed out.

Not her favorite thing. "I could manage for a day. Would you give her away?"

She asked the question without thinking, then remembered Jack and Taryn had been married briefly. She'd gotten pregnant and he'd insisted they do the right thing. When she lost the baby a few weeks later, they'd gotten divorced. As far as Larissa knew, they'd never been in love and the topic of their marriage wasn't the least bit sensitive. At least not on the surface.

"Taryn wouldn't appreciate the idea of being given

or taken," he said. "My guess is if she goes the big wedding route, she'll hustle herself down the aisle."

Larissa began to work on his back. His skin was warm and the oil she used allowed her hands to slide easily. The rhythm of her movements anchored her in place. The music was nice. Soothing, she thought.

"I got another call about the chiweenies," she told him. "They're going to make one more visit to talk to the lady. They're pretty sure it's a hoarding situation. The animal-rescue people are working with local law enforcement to get her to surrender the animals to avoid charges."

"You're not bringing dogs to my house."

She smiled. "Would I do that?"

"In a heartbeat."

JACK DID HIS best to give himself over to the massage. Much of the time, being worked on by Larissa was the best part of his day. His shoulder provided a steady ache and as he wouldn't take drugs for it, he'd learned to live with the pain.

The heat pack she used eased some of it. Later she would dig her needle fingers into the joints, searching out scarring and grinding it into submission. That part wasn't fun, but the result was relief—at least for a few hours.

Her voice washed over him. She told him about her causes and what was happening in town. Sometimes he listened and sometimes he didn't. He'd learned that if it was important, she would tell him again.

But today he couldn't relax. Not the way he usually did. Something was off. Not the massage table. It was the same, as were the sheets and the music. Even the oil she used was familiar.

But there was something. He tried closing his eyes, but that didn't help. Her hands continued to move on his body, sliding down his back. Lower and lower. She worked his shoulder last—leaving it until he was ready to turn over. That way she could attack it from both sides. That's what always happened. She put heat on his shoulder, did the whole back of him, then his shoulder. He turned over, she did the front of the shoulder, wrapped it in heat and then tackled the rest of him. They had a routine. It worked. So what was his problem?

Her hands stroked lower and lower on his back. He knew what was next. She would slide down his hip, then come up to the side of his butt and dig in to some pressure point. She would grind until he was about ready to come off the table, and then suddenly it would ease. Pain would flow out of him as if she'd pulled the cork on a bottle.

Sure enough she started on his right side. He wasn't sure if she used her fingers or knuckles or what, but she unerringly found that damned spot every time and pushed to what felt like the center of his pelvis bone. The pain was sharp and white, almost like a knife. Nerve pain, he thought, recognizing the difference. He began to tense. Just when he thought he couldn't take it anymore, there was a sudden absence of pain and he went limp.

Larissa walked around to the other side of the table

and rested her hand on the small of his back, as if silently telling him she was there. Her fingers slipped down the side of his hip then up to his butt where she dug in again. Her free hand rested on the back of his thigh.

Did she always do that? Rest her hand there? Because it felt nice. She had good hands. Strong. The way she moved them. There was a confidence a guy could get used to. If she would just move that other hand a little higher and toward the center. If he parted his legs a little she could—

The sharp pain grew, but it wasn't enough to distract him, and when it faded, there was a new ache in its place. A growing ache that he couldn't immediately place. It was as if—

Jack silently swore as he realized he had an erection. What the hell? Now? During a massage? What was he—fifteen?

Stop it, he told himself. No way could he be aroused. Not like this. He never had been before. Okay, maybe a couple of times when it had been a long time between women, but then he thought about his relationship with Larissa and knew that was never going to happen. They were friends. He cared about her. He knew better than to sleep with someone he cared about.

The realization had always been enough to take care of the problem. But it wasn't today. The more he thought he shouldn't, the bigger he got. The more he told himself not to, the more he imagined what it would be like. Her hands moving all over him. Him touching her in return. His mouth exploring every part of her before he settled between her thighs and—

Shit!

Without having anything close to a plan, he grabbed the sheet below him and pulled it free of the pad. It came up easily.

"Jack?" Larissa stepped back from the table. "What are you doing?"

"I have to go," he said, scrambling to his feet. He was careful to keep the sheet bunched around his raging hard-on and then bolted.

The locker room was across the hall. He raced inside, then headed directly for the showers. He turned on the cold water, then stepped into the spray.

Ten minutes later, order had been restored in his personal universe. Jack dried off and dressed. He picked up the soggy shoulder wrap and wondered how he was going to explain what had happened to Larissa. Maybe he could tell her he got sick. Would she believe that?

The locker room door opened. Jack groaned and turned, prepared to lie his way out of the problem. But luck was with him and instead of Larissa, he saw Kenny strolling toward him.

"What?" his friend demanded. "Larissa is out there, wringing her hands. She says you ran away without an explanation." Kenny put his hand on Jack's shoulder. "Bro, she's worried. What's up?"

Not the best choice of words, Jack thought, not sure if he was going to laugh or start swearing again.

He dropped the soggy pack onto the bench and settled next to it. He rested his head in his hands.

"I got a boner during the massage," he admitted.

Kenny snickered. "Seriously? That's what all the fuss is about? It happens. It's no big deal."

Jack dropped his hands and glanced at his friend. Kenny's blue eyes were filled with amusement.

"You, too?" Jack asked.

"Sure. Larissa doesn't care. We joke about it. Eventually it goes away. Why did this time freak you out?"

"Because I don't usually have that problem."

"You and Sam," Kenny said. "You make things too complicated. Look, you're not seeing anyone, you're naked and a beautiful woman is rubbing on you. Biology, man. It's all about biology."

Maybe, Jack thought, but that didn't explain why he felt so strange about it all.

"She's out there, worrying," Kenny told him. "Tell her you're fine."

"You do it."

Kenny shook his head. "You're making this more than it is. If you don't talk about it now, you're going to have to explain it later. It's not going to get easier with time."

Jack shrugged. That was a problem he would deal with when he had to. Until he figured out what had happened, avoiding Larissa seemed like a damned good plan.

LARISSA WALKED UP the front walk of Jack's house. The imposing two-story structure was elegant. One of several sleek custom homes on the golf course. The yard was perfectly manicured, the windows large, the paint fresh. Jack was a big believer in hiring the right person for the job and it showed. Everything in his life was well tended.

So not her style, she thought as she crossed to the front door, knocked once and then let herself in. Because the door was almost never locked.

"It's me," she called as she entered. "Jack?"

She knew he was here. His Mercedes was in the driveway. Still, she half expected him not to answer, mostly because he'd been avoiding her all day.

She didn't like that. Didn't like him running out of her massage and then not talking to her. To quote her mom's favorite movie, "There was a great disturbance in the Force." She'd been restless and on edge. Kenny's assurances that Jack was fine hadn't helped at all.

She heard something and looked up. Jack stood on the landing of the second floor. He'd changed into jeans and T-shirt. He looked tired, she thought. And in pain.

She put her hands on her hips. "What?" she demanded. "Tell me what happened. I'm not leaving here until you do."

He walked down the stairs toward her. For the first time in years, she was unable to read his face. How could she not know what Jack was thinking?

"You're scaring me," she admitted. "Are you mad at me or something? We have to talk. This isn't right."

He reached the main floor. He wasn't wearing

shoes, but he was still taller than her. And oddly broad across the shoulders. A guy, she thought. Jack, the guy, made her nervous. She did much better with Jack, her friend.

"Say something," she told him.

He shoved his hands into his jeans pockets and sighed. "I'm not mad."

"Okay." That was good. "So?"

His dark gaze settled on her face. "I got a hard-on during the massage. I don't usually. I didn't know what to do, so I left."

Ran was more like it, she thought before her brain went to a completely different place.

A hard-on? As in an erection? As in arousal? He was still talking but she wasn't listening. Not when there was so much to process.

She knew the women in Jack's life. Not personally, of course. While she met them, they didn't hang out or anything. It probably took too much time to be so beautiful for them to have friends. His women were all models or actresses. There was also the unfortunate two months of him dating a Playboy bunny. She'd been a stunning girl, but not so much in the conversation department.

Larissa got it. Jack liked beautiful women. Why wouldn't he? They were available. Which was probably why she was having trouble with the idea of him being aroused because of her. She knew that she was pretty enough, but firmly in the normal category. He

was used to perfection and she was just kind of…
ordinary. So how could he have gotten turned on by
her?

She supposed it was because he hadn't had a girlfriend for a while. He'd been in Fool's Gold and there
was no sneaking around here.

"…asked Kenny to talk to you," he finished.

She'd missed the middle bit, but figured that was
fine.

"That sort of thing happens," she told him, still
confused but willing to go with it. "They cover it in
massage school. Sam never does, but Kenny's pretty
regular. We joke about it and then it's gone. It's a bio-
logical function. I know it's not personal."

Jack's guarded expression started to relax. "You're
okay with that?"

"Sure. I was touching you intimately. We know
each other. We're friends. You're comfortable. You
got a little too relaxed."

She was saying all the right things. The professional things. But what she was really thinking was
that she kind of wouldn't mind for it to be personal.
She'd kind of like him saying he'd been swept away.

Even as the thoughts formed, she mentally retreated from them. What on earth? Where had that
come from? She and Jack were friends. She liked
him, but not *that way*.

He touched her arm. Just a light touch, but it
seemed to burn all the way to her gut.

"Thanks," he said sincerely. "Why didn't I come
talk to you earlier?"

"You didn't come talk to me now. I came to you."

He flashed her a smile. A sweet sexy smile that made her knees weak.

"Right as always," he told her. "Come on. I'll buy you a glass of wine."

She automatically followed him into his big, open kitchen. He pulled a bottle of merlot from the built-in wine cellar and walked to the drawer that held the opener. She collected glasses. Because they'd done this a thousand times before, they had a ritual. A ritual she liked.

Only tonight she wanted something different. She wanted him to pull her close and kiss her and… Well, she wasn't exactly sure what they would do next, but she wasn't feeling that picky. As long as it was Jack, she was happy.

For the second time in as many minutes, she was mentally backtracking. No, she told herself firmly. They weren't involved. They never had been. She'd learned that lesson early and she'd learned it well. Jack was heartache. Jack wanted the most beautiful woman in the room…for fifteen minutes. And then he was done. He wanted sex and easy conversation—he didn't want to get involved. And she…she didn't know what she wanted but it wasn't that. Was it?

She took the glass of wine he offered and followed him into the big open living room. When they watched movies they went downstairs to the media room. Because Jack had, if not the biggest house in town, then one that was certainly close. Five or six bedrooms, a fully finished basement, a three-car garage. He had space and gadgets and lots of shiny surfaces. But sometimes she wondered if he ever got lonely in his big house.

His place in L.A. had been similar. Maybe that explained all the fast-food women he favored. He got to pretend he was a part of something, even for a few hours, and then didn't have any relationship messiness.

There was a large curved sofa facing a massive fireplace. Paintings hung on the walls. Real paintings of beaches and trees. Not quasi–pop art representations of him playing football.

She spotted a small oil painting by the antique writing desk in the corner.

"Is that new?" she asked. She put down her glass of wine and walked to study it.

The colors were all shades of the ocean and forest. There was a rough sea and an island beyond. She could barely make out the tiny sign by the boats. "Blackberry Island Marina."

"When did you get this?" she asked, turning to face him.

He set his wine next to hers and grinned. "You don't know everything about me."

"I usually do, but this is unexpected." Her smile widened. "You have a secret life."

"I wish. A little privacy in this town would be nice, but I'm not holding my breath."

She returned to stand next to him. "What would you want to keep private? It's nice that we know everything about each other."

"It's a guy thing."

She rolled her eyes. "A convenient fallback statement that has no basis in reality. You're trying to distract me and it's not going to work."

"Larissa, if I wanted to distract you, there are better ways."

He was being fun. Or playful. She knew that, because she knew Jack. But when he made that statement, in a firm voice that was both teasing and slightly sexy, she could only think of one thing.

Her muscles tensed even as her gaze involuntarily settled on his mouth. Breathing was tough and the only thought she could hold on to was an intense desire to have him kiss her. Not on the cheek or the forehead, like he usually did. She wanted him to kiss her on the mouth. Like he meant it.

Jack's startled expression quickly changed to something she couldn't read. He took a step back and held up his arms, as if warding her off. But in the next movement, he grabbed her, hauled her against him, then pressed his mouth to hers.

The contact was unexpected and exactly what she wanted. She went willingly into his embrace. Her hands settled on his broad shoulders as her thighs nestled against his. But the best part was how he kissed her.

Gently, at first. Light, barely touching, then more firmly. His mouth lingered. Her eyes sank closed as she melted against him. Yes, he was definitely lingering, she thought. Lingering and moving back and forth. There was a tenderness, but also a hint of something else. Something more.

Heat began to bubble deep in her chest. It flowed in all directions, making her body warm and sensitive to every touch. His fingers stroked her back, holding her with just the right amount of pressure. Thinking became more difficult and the world reduced itself to this man and what he was doing to her.

His tongue brushed against her bottom lip. She sucked in her breath even as she parted for him. He slipped inside. The kiss deepened and then they were straining against each other. She moved her hands up and down his back, wanting more. Needing him to touch her everywhere. He responded in kind. One hand slipped to her rear while the other slipped around her waist and up her rib cage until it settled on her left breast. His fingers brushed against her tight nipple. Electricity shot through her and she jumped back.

They stared at each other, both breathing hard. Passion darkened his eyes. It made her tremble. She tried to speak, but honest to God, what was there to say? Larissa did the only thing that made sense. This time it was her turn to run.

CHAPTER FOUR

"I KISSED JACK."

Larissa supposed "Hi" or "Can I come in?" was a more conventional greeting, but the words just sort of spilled out. Bailey stared at her a second before motioning her into her small house.

"Wow," her friend said. "I'd been thinking I was going to have a quiet, if slightly boring, evening at home while Chloe is with one of her friends, and then you come along. Well done."

"I'm sorry," Larissa breathed. "Is this an okay time?"

"Of course. Like I said, Chloe's gone. And you are better than anything on TV. Let's go into the kitchen. I have some very cheap wine and I made brownies yesterday."

Another offer of wine, Larissa thought, determined to actually taste it this time.

She followed Bailey into her kitchen. The contrast between the open, modern new space at Jack's place and this tiny, aging but homey one couldn't have been greater. Here the counters were yellow and green tile—a holdout from the previous century. The cabinets had seen better days and there was barely room for a tiny table and chairs.

Yet the room felt cozy. There were dozens of brightly colored drawings held to the front of the refrigerator with magnets. A big, bright calendar dominated one wall. It showed lots of activities and dates with friends.

Larissa inhaled slowly and started to relax. Nothing too horrible had happened. Nothing that she couldn't recover from. Order and balance would be restored. And if they weren't, she would find another cause and lose herself in that.

Bailey unscrewed the top on the wine and poured them each a glass, then set out a plate of brownies. They sat across from each other at the tiny table. Bailey leaned forward and grinned.

"Okay, start at the beginning. How long have you and Jack been kissing?"

Larissa groaned and covered her face with her hands. "We haven't. Ever." She straightened and reached for her wine. "It just happened."

"When?"

"Like twenty minutes ago. We were talking and then we were kissing." At least she thought that was how it had happened. The memory was already blurring. At least the memory of the conversation—not the one of the kiss itself. That had been spectacular.

"It's all my mother's fault," she added.

"Telling Jack you were in love with him?" Bailey's voice was sympathetic. "Yeah, I heard about that. And I can sure see how that would change things. Even if it's not true, you're suddenly aware of everything happening with Jack. It's awkward." She reached for a brownie. "Unless you *are* in love with him."

Larissa grabbed a brownie for herself. "I'm not. I swear. I like Jack. He's a great guy. But like isn't love."

"He's very sexy. Is that the problem? It's not love, but something more...earthy?" Bailey smiled. "I'm trying to be subtle. It's not my greatest strength."

"I can see that." Larissa considered the question. "Do I want to have sex with Jack?"

"You did kiss him and sex is nice."

Larissa stared at her. "Wow. Do *you* want to have sex with Jack?"

Bailey had just taken a bite of her brownie. She shook her head as she chewed. When she swallowed, she said, "No, he's all yours. It's just sometimes having a warm body in the bed can be really great."

Larissa remembered that Bailey's husband had been killed in Afghanistan. While it had been over a year ago, she was sure the memories of the loss were still fresh.

"Is there someone else you want to sleep with?" she asked quietly.

"We're not here to talk about me," Bailey reminded her. "You're the one who showed up and announced the kiss. Speaking of which, how did you leave things with him?"

Larissa took a sip of her wine. She was going to need more than a glass to forget that particular memory. "I ran."

"As in…"

"I just took off. Yeah, not my finest hour. I didn't know what to say. We're not supposed to kiss. We're friends. I depend on him to be there for me."

"Doesn't kissing mean he's totally there?"

Despite everything, Larissa smiled. "Now you're making me feel better and I'm not sure that's allowed." The smile faded. "This is so crazy."

"Why?" Bailey asked. "You work in really close quarters with three hunky guys who run around naked."

The smile returned. "They don't run around naked."

"Practically. I've heard the stories of meetings in the steam room. Taryn talks about it. Plus, you give them massages. I think the real surprise is that it took so long for one of them to come to his senses and kiss you."

"Why do you say it like that?"

Bailey sighed dramatically. "Have you seen yourself? You're this tall, leggy blonde with big blue eyes and a tiny butt. It's discouraging for the rest of us."

The description was so at odds with how Larissa viewed herself that she wanted to turn and see if there was someone standing behind her.

"I'm boring and normal," Larissa pointed out. "I wear yoga pants all the time and never bother with makeup."

"Yoga pants that show off your perfection. I, on the other hand, am carrying around twenty-five extra pounds." She reached for another brownie. "Pounds I have accepted as a permanent part of my life."

Larissa looked at her friend. Bailey was a beautiful redhead with lush curves and a sexy twinkle in her green eyes. She would imagine most of the single men in town were trying to figure out how to get her attention.

"You're sweet, but I'm not all that," she said.

"Uh-huh. We could take a survey." Bailey tilted her head. "Unless you *are* secretly in love with Jack."

Larissa finished her glass of wine and reached for the bottle. "I'm so not and I swear, next time I see her, I'm going to kill my mother."

Bailey smiled. "Unlikely."

"I know." She sighed. "So what do I do about the kiss?"

Bailey considered the question. "What do you want to do about it?"

"Pretend it never happened."

"That sounds like a plan to me."

WHILE KENNY HANDLED company-wide staff meetings, Taryn was firmly in charge of partner meetings. Both of which happened far too often for Jack's peace of mind. Did they really all need to know what the other was doing? Apparently so, which was why he found himself sitting in Taryn's office, listening to her go on about the status of various client projects.

Normally he found this kind of thing interesting, but not today. Not when he was wrestling with the fact that he and Larissa had kissed. What the hell?

He wasn't even sure how it had happened. One second they'd been joking and talking like always and the next she'd looked at him with an expression he'd never seen before. Okay, he'd seen it before, but not from her. And not like that.

She'd wanted him. That had been clear. And being wanted by Larissa had been irresistible. Of course, he'd been dealing with his own crap about the erection, so maybe she'd seen something in him that had triggered her feelings and that had led to the kiss.

He tried to tell himself it was just a kiss; only, could it be just that where Larissa was concerned? As far as he knew, she was careful about who she kissed. Which meant what?

Crap. It was all crap. And if his mind kept running in circles like some damned hamster on a wheel, he was probably going to turn into a woman.

"Jack," Taryn said, her voice cool. "Do you mind joining us for the meeting today?"

He looked up, startled. "What?"

His business partner glared at him. "You're somewhere else. Do you care to share with the rest of the class? There's obviously a problem."

They all knew? How was that possible?

Kenny sniggered. "Jack got a boner during his massage yesterday. It freaked him out."

Jack nearly corrected him by saying the real problem was the kiss, but stopped himself in time.

Taryn rolled her eyes. "Seriously? That's what has you distracted? It can't be the first time it's happened."

"Not in life," Jack said stiffly. "You would know that personally."

She drew in a breath, obviously trying to be patient. "Yes, I'm aware that sexually, you're a functioning male. If only it were true in the rest of your world. I was saying I'm surprised it hasn't happened before during a massage."

"I don't get a boner when I get a massage," Sam said.

Taryn barely spared him a glance. "No one here is shocked by that."

"Hey, what does that mean?"

Taryn's grip on her papers tightened. She looked at Sam. "That you have extraordinary powers of control, Sam."

"Oh. Okay. I accept that."

"It happens to me all the time," Kenny admitted cheerfully. "I'm naked. She's touching me. It's nice."

"And the road from nice to boner is less than three seconds?" Taryn asked.

Kenny grinned unapologetically. "Sue me."

Taryn turned to Jack. "Did you talk to Larissa about it?"

"Yes. We're fine. Let's change the subject."

"Fine by me." She sighed. "I find you all desperately annoying. You know that, right?"

Sam grinned. "It's what keeps us going."

PATIENCE GARRETT HURRIED toward Larissa. The other woman was obviously excited and grabbed both of Larissa's hands when they met on the sidewalk.

"There's been a sighting," Patience announced.

"Of a yeti?"

"What? No. Of course not. Oh, look. There's Isabel." Patience waved, as if to hurry her friend.

About fifteen minutes ago Patience had called Larissa and told her to meet her outside of Jo's Bar immediately. Apparently others had also received a call.

Isabel practically ran up the street. "Is it true?" she asked when she reached them. "There's been a sighting?"

"Of what?" Larissa demanded. "What are you talking about?"

Patience still had hold of her hands. She squeezed them and practically danced with excitement. "Zane Nicholson."

Larissa wasn't one to follow the gossip magazines. From knowing the guys, she understood everything the publications got wrong. But she thought she had at least a working knowledge of most major celebrities.

"I don't know who that is," she admitted.

Isabel pressed a hand to her chest. "Zane Nicholson. Absolutely the sexiest guy in high school. I mean seriously sexy."

Patience released Larissa's hands and nodded. "He was voted 'the guy every girl most wanted to sleep with' four years straight. And the last vote was *after* he'd already graduated."

"You really had that category in your yearbook?"

Isabel grinned. "Of course not. It was a private poll. But still, he totally won." She sighed. "Those eyes. That walk."

"That smile."

Isabel nodded. "Rarely seen and all the more to be treasured. How do I look?"

"Married," Larissa murmured. "You look married."

Isabel brushed off the comment. "I'm not going to sleep with him *now*. I'm just saying, back then, he was totally all that." She turned to Patience. "He's really in Jo's?"

"That's the rumor."

"Then let's go."

Larissa walked with them, not sure if she was being treated to a rare event only locals could appreciate or simply the victim of wrong place, wrong time. So some guy had come into town. Big whoop.

They crossed the street and walked up to the bar.

"My heart is pounding," Patience whispered. "I feel like I'm sixteen again. He danced with me once. At homecoming. I thought I was going to die."

"I remember and I was bitter," Isabel said cheerfully. "He smiled at me once in the hall, but I would rather have had a dance. Or a kiss. Or maybe have given him my virginity."

They giggled at that. Larissa shook her head. "I'm glad you called me," she said as she pulled open the door. "Someone needs to be here to keep you two out of trouble."

They stepped into the bar.

It looked as it always did, with flattering lighting and TVs turned to shopping and HGTV. The only thing out of place was the fact that there was a man at the bar. A tall man with broad shoulders and an air of confidence about him.

Larissa spent her day with three former NFL greats. She understood about power and egos and having a body that was a whole lot better than the average guy's. Most mortals couldn't measure up. This man would be able to hold his own.

Larissa watched Zane and wondered what it was about him that made him different. There were muscles, but it was more than that. Not his clothes, she thought, taking in the chambray shirt, worn jeans and cowboy boots. There was also a straw Stetson on the bar next to him.

Isabel and Patience inched toward the man in question. He turned and saw them, then gave a slow, sexy smile that had even Larissa's toes curling in her flats.

"Ladies."

"Hi, Zane," they said together.

"It's been a long time," Isabel said.

"It has." Patience nodded. "So, what brings you to town? Are you meeting with the mayor about the annexation?"

One dark eyebrow rose.

"Everyone knows about it," Isabel added. "It shouldn't change anything for you."

"So I heard."

His eyes were dark blue and his gaze steady. He wasn't looking at Larissa and a part of her was grateful to avoid all that male attention. She had enough stress in her life with Jack. She wasn't looking for a crush on a taciturn cowboy.

"How's Chase?" Patience asked.

Isabel turned to Larissa. "That's his younger brother," she said in a low voice.

"Good."

"And the, um, steers and everything?"

He nodded, as if to say it was all fine.

Patience and Isabel looked at each other, then back at him.

"We won't keep you," Patience said. "It was good to see you."

Zane nodded again.

The women turned around and left. Larissa trailed after them. When they reached the sidewalk, the two of them hung on to each other and jumped up and down.

"He's so amazing," Isabel said. "He smiled."

"I saw. We talked to him." Patience sighed. "That was so great."

Larissa shook her head. "You do realize he spoke maybe eight words, right?"

"That's not the point," Isabel told her. "I got to be sixteen again. Even if it was just for a minute. That was totally fun. I can't wait to tell Ford. He'll probably remember Zane and tease me unmercifully."

She sounded cheerful at the prospect.

Patience laughed. "Yes, I'm sure Justice will do the same." She hugged Larissa. "Thanks for joining us."

"You're welcome. And you're weird."

"We know."

Larissa waved at them and started back toward Score. She loved the town, but there were elements she would never understand. Like Patience's and Isabel's wild crush on cowboy Zane. But it was sure fun to be a part of it all.

LARISSA RUBBED HER hands across Taryn's back. Her movements were long and slow, designed to relax, rather than heal. Taryn was easy, she thought humorously. While her friend would think she was muscled, compared with the guys, she was a wimp. Not that Larissa was ever going to say that.

She liked working on Taryn. The movements were different and they talked about girl stuff, which was nice. There was no discussion of the latest score for whatever game was in season. And during play-offs, she didn't have to remind Taryn to stay relaxed during the massage. Because the guys always got riled up during play-offs.

Later she would see Jack, then Kenny. By the end of the day, her hands would be tired, but that came with the job.

Her fingers moved against smooth skin. The oil—a calming blend with a nice moisturizer—always left her skin silky.

She liked the differences between her clients. Sometimes she wondered what things would have been like if she'd actually gone into massage therapy instead of going to work for Score. She wondered if she would be at a spa of some kind or out on her own. While her room at the company was hers to do with as she liked, it wasn't exactly the same as having her own business. Of course, the upside of that was she also didn't have to worry about her budget. If she wanted a new table or different linens or new anything, she simply had to tell Sam and he ordered it for her.

But to be her own boss would be a different kind of challenge, she thought. First she would have to get certified. Easy enough. She had the education and the work experience. One day, she told herself. One day.

She pressed in around Taryn's scapula. The tension there surprised her.

"Why aren't you relaxing?" she asked.

Taryn sighed. "Sorry. I have stuff on my mind."

"Like?"

"The wedding."

"I thought Dellina would be handling the details. No one plans a party better."

"It's not the planning. It's the having." She raised her head and looked at Larissa. "I can't decide. On the one hand a big wedding would be nice, but doesn't a small one make more sense? It's not like Angel and I are twenty."

"All the more reason to do what you know you want. Taryn, seriously, you don't do anything small. It's not your style. Have a dream wedding that makes us all envious and wear a killer dress. We need that in our lives. You're our inspiration."

Taryn smiled, then lowered her head. "You're very good to me."

"I'm your friend. Be happy. March your skinny-assed self down a long aisle somewhere fabulous. Have a band and your Acorns as bridesmaids."

"They're Sprouts."

"What?"

"The girls. They were Acorns last year. They'll be Sprouts this year." The Acorns, or Sprouts, were part of a group called Future Warriors of the Máazib. It was Fool's Gold own version of scouting, based on the ancient tribe that had first settled in the area.

"Whatever. Have your Sprout bridesmaids and little tuxedo-decorated truffles as favors for the guests. Go for it—just because you can."

Taryn raised her head again. "How do you know about tuxedo decorated truffles?"

Larissa grinned. "I have two married sisters. I went through all this twice. When it comes to a wedding it's all about the dress and the details."

"I guess. It just feels weird."

"Because you never thought you'd fall madly in love."

Taryn put her head down. "Maybe. Mostly." She sighed. "Angel is so amazing."

"Yes, he is," Larissa said, thinking that he was also a tiny bit scary. Taryn was his equal. There weren't many women who could say that.

She moved down her friend's back. "Jack won't mind if you have a big wedding," she said quietly.

Taryn tensed, then relaxed. "I hate it when you read my mind."

"It doesn't take a lot of skill. You're family, which is sweet, but you were also married before. That makes it weird."

"A little," Taryn admitted. "You know how much I

love him, just not that way. I never did." She paused. "He was good to me. I was able to trust him and I don't trust easily. Our wedding was like our marriage. Very quick and purpose driven."

Larissa knew that Taryn had gotten unexpectedly pregnant. Jack being Jack had insisted they marry.

"Would you have stayed with him?" she asked. "If you hadn't lost the baby?"

"I have no idea. Probably not. One of us would have gotten restless. I was still in shock about being pregnant and then married. I hadn't figured any of it out. Before I could, the baby was gone."

"That must have been hard," Larissa said, thinking she would be crushed. No matter how her mother made her crazy, the other woman was right about one thing. Larissa did want to get married and have kids. The problem was she couldn't see a way to get from where she was to there.

"It was," Taryn murmured. "I felt so guilty for getting pregnant in the first place. Then to lose the baby.... I filed for divorce the same day."

Larissa knew the rest of the story. Taryn had been a junior PR person for the L.A. Stallions. When management found out that their star quarterback was getting a divorce, they did everything they could to make the situation easier. That meant firing Taryn so she wasn't around to make Jack uncomfortable. Jack had protested. The last thing he'd wanted was for Taryn to lose her job. But the team had stood firm.

Not knowing how else to help, Jack had given Taryn the money to start her own firm. He'd been a silent partner and had thrown plenty of business her way. She'd thrived and had reached the point where she was going to buy him out when Kenny had taken that last hit. Jack had decided it was a good time to retire, as had Sam. Suddenly Jack and his friends had lots of free time on their hands. Then Jack had remembered he was half owner of a PR firm. They'd joined Score and the rest was history.

"I would love to have been a fly on the wall when Jack came to tell you he and Kenny and Sam were joining Score," she said.

Taryn groaned. "There was a lot of swearing. I felt invaded and manipulated. I was not happy."

"Still, it worked out."

"It did. But you can't tell Jack."

Larissa chuckled. "I think he already knows."

She wondered how things would have been different if there *had* been a baby. Imagining that made her chest tight, which was strange. Jack would be a good dad, she thought wistfully. Despite the fact that he pretended not to care, she knew things touched him deeply. His goal was to keep the world at bay and he mostly succeeded.

He'd lost so much already. His brother. After his brother's death, his parents had gone away. Both physically and emotionally. Then his child with Taryn. She understood why he protected himself. She enabled that, she knew. Her causes became his causes. He could be a part of things without ever truly being touched by the circumstances.

They were a team. Maybe one that could do with

a little therapy, but a team all the same. She counted on that. Needed it. As far as she was concerned, nothing was going to get in the way of their connection. Not her mother's crazy statements or a kiss she still couldn't quite explain.

CHAPTER FIVE

JACK HOVERED IN the hallway. Taryn's massage had ended ten minutes ago and now it was his turn. He liked his turn. He liked knowing that in ninety minutes, his shoulder wouldn't hurt and that he would sleep better that night because of it. He liked that he could completely relax because Larissa knew what she was doing and she always took care of him.

Except relaxing today seemed impossible. He and Larissa hadn't spoken since that kiss. If he didn't know better, he would say they'd been avoiding each other. Which meant they were going to have to talk now and he didn't want to. Talking about kissing would remind him of the act, and going down that road was dangerous. Not to mention humiliating.

He was determined to keep things under control, so to speak. Which meant vigilance. He couldn't allow his mind to wander. He had to stay focused on the pain. On staying ahead of his body. Because if he wasn't careful, he would start to think about her hands on his body. Or worse, that damned kiss. And they all knew what would happen then.

The door opened and Taryn stepped out. She

smiled at him. "Larissa's on her A game today, big guy. Enjoy."

He nodded and waited for her to walk past him. Then he started toward the half-open door, only to stop. He was naked, he thought suddenly. Buck-naked, except for the robe he would take off as soon as he got into the room. Naked and alone with a beautiful woman. Under what circumstances was that a good idea?

He swore under his breath. Why hadn't they hired some guy to do the massages? It would have made all their lives easier, especially his. But it was too late now. Everyone liked Larissa and there was no way he wanted to replace her. It was just, dammit all to hell, why couldn't he shut off his brain?

He walked purposefully toward the door and flung it open. Larissa looked up and smiled at him.

"You are not my last massage of the day," she said. "A couple of days ago I was trying out some techniques on Dyna and she loved them. Now I get feline requests in the evening. I give her a kitty massage, then brush her. It's becoming a ritual."

Jack nodded because he couldn't seem to speak. Had the massage table always looked so suggestive—with the top sheet pulled back? And what was up with the soft, sexy music? He glanced around the room, half looking for an escape, then told himself to suck it up. As long as he stayed focused, everything would be fine.

She looked at him, then away. Her shoulders rose and fell with a sigh. "It doesn't mean anything. It just happened. I'm going to ignore it and I think you should, too."

At first he thought she meant his erection. While ignoring it made the most sense, a part of him felt a little snubbed. Only then he realized she was talking about the kiss.

The one that had rocked his world and left him hard for the rest of the night. Kissing Larissa had been an impulse—one he couldn't regret. Not that he would repeat it. Because that led to yet another dangerous place.

"You're right," he said. "Ignoring it would be best."

"Good. Then let's get on with it."

She politely turned her back, as she always did. He shrugged out of his robe and hung it on the back of the door, stepped out of his shower shoes, then walked to the table. He stared at it for a second.

"I want to start on my back," he said.

"Sure."

He figured he would have a better shot at staying in control during the first half of the massage, when he wasn't so relaxed.

"I want you to really dig in on my shoulder."

"Is it bothering you more than usual?"

"Yes," he lied, hoping the pain she inflicted would help.

He got on the table, faceup, and draped the sheet over himself. Larissa moved next to him. She already had the moist pack out of the hot water. She draped it across his shoulder, then tucked it under. The warmth immediately went to work. He began to relax.

"Should I leave the sheet on or put on a towel?" she asked.

Because she always draped a towel across his groin, he thought. "The towel is fine."

She crossed to the cabinet and pulled out a towel. He closed his eyes and thought about the last offensive play of the regular season game during the 2010 season. The Stallions had been on the twenty yard line with fifteen seconds left. They'd been down by three and—

She pulled off the sheet. Truly pulled it so that yards and yards of warm, soft linen rode against his penis. It was like silk, he thought, enjoying the sensation. Not as good as Larissa touching him, but still nice. What would make it better was if she was pulling it away to crawl in next to him. Then they would—

He swore silently and opened his eyes. Larissa draped the towel across him, then turned away. She pumped oil onto her hands, as if she hadn't felt anything. Which she hadn't, he reminded himself. He was the only idiot in the room.

He forced his brain back to the game, reliving the entire play. He'd thrown a perfect pass to Kenny who had caught it, scoring the winning points. As he remembered the elation of the moment, Larissa slid her hands across his chest.

She'd done it a thousand times before, to stay connected as she moved from one side to the other. It was normal and expected and not in the least bit sexy. The only problem was the light touch was just enough to get his blood pumping a little too fast.

No way, he thought, grinding his teeth together. He would *not* be controlled by his dick. He was a bigger man than that. Only thinking the word *bigger* wasn't his smartest idea.

Sports, he thought frantically, as his blood heated and the familiar growing ache began. Ah, a game they'd lost. Right. Against Dallas. He'd been intercepted in the third quarter and it had all gone to shit after that. He relived the play and the subsequent disaster. It seemed to be enough to cool himself down. He breathed a little easier.

She massaged both arms. She would do his right shoulder before he turned over, so it made sense that her next move was his legs. She walked around the table and put her hands on his left thigh. As her thumbs dug in, her fingers slid along his skin and by the time she got to his knee, he was hard as steel. He had to give Larissa points. She never faltered in her work. Even though his dick formed a good-size tent in the towel. Heat burned in him—half from arousal, half from humiliation.

"I'm ignoring it," he said at last.

"Me, too."

He couldn't tell for sure, but it seemed like her voice was a little strangled. Humor or mortification? He wasn't sure he wanted to know which.

She continued to work her way down his leg before circling the table and starting on his other leg. She half turned to reach the oil. As she moved, the towel got caught or something because he suddenly felt it sliding off. He opened his eyes and started to sit up. Instinctively he reached for it, just as she did the same. He grabbed and she stretched and their hands met, right on his erect penis, her hand trapped beneath his, his long, hard shaft below that.

For the first time ever, Jack got the real appeal of a "happy ending." In that split second, all he could think was how much he wanted her to touch him there. With her hands or her mouth—he didn't much care which. As long as they stopped before he came so he could please her as much and then they would finish the whole thing with some old-fashioned intercourse.

Which was not to be, he thought, instantly releasing her hand and half expecting her to jump back and shriek. She didn't jump or yell, instead she studied him.

"If you want to go take care of that, I can wait," she said.

It took a second for the meaning of her words to sink in and when they did, he deflated like a popped balloon.

"Excuse me?"

She shrugged. "It would solve the problem."

She expected him to go masturbate? Like some kid? "No," he said firmly, gathering the towel and his dignity as best he could and sliding off the table. "No."

He crossed to his robe and pulled it on. Only then

did he let the towel drop to the floor. He slid into his shoes and stalked out of the massage room.

It was only when he was back in the relative safety of the locker room that he realized she probably thought he'd retreated to do just what she'd suggested. And there didn't seem to be a way to tell her otherwise.

LARISSA FINISHED CLEANING up her massage room, then turned off the lights and walked toward her office. Jack's inexplicable behavior still had her shaking her head. She didn't like that he was making a habit of running out on her. Plus, she hadn't finished her massage, so she knew he would be in pain. Her job was to prevent that. They had a really big problem—all penis puns aside—and she didn't know how to fix it.

Yes, the whole erection thing had been a bit awkward. Personally, she'd found it difficult to think about anything else and she would guess he'd had the same problem. While she wanted to take credit for his aroused state, she had a feeling it was a lot more about circumstances than any allure on her part. She also knew exactly who was to blame.

She walked into her small office only to find her cell phone ringing. A single glance at the screen warned her the caller was the person who had started all this mess.

"Hi, Mom," she said when she answered.

"Larissa, dear, I'm checking in. How are things?"

Complicated. Embarrassing. Confusing. There were so many words, she thought, not sure if the situation was comical or tragic. Probably a little of both, she thought.

"Things are good," she said, taking the easy way out. "How about with you?"

"The usual. Your sister is finally admitting she's pregnant."

"The baby's due in a couple of months."

"You know that and I know that, but she's been avoiding the truth. Your stepfather and I are going over this weekend to help with the nursery. A little paint, some new bedding and they'll be ready."

Larissa settled in her chair. "I'm sure they appreciate your help."

"I'm sure they do. How are things with Jack?"

Larissa caught her breath. "That was subtle."

"I wasn't trying to be. He told you I talked to him."

"Yes, and what you said."

"I'm not wrong."

Larissa drew in a deep breath and told herself to stay calm. "Mom, I'm not in love with Jack."

"Really? When was the last time you went on a date?"

"I haven't met any single guys here, yet. I've only been in town a few weeks." It was more like months, but why say that. "I've made lots of girlfriends and that's more important right now. I want a support network."

"Why? You have a loving family, but fine. Have your girlfriends."

"Gee, thanks."

"Oh, Larissa, I'm not trying to be difficult."

"Maybe not, but you embarrassed me, Mom. You shouldn't have said what you did to Jack. He's my boss."

There was a pause. "All right. You might be right about that, but I only did it for your own good."

"Trying to get me fired so I can move back to L.A.? How does that help me?"

"You need more than your feelings for Jack and your causes. You're so busy trying to save the world, you never have any time for yourself. Jack exacerbates the problem. You're so close that you're getting most of your emotional needs met, but you're not actually in a relationship. It's a dangerous situation. You're not thinking about your future. Don't you want to get married and have children?"

Talk about blunt, Larissa thought, telling herself that her mother was wrong about all of it. She had to be. "Eventually. What I don't want is to do it on your timetable."

"I know, honey, but I'm terrified you're making choices for the wrong reasons. That you're hiding behind your so-called good works. Yes, saving animals is important, but so is saving yourself. You don't have to say anything, just promise me you'll think about it."

"Only if you promise to never pull anything like that again."

"I promise."

"Me, too."

"Good. Now let me know when you plan to come for a visit. Your stepfather recently hired a couple of very nice, single accountants in his office. I think you'd like them both very much."

And the conversation was going to end the way it started, Larissa thought, not sure if she should laugh or scream.

"I'll talk to you soon, Mom."

"All right. I love you."

"I love you, too. Bye."

JACK WALKED TO the break room. He needed coffee. Actually what he needed was a drink, but it was too early in the day. He had plenty of vices without going down that particular path. But even without drinking, he was a mess. He couldn't focus and he knew the cause. But what was he supposed to say to make things right?

He poured himself a large cup of coffee then rummaged around in the cabinet. There were plenty of cookies and chips, along with protein bars and other healthy alternatives. But he wasn't hungry.

"Hey," Sam said as he walked into the break room. "What's going on?"

"Not much," Jack said with a silent wince.

For a second he thought about asking Sam to tell Larissa that he didn't masturbate, but he stopped himself. Seriously, how was that going to work? First, he could never have that conversation with anyone and second, Sam would never pass the news on to Larissa. Even worse, Jack would hear about it for the rest of his life. No, better to suffer in silence.

"Taryn has some campaign ideas she wants feedback on," Sam told him. "Stop by her office when you get a chance."

"Sure thing," Jack said.

He went to see Taryn and faked his way through a conversation on which colors popped more on a new rum campaign, then wandered back to his own desk. He was both hoping to see and dreading running in to Larissa. They had to get their problem worked out. Of course, that would first require him knowing what the problem was and *then* fixing it.

By four he was ready to be done for the day. He'd accomplished little and there didn't seem to be much hope for improvement. He was going to go home, have some quality time with a merlot and a few high-light reels, then come up with a plan to fix things with Larissa. He had plenty of women he could call. Maybe a wild weekend with one of them would cure what ailed him.

He turned to shut down his computer just as Larissa walked into his office. Her shoulders were slumped and tears filled her eyes. He was instantly on his feet.

"What?" he asked, circling his desk toward her.

She drew in a shuddering breath. "Mary died. Early this morning. I just got the call."

He held out his arms even as he wondered who Mary was. With Larissa there was an equal chance that Mary was a kid or an orangutan.

"Mary had the liver transplant last year," she said, shaking slightly as she stepped into his embrace. "I told you she wasn't doing well and that we were concerned."

He wrapped his arms around her and stroked her back. While the stupid side of him noticed how well they fit together and the way her body pressed against every inch of his, the more mature areas of his brain understood this was a moment of grief and allowed him to act appropriately.

"You just sent them that book," he said, remembering their recent conversation about the girl. "I'm sorry she died. Her family must be devastated."

"They are. We were all so hopeful."

"Because a transplant usually works." Although not always. Because sometimes the body didn't want to be saved. That was his theory, anyway. Whatever the spirit might wish, there were other forces at work. He knew that pain personally.

He tugged on the end of her ponytail until she looked up at him. "You know you're not to blame, right?"

Her cheeks were damp and slightly flushed. She sniffed once, then nodded. "I know."

"I'm not convinced."

She swallowed. "There's nothing I could have done to save her. I'm just sad she's gone. She was a great kid." She rested her head on his shoulder and began to cry again.

He held on to her. For as long as she cried, he wouldn't let go. He wasn't sure how this had started, but now it simply was. When they lost one, and with transplants the possibility was always there, Larissa came to him and he was there for her. No matter what.

He remembered getting a call while he'd been in Hawaii with a former Victoria's Secret model. Eight hours later, he'd landed at LAX and gone directly to Larissa's house. He'd stayed with her until she'd finally fallen asleep, and in the morning he'd helped her find the right way to celebrate the child's life.

"Think about what you want to do in Mary's name," he said softly. "Maybe American Girl dolls for every patient in her hospital."

Larissa looked at him. "I don't think the boys would appreciate that."

"You're right. We could get them something else."

"Maybe," she murmured. "Let me think about it."

He kissed her forehead, then grabbed his car keys. "Come on. I'm buying you dinner."

"I'm not hungry."

"I know, but you will be."

LARISSA GLANCED AROUND the restaurant. Margaritaville had been pretty quiet when they'd arrived, but it was filling up now. There were plenty of locals, but also lots of tourists, which was good for the economy.

Her initial grief had passed. It was always like this, she thought sadly. When one of the children they helped died. She hated the loss and the pain, and knew that whatever she was feeling, the families were suffering so much more.

Jack pushed the chips toward her. He'd ordered

tableside guacamole and chips to start, telling their server they would get to food later.

"If you don't eat something, you're going to feel crappy in the morning," he pointed out.

"I know." She reached for a chip. "It's the margaritas. They're really strong."

"Such a girl drink."

She glanced at his glass. "Because beer is so masculine?"

"You know it."

"Monks invented champagne."

He grinned. "We're not drinking champagne."

She smiled back at him, only to remember what had happened. The smile faded.

"Mary was a sweet girl. So happy." Larissa had only met her once, but she'd emailed a lot with her mother. "The transplant gave her an extra year. That's something, right?"

"Yes, and it gave her hope. She and family were allowed to imagine a better future. You do good work, Larissa. You have to remember that."

"You're the one who has the money to give them," she pointed out.

"Yeah, but you're the one with the open heart. Don't discount that. Heart trumps just about everything."

Larissa wished that were true. She leaned back in the booth and chewed on her chip. Food probably was a good idea, she thought. After all, this was her second margarita.

"I talked to my mother today," she said when she'd swallowed. "She still wants me to come back to L.A."

Jack's expression was carefully neutral. "What did you tell her?"

"I said she'd been wrong to tell you what she did." She wrinkled her nose. "She promised to never do that again."

"Do you believe her?"

"Yes. But in return I had to promise to think about what she said." She turned to him. "Do I hide behind my causes?"

Jack cleared his throat. "Why no, Larissa. I'm shocked you'd ask."

She managed another small smile. "Very funny. I'm being serious."

"I am, too. You've always had your causes. They're a part of who you are."

Maybe, but there was a difference if she was truly using various charities to avoid her personal life. Something to consider when she wasn't feeling the buzz that only tequila could bring.

He put his hand over hers. "You make me a better person and it's not wrong to want to save the world."

"Thank you. Now enough about me. Please distract me with an unexpected football fact."

He gave her a quick smile. "You know that committee Mayor Marsha wants me on? To find Cal U Fool's Gold a new football coach?"

"Uh-huh."

"They don't have a team."

"What? They don't play football?"

"Not officially. They're in the Western Athletic Conference, which is a nonfootball conference."

"I've never heard of anything like that."

The smile returned. "There are other sports."

"I find that so hard to believe. So why did she want you to find them a football coach?"

"From the research I've done, they're thinking of building a team."

"Can they do that?"

"I guess. You start with a group of kids and grow from there. It'll take a while and it's a big commitment for the university. They're going to have to sink a lot of money into the program."

"That's probably more than you'd planned to take on."

"A circumstance I deal with frequently." He leaned toward her. "Want to hear what I think about the Stallions' chances on opening day?"

"There's nothing I would like more."

JACK DROVE THROUGH the quiet streets of Fool's Gold. The days were noticeably shorter than they had been just a few weeks before. Summer was nearly over and fall would be here soon. He couldn't begin to imagine what the festival-loving town would be like through the holidays, but he was looking forward to finding out.

Larissa sat next to him. Despite her claims of not being hungry, she'd polished off the entire taco platter without help and now looked out the passenger's window. She was quiet—no doubt thinking about Mary. But at least she wasn't crying. He hated to see her cry.

"Pull over!"

He hit the brakes. "What?"

She pointed to the side of the road. "Pull over."

He'd barely reached the curb when she jumped out of the car and bolted across the street and into the park. Jack leaned back in his seat and sighed. There was no point in speculating, he reminded himself. Larissa had obviously seen some kind of creature in need of aid. As it could be anything from an endangered leaf to a three-legged moose in need of antler care, he would simply wait it out. When the time came, he would figure out how to lessen the impact on his life.

She was back in less than five minutes, dragging a lanky dark-haired teenaged boy behind her. The kid was tall and skinny, with a medium-dark complexion and a wary expression.

Jack sighed heavily and got out of his Mercedes. He could feel the beginnings of a headache starting around his temples.

"Larissa," he began, his voice warning.

She cut him off with a cheerful smile. "Jack, this is Percy."

Jack nodded at the kid.

"Percy's from Los Angeles and he turned eighteen a couple of weeks ago. He spent the summer at End Zone for Kids. That's Raoul Moreno's summer camp."

"I know what it is," he told her. He turned to the teen. "You miss the bus, son?"

Percy shook his head.

Larissa put her hand on Jack's chest. "He aged out of foster care, Jack. Percy doesn't have any family and he didn't finish high school. He has nowhere to go, so he made his way back here. He thought Fool's Gold would be a good place to spend the winter."

Obviously the kid had never taken geography, Jack thought grimly. Winters in L.A. barely dipped into the fifties. Fool's Gold got snow. This was not a well-conceived plan. But he wasn't even surprised.

"You were gone three minutes," he said to Larissa. "How did you get all that information?"

She smiled up at him. "I have my ways." Her blue eyes locked on his. "Jack," she said slowly.

Then he got it. Right. Because the kid was eighteen, there was no social worker to call. Also no family. And he couldn't go home with Larissa. Her tiny apartment barely had room for her cat.

"I'm sure we can get him a hotel room."

Her gaze stayed on his face.

"Or not," he grumbled, bowing to the inevitable. He looked past her to the teen. "Let's go to my house and we can all chat."

Percy's expression tightened. "Why would you do that, man? You don't know me. What if I murder you or rob your house?"

"Are you going to?"

"No, but you have to ask about that kind of thing. You have to be careful."

A handful of sentences that told Jack a lot about the kid. One of these days Larissa was going to bring home a serial killer, but apparently not today.

"Right back at you," he said.

Percy frowned. "What are you talking about?"

"I'm not going to murder you, either."

Percy's mouth curled. Jack had a feeling it was in humor rather than appreciation for the assurance. No doubt the teen figured no middle-aged guy from a place like Fool's Gold was a threat. He was probably right about that.

Jack glanced from Larissa to the kid. She didn't usually take on people projects, he thought. But Mary had died today. He would guess she needed to help Percy as a way to heal. Jack knew he wasn't going to get in the way of that.

"Let's go," he said, getting back in the car.

Larissa and Percy spoke for a couple of seconds before she climbed in next to him and Percy settled in the backseat.

The trip to his house took less than five minutes. Jack parked in the driveway. Percy let out a low whistle.

"You live here?"

"Uh-huh."

"Are you rich?"

"Not in privacy," Jack muttered as he climbed out of the car.

Larissa was already guiding the teen up to the front door.

"Jack has a guest room upstairs," she was saying. "It's very comfortable. Have you eaten today?"

Jack followed them, his gaze involuntarily taking in the kid's too-lean frame. Sure, baggy jeans could be a fashion statement, but he suspected Percy had earned his low-riding pants the old-fashioned way.

"I, ah, sure," Percy mumbled. "I'm not hungry."

"Well, I am. Come on. Let's go raid the refrigerator."

Jack left them to forage through his leftovers. He was pretty sure there was a frozen pizza or two in the freezer, but Larissa would already know that. He made his way upstairs where he dropped his key fob and wallet on the wooden tray in his big closet.

He went to the opposite end of the hall and checked out the guest room. It looked clean enough. He had a weekly service that did things like change sheets, handle his laundry and keep food in the house. He walked into the attached bathroom and saw there were towels.

By the time he'd returned to his room and changed his clothes, the smell of pizza dough wafted upstairs. He headed for the kitchen.

Larissa and Percy sat at the eat-in bar by the main island in his kitchen. The teen had already polished off a banana and was munching his way through an apple. The timer showed less than two minutes on the pizza.

Jack walked to the refrigerator and pulled out a beer. He opened it and took a swallow, then leaned against the counter.

"Tell me about yourself," he said.

Percy stared at him before standing and squaring his shoulders. "Sure. What do you want to know? I don't have a record, if that's what you're asking. Not all black men have a record."

"Never thought they did."

"Jack," Larissa began.

Jack cut her off with a shake of his head. If Percy was going to be living in his house, they had to come to terms. An eighteen-year-old was a whole lot more complicated than butterflies.

He continued to study Percy, who stared back at him. Finally the teen shrugged.

"I never knew my dad. My mom was a waitress who cleaned houses on her days off." Percy's chin came up. "She was shot. You know—wrong place, wrong time? It was a drive-by shooting."

Jack didn't allow himself to react, even as Larissa touched Percy's arm.

"I'm sorry," she murmured.

"How old were you?" Jack asked.

The chin went up more. "Fifteen. That's when I went into foster care."

Hell of a thing to have happen, he thought. "You bounced around a lot?"

"Some. I got by."

"I told him he would be safe here," Larissa said. "That we would help find him a home and get him moving toward his bright future."

She spoke earnestly, he thought, watching the determination fill her blue eyes. She believed there was a "we" in all this. But Jack knew the truth. He would provide the means, but Larissa would be the heart and the drive of whatever mission was to be called Percy.

She would save Percy and then move on to another project, dragging them all along in her wake. She was unstoppable and endlessly optimistic. He supposed that was one of the reasons he couldn't resist her. Larissa still believed.

Jack turned back to the boy. "If you want to stay, you can."

Percy frowned. "Just like that?"

Jack smiled. "Yeah. Just like that."

CHAPTER SIX

JACK STEPPED OUT of his shower and reached for a towel. He'd slept well the previous night. No doubt the aftereffects of his good deed. His wallet and cell phone were where he'd left them, also a good sign that he hadn't been completely idiotic to let some teenager he didn't know spend the night in his house.

He dressed and made his way downstairs. Percy was already in the kitchen, eating cereal from a bowl. The two males stared at each other. Jack had a feeling that if they were elks or gazelles or something and in the wild, they'd be butting antlers. And if one of them got hurt, Larissa would show up and take him home.

He walked over to the Keurig and turned it on, then dropped in a pod, shoved a mug into place and waited for the magic to happen.

"You sleep okay?" he asked, knowing he was the grown-up in the room and therefore the most likely one to start the conversation.

"Mostly. It's real quiet here."

Jack wasn't sure if Percy meant in the town or the house, then decided it didn't matter.

The Keurig poured out the elixir of life. When the

mug was full, Jack carried it over to the table and sat across from Percy.

The kid was wearing the same clothes he had the previous night, although he'd obviously showered and shaved. There was a small cut on his chin. He thought about the backpack Percy had been carrying and held in yet another sigh.

"All right, let's start at the beginning," he said. "Where are you from?"

"Los Angeles. South Central."

Jack had lived in L.A. for years, and parts of South Central L.A. were not to be messed with. "Tell me about your mom."

Percy looked startled by the question. "Why?"

"Humor me."

"Okay. She got pregnant in high school. Her boyfriend ran off and her family kicked her out. I don't remember much about when I was little. We lived in a shelter mostly, but we got by." Percy's mouth tightened, as if he were holding in emotion. "She was real good to me. Always looking out for me and telling me not to get into trouble. When I was seven, we moved in with my grandma and things got better. Mom got a steady job and we stopped moving around so much. When my grandma died, we couldn't afford her nice apartment anymore. That's when we moved again and it was harder. My mom worked a lot and that meant I was on my own."

Percy stared at his empty cereal bowl. "I got jobs in the neighborhood, to help out, you know? But she made me promise to stay away from the gangs and if you're not tight with them, it's hard to find work. Then she was killed and I got into the system. I was bounced around every couple of months. Then I ended up here."

Percy looked at Jack. "She was a good person and she tried real hard. I didn't want to let her down."

"Sounds like you didn't," Jack said, thinking that the difference between making it and not was so narrow. How many other kids had suffered Percy's fate and made the easy choice to join a gang? He knew from a few of his former teammates that not only did they provide a sense of security, there was also belonging. A social structure. Of course, it came with a heavy price.

"You have ID? A social security card, stuff like that?"

"I have a social security card and a copy of my birth certificate," Percy said slowly. "Why?"

"You're going to need them in life. So tell me what you want, Percy. A good job? A college education?"

Percy frowned. "I don't understand, man. What are you asking?"

"That lady you met last night? Larissa? Well, think of that meeting as winning the lottery. Larissa is going to take care of you. So what do you want? Any dreams? Becoming a navy SEAL? Learning how to work on cars? Going to college and studying to be a doctor?"

Percy scowled. "If you want me to leave, just say so."

"Why would I want you to leave?"

"You're messing with me."

"I'm not. I'm saying you have an opportunity. You've spent your whole life making your mother proud of you. You resisted the easy road. Because joining a gang would have been easy, right?"

Percy nodded, even as he crossed his arms over his chest. "So?"

"So there aren't any gangs in Fool's Gold. Hell, I don't think there's any crime. You made a good choice coming here. Larissa likes to help people in need. Right now that's you. Let's start easy. How about a few classes at community college and a part-time job?"

Percy stared at him. "For real?"

"Yeah, for real."

The teen seemed to shrink in his seat. For one horrifying second, Jack thought he might cry. Then Percy swallowed and shook his head.

"I can't."

"Go to college?"

The teen stared at him. "I'm not a charity case. Anyway, I never graduated from high school." He darted a glance at Jack. "I'm not good with study-ing and stuff."

The last couple of words were barely audible and spoken in a tone that implied both humiliation and shame.

Jack finished his coffee and wished it were later in the day because getting drunk seemed like a fine idea right about now.

He drew in a deep breath. "Can you read?" he asked flatly.

Percy pressed his lips together. "Sort of."

For a second he thought longingly of the fighting dogs that Larissa had left in his house. Because with them, he'd been able to escape to a hotel.

"You have any other luggage stashed somewhere?" he asked.

Percy shook his head. "I have everything with me. I like to travel light. You know, in case I have to take off or something."

Of course he did. "Percy's an unusual name. Any reason your mom picked that?"

"Yeah." The teen gave a shadow of a smile. "It was the name of her favorite teacher in high school. The one who was helping her apply to college when she got pregnant. She said naming me Percy reminded her that there were possibilities. She wanted that for me. That's why she made me promise about the gangs."

Jack nodded. "Give me a second." He pulled out his cell phone and scrolled through his contacts. Seconds later, he was connected with Taryn.

"Hey," he said. "I need your help."

Taryn swore. "I knew it! When I saw Larissa a few minutes ago, she practically ran in the other direction. What has she done now?"

Jack looked at Percy, who was watching him. "I have a guest for a few days. Maybe longer. His name is Percy. He's eighteen and needs some new clothes. Is there a store in Fool's Gold where we can go?"

Sacramento was an option but not today. He had

to get Percy settled and in the afternoon he had his first committee meeting at Cal U Fool's Gold to help with the coaching search.

Taryn laughed. "Really? Haven't you ever seen that giant Target on Forest Highway, by the college?"

Jack probably had, but why would he remember? It wasn't as if he shopped regularly. "Great. I'll take him there and then bring him to work."

She stopped laughing. "No way. You're not dumping him on me."

For the first time that morning, Jack smiled. "Would I do that?"

She was still calling him names when he hung up.

Jack looked at the kid. "All right. We're going to Target and then to my office. We'll put you to work until we can figure out the next step." One of which was going to have to be assessing Percy's reading ability. Because until that was up to speed, he couldn't possibly get a GED.

Percy looked both hopeful and suspicious. "You're gonna help me?"

"Apparently."

"Because of Larissa?"

"Mostly."

"Okay, but I'll pay you back. My word is bond." He took his bowl to the sink. "You're not going to tell her I can't read, are you?"

Jack sighed. "No."

"Good. Because I don't want her thinking bad about me."

"Trust me," Jack said as he led the way to the front door. "That could never happen."

Two HOURS AND a few hundred dollars later, Jack drove Percy to the Score offices. The teen now owned a couple of pairs of jeans, several shirts and sweaters, shoes, toiletries, a cell phone and basic school supplies. Jack figured that wherever they were starting on Percy's education, he would need paper, a couple of notebooks and pens and pencils.

"So where do you work?" Percy asked, as he ran his hands up and down his new jeans.

"At a company called Score. It's a PR and marketing firm."

"What's that?"

"We promote companies. Get them publicity and advertising. We design campaigns, help get them sponsorships at different kinds of events."

"Do you like it?"

"Mostly. I work with my friend Kenny on getting new clients. There are four partners in the company. Sam, Taryn, Kenny and me."

Percy seemed to be digesting that information. "What about Larissa?"

"She's my assistant."

They pulled into the parking lot. Jack drove into one of the free spaces, then shut off the engine and turned to Percy. "You can leave your stuff in the car," he said. "We'll take it home after work. You'll fill out some paperwork to get on the books as an employee.

The job will be part-time while we figure out how to get going on your GED."

Percy studied him. "Why are you doing this, man? You don't know me."

"Maybe not now, but I will eventually. Look, Percy. You have to take a leap of faith on this one. No one's going to hurt you."

"Foster parents are usually nice. At first."

Jack would guess that was true. "You're saying you expect this to change?"

Percy nodded.

"Fair enough. If it gets bad, you don't have to stay. Until then, let's see where this all goes."

The teen nodded and got out of the car.

They walked in the main entrance of the building. Jack started down the hall. Halfway to Taryn's office, he realized he was alone and turned around.

Percy stood in the middle of the foyer, head back, staring up at the larger-than-life pictures of Jack, Kenny and Sam in uniform during various games. Each of them had an action shot, along with several posed pictures. There was also a photo of the four partners together, with Taryn looking totally in charge.

Percy slowly lowered his head. "That's you," he said, his voice disbelieving.

"That's me."

"You played football."

"Uh-huh. For the L.A. Stallions. I was the quarterback."

Percy looked between him and the pictures. "It's cool, I guess. I'm more into basketball."

Jack bit back a laugh. "Of course you are. Come on. I'll introduce you to the dragon lady. Don't let the high heels fool you. She could take both of us without even breaking a sweat."

JACK'S WORK WITH coaches had always come as a player. There were coaches he'd liked and those he'd hated, but he'd never had anything to do with hiring one before. He hadn't even been sure of the exact process. He knew there were interviews and that after a winning or losing season, coaches often moved on, but he'd never given it any thought beyond how it had affected him as a player.

Hiring a coach would be different. He would need to look at the process from the university's point of view. Do what was best for the organization. The switch in sides was going to take some doing, he thought as he drove out to the Cal U Fool's Gold campus.

The university sat on nearly a hundred acres just northeast of downtown. The buildings were a mix of old and new, as if the campus had grown over the years. It was still a few weeks before classes started, so there weren't any students around. Jack found parking in the visitors' lot and made his way to the main administration building.

The stadium and practice field were closer to the mountains. By late August the team should have already started their preseason games. If there was a team playing football. Something he was going to discuss with Mayor Marsha when next he saw her. Or perhaps not. He was tough on the field, but not known for his ability to take down old ladies.

The research he'd done on the athletic programs at Cal U Fool's Gold had told him that the university had an excellent baseball team, a surprising number of successful programs for women's sports, including golf, but that they'd ended their football team nearly a decade before. So why start now? Something he was going to find out.

He walked into the conference room and greeted the other people there. The president of the college was easy to spot. She was a woman in her late forties, well dressed and confident. The athletic director, who had the unfortunate first name of Tad, was about Jack's age, and way too cheerful. Introductions were made. A few more people came into the room, then they all took their seats around the large table.

"Thank you all for coming," Kristan Newham, the college president said. "We're here to discuss the feasibility of restarting the football program here at Cal U Fool's Gold. The students are interested, the regents are open to providing us with some of the funding, although we'd have to get the rest of it from alumni and outside donations. The questions I want us to explore are should we and what would it take?"

Tad shrugged. "There's no point in discussing what it would take if we're not interested in bothering in the first place."

Jack bristled. "And you're not interested?"

"It's going to be a lot of work. We'll have trouble getting players. Good ones, I mean. Sure, there's student interest, but students are fickle. Tomorrow there will be some rock band blowing through town and no one will show up for the game. It's expensive and time consuming and it also distracts from the other sports."

Jack studied Tad's lean build as he processed the heresy of not wanting a football team. "You didn't play team sports in college, did you?" he asked easily. "Let me guess. Golf?"

Tad flushed. "Tennis and it's a team sport."

"Competing individually. Or at best, in pairs."

"I played singles."

"Of course." Jack leaned back in his chair. "Sorry to interrupt."

Tad glared at him. "I don't think football is worth the trouble. We have a regional championship baseball team. Our basketball team is better every year. Two of our graduating seniors in women's volleyball have a shot at making the Olympic team. That's enough."

"It's good that the scientists working with antibiotics didn't have your 'it's enough' attitude when they discovered penicillin," Jack murmured.

President Newham glanced between the men before her gaze settled on Jack. "You want to make a case for a football team?" she asked.

"Sure. Football is America's game. People like it. It teaches discipline and teamwork. It teaches life." He paused, then smiled. "On a more practical side, college football brings in money. The Texas Longhorns football program was recently valued at $805 million dollars. That's just football. Superstar athletes bring in five or ten times what their scholarships are worth."

"In ten years maybe," Tad muttered.

"Another one of your long-term views. I'd love to see your five-year plan for the college," Jack murmured. "I had a coach once who used to say you're either part of the problem or you're part of the solution." He turned to President Newham. "Ma'am, it's not an easy decision to make. There will be costs and starting a team is a long-term proposition. People may argue that the money is better spent elsewhere. But even if you only end up with an average team, you'll be bringing in multiples of what you spend to get it up and running. Plus, a good football team is great advertising for the college. Who in America hasn't heard of UCLA?"

"That could be because of the medical center," Tad pointed out.

"Yeah, it could," Jack said easily. "Except every one of those people know they're the UCLA Bruins and the USC Trojans and the Notre Dame Fighting Irish. You don't learn that from a medical school." He paused. "Or a tennis team."

Tad started to rise from his chair. Jack was kind of hoping the man wouldn't have second thoughts because every now and then a fight seemed like a good idea. Of course, that belief only lasted until he landed the first blow—which always hurt like a son of a bitch.

"Am I going to have to separate you two?" the university president asked.

Jack grinned. "Probably a good idea."

She surprised him by smiling back. "All right, Mr. McGarry. Convince me you're right. Tell me all the reasons Cal U Fool's Gold *should* have a football team."

Jack nodded slowly. "Sure thing. How much time do you have?"

LARISSA WALKED INTO the project room. It was a big open office with long tables pushed together to form a square. There were huge dry-erase boards on two walls and corkboards on the other two. A screen could be pulled down for computer presentations. Low cabinets held every kind of office supply and craft material. Because the project room was where the magic happened. Mock-ups began here, as did the brainstorming sessions.

Percy sat at one of the long tables, stacks of magazines in front of him. He had one open and was carefully measuring a page with a ruler.

"Whatcha doing?" she asked as she approached.

He glanced up and smiled at her. "Hey, Larissa."

"Hey, yourself. I see Taryn already put you to work."

"She did." He pointed to the magazines. "There are client ads in each one. I'm making sure they're the right size and in the right part of the magazine."

He showed her the cover sheet for the ad approval form. It listed the size of the ad—full page, half page and so on—the name of the magazine, the issue number and the page number the ad should be on. At the top of each cover sheet was a small picture of the magazine itself, making the referencing easier.

"The pictures tell me which magazine to look for. Then this number is the page number and the size of the ad is right here. When I've checked it all, I put my initials in this box here." He pointed to the form.

He sounded proud of the work he was doing, she thought happily. "You like working here?"

"Yeah. It's real interesting. I've had jobs before, but not in a place like this. I'm usually sweeping up or cleaning the bathrooms. I worked for a moving company for a few months." He wrinkled his nose. "This is better." His smile returned. "Kenny came by a little bit ago and introduced himself. He's a big guy."

"He is."

"He's taking me to lunch. He said there's a Mexican restaurant with enough food that I won't be hungry for hours." His expression turned wistful. "That's a nice feeling, not to be hungry." He glanced at her, then away. "Not that I care about that kind of thing. But some people do."

Her heart cracked a little as she wondered how many times the teenager had gone to bed without anything to eat that day.

"You'll like Kenny. He's a great guy." She pulled out a chair and sat next to Percy. "I hope you'll think about what you want to do for your future," she said. "Maybe college."

Percy turned his attention to the magazine in front

of him. "Jack talked about that this morning. I need to get my GED first. He's, ah, gonna help me with that."

"Good."

"Are you two, like, engaged?"

Larissa jumped to her feet. "No. Of course not. What a silly question. Why would you ask that?" Before he could answer, she was heading for the door. "I'll check in with you later," she called over her shoulder.

Engaged? That would never happen. Jack didn't want a permanent relationship and she wasn't interested in one now, either. Certainly not with him. Jack was the kind of man who…

She walked down the hallway. Jack was nice enough, she reminded herself. Good-looking. Successful. He cared about people and she trusted him. But he was also into his bimbo of the week. His idea of an in-depth relationship was one that lasted two weeks. She would know. She bought the parting gifts he gave his lady friends.

Her and Jack? Ridiculous. They were friends. Good friends. Good friends who had kissed that one time, she thought with a sigh.

She wandered into Taryn's office only to see her friend jump in her chair.

"What?" Taryn demanded. "Why are you here?"

Larissa held up both hands in a gesture of surrender. "Why are you crabbier than usual?"

Taryn sighed. "Sorry. That was guilt."

Larissa looked at the computer. "Seriously? Are you on a porn site or something?"

Taryn turned the computer to show Larissa the display. "No, wedding gowns."

Larissa stared at a beautiful dress that was fitted to the waist, then flowed down in a cascade of fabric and lace and flowers. "If there's rain we can all take cover under the skirt."

Taryn's mouth twitched. "Shut up. You don't know anything about fashion."

"Which works out because you know enough for both of us. Do you like that?"

"Sort of. I worry it's too much for this damn town."

"You're too much and yet you love it here."

"I know. Life has quite the sense of humor." She leaned back in her chair. "Isabel is getting me some samples to try on. If I go with something couture, it's going to be months before it's ready."

Larissa sprawled in a seat on the visitor's side of the desk. "What about the designers Isabel already works with? You've said there are several you like. Ask them to design you a gown. If it's just a drawing, you're not committed or anything. And it would be faster than some famous designer."

Isabel had a clothing store and a bridal gown store in town. For a sleepy little tourist town, Fool's Gold had some great shopping.

Taryn's blue-violet eyes widened. "That's a brilliant idea."

"Please don't sound surprised. I can be intelligent."

"You always are. And that's great. I'll talk to Isabel and see what she thinks." Her eyes narrowed slightly. "Why are you here?"

"You mean your office, right? Because if we're going to talk about the metaphysics of life on earth, I need a cookie."

"Why are you in my office?" Taryn clarified.

"I'm bored. Jack's at a meeting and the guys are all doing different stuff. Want a massage?"

"I just had one."

Larissa shrugged. "See? I have no responsibilities."

"Speaking of taking charge and being left to handle the work, what's up with the kid?"

"His name is Percy."

Taryn waved away the information. "Your latest project?"

"Jack and I found him last night. He was homeless. He's just eighteen and he needs help."

"You found him?"

"Uh-huh."

"Why isn't the rescue cat enough?"

"Dyna's lovely. This is different. Besides, he's not living with me. He's with Jack."

"Of course he is. What are you going to do with him?"

"I don't know. Jack and I are working on that."

Taryn's expression turned knowing. "You're always going to try to save the world, aren't you? I can't figure out if you're truly that good or if you're simply distracting yourself."

"Ouch," Larissa said. "I have feelings and I care about people and creatures in trouble."

"Just a little bit more than the rest of us do," Taryn told her. "I think you're hiding."

Something Larissa didn't want to hear. It was too close to what her mother had mentioned to her. They meant it in different ways but the ultimate message was still the same.

"I'm fine," she insisted.

"Do I look convinced?" Taryn asked.

"Yes."

Taryn raised her eyebrows. "I worry about you. You're so busy taking care of everyone else. Who looks after you?"

Jack, Larissa thought, but instinctively knew that wasn't a good answer. Not in these circumstances. "I can take care of myself. I don't need saving."

Taryn shook her head. "Some days we all need saving. You should know that."

CHAPTER SEVEN

DYNA'S PLAINTIVE CRIES made Larissa rethink her plan. The sweet-faced Ragdoll cat was obviously unhappy with the evening's events.

"I think you'll like it when we get there," Larissa said as she grabbed the carrier, along with the big bag of takeout she'd picked up on the way over. "And Percy is nice. You'll enjoy him."

Dyna meowed again, making it clear she wasn't on board with the program. Larissa did her best to not feel guilty as she walked up the walkway to Jack's front door.

Jack opened it before she got there and stared at the carrier. "Dyna?" he asked, taking the food from her.

"I thought she'd like Percy. Pets are important in a family."

"Uh-huh. I don't have a litter box."

"Yes, you do. From when you had those kittens."

A couple of months ago, a litter of feral kittens had been in danger of dying when their mother had been killed by a car. They'd moved in with Jack until they'd been adopted.

"Right," he said. "I'd forgotten. I have no idea where it is."

"Not a problem."

Larissa made sure the front door was securely closed, then opened the carrier. Dyna stepped out with the dignity only an offended cat could muster.

"I keep making backward progress with her," she murmured.

"I'll tell her she's a fool not to adore you," Jack told her. "Come on. Let's eat."

Percy clattered down the stairs. He was all arms and legs, still growing, Larissa thought as he stepped into the living room. But his new clothes looked good on him.

"Hey, is that a cat?" he asked, seeing Dyna. "She's a real beauty."

He bent over to pick up the feline. Larissa started to warn him that Dyna could be standoffish, only to watch while the cat relaxed into his arms and began to purr.

"That just figures," she said with a sigh, then went off to the storage area by the utility room. Sure enough, the cat box and extra container of litter were just where she'd last seen them. She filled the box and set it by the washer, then returned to the living room.

Percy stood cradling the cat as he stroked her. She had her big blue eyes half-closed in pure bliss.

"I've never had a cat," he admitted. "I didn't think I'd like them, but she's nice."

Larissa thought of the dogs, cats, fish and hamsters she'd grown up with and briefly wondered how many other Percys were out there, barely getting by.

"Let's show her the litter box," she said, motioning

for him to follow her. "Then eat. Jack gets crabby if his meals are delayed."

"I heard that," Jack yelled from the dining room.

Percy grinned.

After showing Dyna her facilities, Larissa and Percy detoured by the kitchen. They both washed their hands and collected cans of soda before walking into the dining room.

Jack had set out plates and serving spoons. He'd unpacked all the cartons and opened them. Larissa handed him a soda and sat across from him. Percy sat next to Jack and a few seconds later, Dyna sat in the chair next to Percy.

"Traitor," she told the feline. "I'm the one who saved you."

"There's no accounting for who you fall for," Jack said, and handed Larissa a carton. "Have an egg roll. You'll feel better."

There were plenty of choices for dinner. She'd gotten all of Jack's favorites, along with the crispy spicy shrimp she liked, then added a few things for Percy. She preferred chow mein and Jack preferred rice, so they usually alternated. But with a teenaged boy in the house, she'd gone for both.

For a few minutes there was only the sound of chewing, accompanied by Dyna's soft purr. Then Percy surfaced long enough to say, "I had Mexican food for lunch. It was good, too."

"That's right. Kenny took you out." Larissa smiled. "You had a nice time with him?"

"Yeah, he's cool. He really likes football, though."

Larissa felt her lips twitch. "Could be from being a professional and all."

"I guess. But it's just a game, man." The teen glanced at Jack. "No offense."

"None taken." Jack put down his fork. "Basketball is more your game?"

"Uh-huh."

Larissa saw where this was going. "No," she said firmly. "No way and no. You can't."

Percy's dark eyes widened slightly. "Can't what?"

"Invite you to play with his friends."

"Why not? I've got game."

Jack's expression turned smug. "Yeah, Larissa. He's got game."

"They're grown men," she told the teen. "Some of them are dangerous. This is basketball with blood."

"Only sometimes," Jack pointed out. "Percy, we play three days a week. If you want in, you're welcome to join us."

"I'm in," Percy told Jack. They exchanged a high five.

It was a part of the male psyche she would never understand, she thought. The need to be so competitive about everything. On the bright side, at least Percy and Jack were connecting.

She accepted the inevitable and picked up her fork. "How was your meeting at the college?" she asked Jack.

Jack's expression shifted to a scowl. "The athletic director is against starting a football program at the school."

"Then he's stupid," Percy announced. "Football isn't my thing, but even I know that it brings in the big bucks. Right? Money that pays for other stuff in the school. You know, like the library. Important to the students, but not exciting, like a football game."

Larissa blinked at him. "You're right. That's very insightful."

Percy sat a little straighter in the chair. "I'm an insightful guy."

"I see that."

"Don't get too cocky, kid," Jack told him. "Not until you've proved yourself on the court."

"You'll see."

"Uh-huh." He turned back to Larissa. "I'm with Percy. They're idiots. They have the support of the regents and you know the alumni would be on board. The amount of money they could pull in is staggering, but you can't push a rope. If they don't want it, they shouldn't do it."

"Is that what you told them?"

"Among other things."

"I'm sorry the meeting was frustrating."

He shrugged. "I told them what I thought and now they'll make their decision. I'm out of it."

She wondered if he really was or if that was wishful thinking on his part. Jack wanted to get involved and pull away in equal measures. Conflicting emotions with a significant cause. No one could go through what Jack had and not have those events change a person. Some people would have gotten angry or depressed. Jack had moved on, but with emotional protection carefully in place.

He'd been nearly eighteen when his brother, Lucas, had died, but he'd been much younger when his twin had gotten sick. She would guess his life had been defined by Lucas's illness. She knew his personality had been molded by it. While other kids were free to act out or be irresponsible from time to time, Jack never could. Lucas needed all the family's attention. Jack had learned to do the right thing, to stay out of trouble and not call attention to himself.

Larissa understood and respected his boundaries. She knew he was a good guy and that was enough for her.

Conversation shifted to what was going on in town. The Máa-zib Festival was the following weekend and Larissa was excited to see all the activities.

"I don't get it," Percy said, after finishing his third serving of food. "There's a dancing horse?"

Jack leaned back in his chair. "That's what has you confused?" he asked. "Did you hear the part about some guy getting his heart cut out?"

Percy waved off the comment. "That's not real, man. It's like the movies. A fake knife and red food coloring. But the horse dancing is actually horses dancing? I didn't know horses could do that."

"I've never seen it," Larissa told him. "We'll have to go check it out."

Percy started to say something but the word turned into a huge yawn. Larissa glanced at the clock. It was barely after eight, but she would guess the teen hadn't slept much in the past few days. He'd been making his way back to Fool's Gold and then last night he'd been in an unfamiliar place.

She stood. "Okay, go on."

"What?"

"To bed."

"It's too early," Percy protested. "I'm not a baby."

"No. You're exhausted. At least go lie down. You can watch TV or something." And fall asleep in fifteen seconds, she thought, holding in a smile.

Percy yawned again. "Okay. Maybe I'll go watch a show."

He rose and reached for his plate. After carrying it to the kitchen, he returned and patted Dyna.

"Thanks for everything," he said, staring at the cat.

"You're welcome," Larissa told him. "We'll see you tomorrow."

He nodded and headed for the stairs. Jack got up and started clearing food. Most of the cartons were empty but a few still had a bit in them.

"Worth saving?" he asked.

"Might as well. Percy will eat them for a snack. Or breakfast."

"I'm sure he will." Jack grinned. "He's a good kid. You have a knack for finding good people."

A compliment that warmed her from the inside out.

Together they put food in the refrigerator, threw away cartons and loaded the dishwasher. Dyna checked out a few of the leftovers they offered her and daintily took a piece of chicken. When the cleaning was done, Larissa walked to the freezer.

"I think there are some brownies in here, unless you ate them all."

She searched behind frozen roasts and single servings of her crockpot chili before finding a package of brownies, then bumped the freezer door closed with her hip.

"Perfect," she said. "These won't take too long to thaw."

She put them on the counter and unwrapped them, then turned to get a plate, only to find Jack was right behind her.

Momentum carried her forward a half foot or so, until she was nearly touching him.

Everything about the moment changed. The easy, lighthearted evening they'd been sharing shifted until the atmosphere was so thick, she could nearly touch it. Her breathing stopped as she stared up into his dark eyes. Her skin heated, her heart rate increased and the world shrank to hold only the man in front of her.

They stared at each other for what felt like an eternity. Unexpected need pulsed through her, making her want to close the small distance that still separated them.

This was Jack, she thought, confused and determined at the same time. She knew every inch of him. Knew the feel of her hands on his skin. She wanted that now, but not in the usual way. She didn't want to give him a massage—she wanted to be touching him the way a woman touches a man. She wanted to be next to him, exploring him as he explored her.

The sexual image was powerful enough to make

her knees weak. She sucked in a breath and waited
for whatever would happen next. Did he sense the
tension between them or would he simply joke about
the brownies and suggest they find a baseball game
on TV?

His dark eyes were impossible to read. For several
long seconds, he didn't move at all, then he raised his
hand and cupped the side of her face.

"Larissa."

The single word was spoken on a whisper of air.
Before she could know what it meant, he bent down
and kissed her.

The feel of his mouth was heaven. Gentle, with
only a hint of passion. Then the hint grew as the pressure increased. He drew her along with him, building
need inside of her.

Without thinking, she raised her arms and wrapped
them around his neck. He put his free hand on her
waist and drew her against him. They were touching
everywhere, hard to soft, male to female. She surrendered to his strength and melted against him, even as
their kiss stayed chaste.

He brushed his lips against her cheek, then her
closed eyelids. He nuzzled her ear before touching
the tip of his tongue to the sensitive skin below her
lobe. When his mouth returned to hers, she parted
immediately and felt the sizzle that accompanied the
first stroke of his tongue against hers.

Heat poured through her, settling low in her belly.
Wanting exploded, surprising her at first with its presence, then with its intensity. She had to consciously

keep from grinding into him—pelvis to pelvis. At the same time her breast ached for his skilled touch.

The kiss continued—a passionate game of tag, where losing was delicious and winning meant going into overtime.

Jack put both hands on her waist, then slowly slid them up and down her back. On the second pass, he slipped down over her hips. He moved slowly, exploring unfamiliar territory. Anticipation built. Her nipples hardened.

More, she thought, ready to go wherever this led. Definitely more.

But instead of reading her mind, he drew back enough to break the kiss and put space between them. They stared at each other, both breathing more quickly. She felt as wide-eyed as he looked. Emotions flooded his eyes. Confusion, affection and, most of all, desire. Exactly what she was feeling. Because while she'd always liked Jack, until recently she hadn't thought about *liking* Jack.

Indecision had her biting her bottom lip. Because this night could go in two very different directions. While wanting him was great and making love would probably rock her world, what would happen the next morning? What would she have lost?

She nearly stomped her foot. This was all her mother's fault, she thought bitterly.

"I have to go," she said suddenly, darting around him.

"Larissa, we have to talk."

"We don't. Not really."

She found Dyna curled up on the sofa. Her cat didn't take kindly to being disturbed, but allowed her regal self to be placed in the carrier.

"I'll see you tomorrow. At work."

With that, she raced for the front door and didn't allow herself to relax until she was safely in her car. Before starting the engine, she drew in a few breaths and told herself living in a state of denial wasn't all that bad. People did it all the time and she could, too.

JACK CHECKED ON Percy and found the kid was out like a light. After that, he wandered through his too-large house, then tried to find something interesting on TV. When that didn't work, he grabbed his phone and scrolled through the numbers, looking for a way to ease his troubles.

A woman seemed like the best solution, he told himself. A safe nonLarissa kind of woman. A woman who understood who he was and that he wasn't looking for more than a night. But after two passes through the names, he couldn't find a single one he wanted to talk to let alone have sex with.

He tossed the phone onto the coffee table and sighed.

What the hell? When had he and Larissa started kissing? This was the second time and like the first, he had no idea how it had happened.

Sure, she was pretty, and sure, he liked her, but so what? She was Larissa. His assistant, his friend. She mattered to him. A guy didn't mess that up for some-thing as meaningless as a night of sex. He could get that anywhere. What he couldn't replace was her. So what had he been thinking?

Only he hadn't been thinking. He'd been minding his own business, helping in the kitchen when bam— she was in his arms and he wasn't holding back. The thing was, no matter how he tried, he couldn't figure out the steps that had made it happen. It was as if those seconds had never existed.

He stood and grabbed his phone. After starting for the door, he turned around and sat on the couch. Thirty seconds later, he was walking out into the night. But instead of heading over to Larissa's place, he went in the other direction. When he reached the small house with the motorcycle parked in the driveway, he turned up the walk.

Angel answered the front door. He was wearing jeans and nothing else. Jack stared at him for a second before putting the pieces together.

"Were you having sex?" he asked before he could stop himself.

Angel raised an eyebrow. "Not your business and if you're asking to join us, the answer is no. Any threesome would go the other way."

Angel walked off but left the front door open. Jack stepped into the foyer and waited. A couple of seconds later Taryn appeared. She wore a T-shirt over jeans and was barefoot. Her long blue-black hair hung straight and she didn't have on any makeup.

"Sorry," he said, immediately turning away.

She grabbed his arm and drew him back. "It's fine.

Don't leave." She studied him for a second. "What's up? Are you okay?"

"I'm fine."

"You're lying and not very well."

She linked arms with him and led him to the kitchen. An open bottle of red wine sat on the counter. She poured them each a glass and handed him one, then moved into the living room.

"Angel isn't joining us?" he asked.

"Probably not. I think he still worries about you. Well, us, really. The 'you and I' us."

"Why? We work together. We're friends." Taryn was his best friend, except maybe for Larissa. The relationships were different, though.

"We used to be married," Taryn reminded him.

They sat on the sofa. She angled toward him and tucked her feet under her.

"Our marriage was a long time ago," Jack said, then sipped the Cab. "It's not like we were in love."

Taryn's gaze was steady. "What's really bothering you, Jack?"

A polite way of asking why he was there, he thought.

"I don't know," he said, telling the absolute truth. "Cal U Fool's Gold isn't looking for a coach. They're deciding on whether or not to start a football team. I don't know anything about that."

"I'm sure you have strong opinions."

He shrugged. "Sure. Of course they should have a team. But why put me on the committee? I don't have any skin in the game."

"Mayor Marsha, like God, moves in mysterious ways."

"She's a scary old broad."

"Tell me about it." She cupped the wineglass in her hands. "What else?"

"That kid."

"Percy? He seems nice. Considering what he's been through, he could be dealing drugs right now. He wants to do the right thing. I find that admirable."

"He never graduated from high school."

She smiled. "You say that as if you're surprised. Larissa's projects are rarely easy. So you'll help him get his GED. Talk to Sam and Kenny. They'll be on board with it."

"He can't read. He doesn't want Larissa to know."

Taryn's carefully groomed eyebrows rose. "Seriously?" She held up her free hand. "Don't answer. Okay—the lack of reading skills adds a challenge, but not an insurmountable one. Sam and Kenny will still help."

She stretched out her feet until her arches rested on the side of his thigh. "None of this is the problem."

"It isn't?"

"No. The town is sucking you in and you don't want to get involved."

She was right about that part of it, although the bigger issue was Larissa.

"You think you're so smart," he said by way of distraction.

"I *am* smart." She poked him with her toes. "You know I'm right. Jack, you and Sam and Kenny were the ones who wanted to move here. Getting involved is a consequence of that. Just surrender to the mob and learn to like it. You'll be happier if you let them in."

"I don't need them in my life."

"You need some of them. Despite what you want us all to think, you do need people in your life."

"Maybe," he conceded.

"More than maybe."

He didn't bother answering. They both knew that she was right.

JACK DIDN'T SLEEP much that night or the next. He couldn't say exactly what was on his mind, but whatever the topic, it wasn't restful. Everyone knew that when he didn't get enough sleep, he got grumpy. So he did his best to avoid everyone in the office.

Which was why he went into the lunchroom at eleven-thirty—before the rest of the staff would descend. He pulled out a soda and swallowed half of it in a single gulp, then wondered what to do with the rest of his day.

The problem was they weren't looking for clients and that was what he did best. He liked the thrill of the chase. The initial meetings, the presentations that blew away their expectations, the satisfaction of watching them sign on the dotted line. Only, he and Kenny were so good at their jobs that Score was at capacity. Taryn had hired an extra graphics person and was currently torturing three interns from Cal U Fool's Gold in addition to all the permanent staff.

Sam was busy with whatever it was he did with the financial stuff. Kenny didn't mind not hunting down clients for a few weeks. Only Jack seemed to notice there was nothing to do.

He returned to his office and checked his email. Nothing had appeared in the past ten minutes. He could work out, except he already had. He'd also checked on Percy, read the sports section of two papers and had played computer games for the better part of an hour. Talk about sad.

Maybe he could work on plays, he thought. Design a few new ones, write down some favorites. Just in case Cal U Fool's Gold ever added football back to their sports program.

He searched for a big pad of unlined paper. There were always several around the office. When he didn't see one in his office, he headed for Sam's.

Just to pass the time, he took the long way, by the locker rooms and around back. Which put him near Larissa's massage room. His steps slowed.

The door was closed, which meant she was busy with someone. As Jack had just seen Taryn a few minutes before, he knew it had to be Kenny or Sam. Because she worked on both of them. It was her job.

As he approached the door, he heard gentle laughter. Larissa's laugh, he thought, coming to a stop. That was followed by a male voice. A low male voice he recognized. Kenny's words were a quiet rumble. He couldn't catch exactly what his business partner was saying but it wasn't hard to figure out where the conversation was going. Kenny was coming on to her.

Right now he was probably picking her up in his big beefy hands and pulling her against him as he—

Jack grabbed the door handle and turned. He swept into the room, prepared to do battle. Although he couldn't say for what.

But instead of a lover's tryst, he found Kenny lying facedown. Larissa was standing by his feet, digging her fingers into Kenny's calf muscles. They both turned to look at him.

"Oh, sorry," he said, feeling like a prize idiot. "I, ah, didn't know you were with someone."

Larissa drew her eyebrows together. "The door was closed."

"Was it?" Jack tried to smile and had a feeling it didn't go well. "Sorry. I'll catch you later."

He started to leave, then turned back to Kenny. "We need to talk about the kid. Later, maybe."

"Sure," his friend said, relaxing back on the massage table. "You know how to find me. Obviously."

CHAPTER EIGHT

"WHAT THE HELL is wrong with you?" Kenny demanded an hour later as he stood in the doorway to Jack's office. The question was asked in a friendlier tone than Jack deserved and with only mild interest.

"Nothing," Jack said, still embarrassed by his behavior.

Kenny pushed off the door frame and walked over to the desk. He claimed one of the visitor chairs and sat down.

Kenny's blond hair was still damp from his shower and Jack would guess he'd come here directly from the locker room.

"Larissa was fooled," Kenny told him. "But I wasn't. What did you expect to find, bursting in like that? Us doing it on the massage table?"

That was exactly what Jack had been imagining, but hearing Kenny say it made him sound stupid. Or worse—needy.

"No. Why would you even ask?"

Kenny shook his head. "Like I said before, what's wrong with you, man?"

Jack surrendered to the inevitable. "It's Larissa's mother."

"What?"

"When she was here a few weeks ago, she came to see me."

Kenny still looked confused. "If she said I'm sleeping with Larissa, she's wrong. Larissa is gorgeous, but jeez, she's like my sister." He shuddered. "There's no way."

Despite everything, Jack smiled. "No, that wasn't her point. She said..." He swore, not wanting to repeat the words. "She said I should fire Larissa so she would move back to L.A., find some guy and get married."

"Why can't she do that here?"

"Her mother thinks she's in love with me."

Kenny gave one long whistle. "Hell."

"Tell me about it."

"Is it true?"

"What? No. Of course not. We work together." When his friend didn't look convinced, Jack added, "She knows me."

Kenny grinned. "You got a point there. And knowing you, she should know better." He chuckled at his joke. "So what's the problem?"

"There isn't one."

"Try again, because I'm not buying that."

Jack considered his options. "Having her mom say that made things strange between us," he said, hedging with facts while avoiding the whole I-kissed-her reality. "We're still settling in."

Kenny's grin widened. "So that's why you got a boner. You're seeing her in a whole new light."

"Shut up."

Kenny chuckled. "Yeah, poor Jack. Falling for the woman right under his nose."

"I'm not falling for her. We're friends. I care about her. That's different."

"Be sure you keep it to friendship," Kenny said, his humor fading. "She's part of our family. You don't get to mess that up."

"I won't. And thanks for taking my side."

"Screw your side. This is for the greater good. So nothing's happened, right?"

Jack hesitated a nanosecond too long.

Kenny slapped his large hands on the desk. "What?" he demanded. "What did you do?"

"Nothing."

"Like hell it was nothing. Tell me."

Jack groaned. "We kissed."

"You *kissed* her?"

Kenny's voice echoed off the walls.

Jack glared at him. "Keep it down. You want everyone to know?"

"They're going to find out when they ask why I pulverized you."

"You're not going to hurt me," Jack told him. "And it was just one kiss. Twice."

"You kissed her twice?"

"Yes, but I can't say how it happened. One second we were talking and then—"

Kenny stood up. He swore loudly as he walked to the door and slammed it shut, then he stalked back to the desk and leaned over it menacingly.

"You kissed her?" he demanded.

Jack nodded.

"Twice."

Another nod.

"Two kisses as in two different times and places?"

"Want me to draw a diagram?"

Kenny glared at him. "Don't you try any attitude on me, McGarry. I'm protecting my own here, even from you. What were you thinking? Oh, wait. Let me guess. You weren't. Jesus, Mary and Joseph. You're an idiot. Worse."

Jack almost felt relieved to be yelled at. Maybe now he wouldn't have to feel so guilty.

"We only kissed," he said quickly. "There was nothing else."

"Like that makes it okay?" Kenny straightened. "I have to think."

"There's nothing to think about. It won't happen again."

"Where have I heard that before? Besides, there's something going on, even if it's just in your pointed head. Look at how you burst in on me before. You thought I was making a move on your girl."

Jack started to protest, only to stop. No, he told himself. It couldn't be that. He wasn't interested in Larissa that way. He couldn't be. He needed her in his life. If they took things any further, it would all go to hell and she would walk. Because his relationships always ended. Usually sooner rather than later.

Kenny nodded slowly. "I see the wheels turning. I'm glad you're coming to your senses. You're right—

you can't screw around with her. Literally or figuratively. She's part of us. Now tell me you're going to back off and never go there again."

"I'm backing off," Jack said, knowing he had to. "You're right. It's too big a risk. For all of us."

Kenny stared at him for a long time before nodding. "You're making the right decision. Stick to it or I'll kill you."

Jack started to say he'd have to catch him first, then remembered who he was talking to. Back in the day, Kenny could outrun all of them down a football field. He would guess that hadn't changed overmuch.

"Point taken," he said grudgingly.

"Good. Now about Percy—we're going to need a plan. He said he didn't graduate from high school."

Jack nodded. "He also said he doesn't read really well. By the way, he doesn't want Larissa to know that."

Kenny's grin returned. "You have competition. Good to know."

"I'm pretty sure I have a leg up on Percy."

"I don't know. He's young and probably virile. Oh, wait, that's not one of your problems." Kenny snickered then drew in a breath. "I can help with English requirement and some history. Sam will take math, but you're going to have to get him reading."

"Will do," Jack said, wondering if they would flip a coin over the science information the kid would need to know. "Any suggestions on how to start him reading?"

"No. Go online."

Jack perked up. "Great idea. You can find everything on the internet."

"Good. Entertain yourself. Just stay away from
our girl."

PAPER MOON HAD started life as a bridal boutique. At
least Larissa was pretty sure that was the more sophisticated way to refer to it. In her mind, it had been
a wedding-gown store. Then about a year ago, Isabel had decided to open a fancy clothing store in the
adjacent space. There had been lots of remodeling, a
grand opening and now Paper Moon served women
at every stage of their lives. Well, not while pregnant,
although there was a store for that in Fool's Gold.

Paper Moon wasn't Larissa's kind of place. Not
only wasn't she interested in a bridal gown, she didn't
wear designer clothes. Her idea of dressing up was to
wear jeans instead of yoga pants. She never curled her
hair or bothered with makeup. About once a month,
she had the thought she should spend more time on
her appearance, maybe try another style with her hair
or put on mascara. But the impulse usually passed
and then she was fine.

Although she could make a case that shopping in
the fancy places was really nice. Especially when
champagne was involved.

She took another sip of the bubbly liquid and settled more comfortably in the very cushy love seat on
the bride side of the store. In front of her was a platform and a half circle of eight mirrors. The platform
was big enough for a bride in the most ridiculously

huge dress and half her family. Larissa supposed the mirrors were there to reflect the magnificence of it all.

Taryn walked around in a robe and bare feet. She was pale and shaking.

"This is totally ridiculous," she announced, picking up her champagne glass, draining it, then putting it down again. "Why am I even here? I could be at work. Being productive."

Isabel, a beautiful blonde with a curvy figure, rolled her eyes. "I knew you were going to be difficult, but this is completely over-the-top." She glanced at Madeline, her assistant. "It's time."

Madeline grinned. "Really?"

"What?" Taryn demanded. "I hate this. I'm going to punish all of you later." Her gaze landed on Larissa. "Not you. You're here for moral support."

"And to help the men in white coats with the restraints," Larissa murmured.

Taryn glared at her. "Funny," she said, her tone icy. "Very funny."

Madeline nodded. "You're right. It's necessary." She walked to the front of the store and locked the front door, then turned the sign to show the store was "closed for a private event."

"Better?" Isabel asked. "No one will come in or out. I've closed the door between the two sides of the store, so you have complete privacy."

The normally unflappable Taryn sniffed twice, then covered her face with her hands. "I'm a wreck."

"Yes, you are," Larissa said cheerfully. "But impressively so."

Taryn straightened. "Fine. Mock me all you want. This is really hard for me." She drew in a breath. "All right. Go get them."

Isabel nodded at Madeline who disappeared into the back of the store. Isabel then led Taryn to a straight-backed chair in front of a small dresser.

"Let's get you ready," she said gently.

"I'm ready," Taryn told her, obviously reluctant to sit. "What? I'm wearing makeup."

"Just sit."

Taryn did as she was told. Isabel opened a couple of drawers and pulled out a brush, a few pins and a sort of knit-crocheted thing with beautiful ivory roses along one side.

"What is it?" Taryn asked.

"A snood. It's to hold your hair up while you're trying on dresses."

As she spoke, Isabel ran a brush through Taryn's dark hair. She loosely braided it for about three inches, then picked up the snood and slipped it around the ends. A few pins later, it was secure, with the row of lace roses acting as a decoration.

The snood captured all her hair, but in a soft, almost old-fashioned kind of way. Taryn suddenly looked younger and more approachable.

Madeline returned with a rolling rack filled with wedding gowns. Larissa stared at the confections of lace and silk and knew this was going to be a fashion show like no other.

"These are samples," Isabel said, walking toward the dresses. "That means they're around a size ten, so they'll be falling off your bony butt. Something I find intensely annoying."

Taryn looked away from her reflection and studied the dresses. "You got the ones I mentioned to you?"

"Yes, and a few others. I also have two couture dresses. They are literally one of a kind, so I practically had to give them a kidney to get them. You will notice a significant charge on your credit card for the privilege of trying them on." Isabel grinned. "The charge will be refunded if you don't want the dresses, of course."

"You know you don't have to pay a deposit when you buy retail, like a normal person," Larissa teased.

Madeline walked over and sat next to her. "It was really tough to get them." She lowered her voice. "I didn't know credit cards could have a limit that high."

"Taryn has a unique relationship with clothes," Larissa said. "I think it's fun to look at it like a show or something. You know—Broadway. But without the singing."

Taryn walked over to the dresses and touched the first one. Her mouth twisted and Larissa knew her friend was fighting tears. Because weddings were always complicated, she thought. She'd been through two with her sisters.

Always a bridesmaid, she thought as she sipped her champagne.

It wasn't that she didn't want to get married, she thought wistfully. Of course she did. And have a family and all that went with it. It was just there wasn't anyone who made her believe that forever was possible.

She had a feeling Taryn would tell her that was because she didn't put herself out there. She was too busy saving the world to save herself.

Her friend might have a point, Larissa admitted to herself. Her causes were a distraction and sometimes that was a good thing.

Taryn dropped her robe, revealing a perfectly toned body in a flesh-colored thong and strapless bra. "Let's do this," she said.

Madeline stood and walked over to the rack. Together she and Isabel removed the dress from its hanger and carried it over to the platform.

"For some of them, stepping in is easier than trying to pull it over your head," Isabel told Taryn.

The pile of lace and silk pooled on the carpeted platform. Taryn carefully stepped into the middle and the two women drew it up around her.

Larissa hadn't gone dress shopping with her sisters. She'd shown up for her fittings and had been in both weddings. But the whole bride-marriage thing hadn't been that interesting to her. Now she wondered if she'd missed out on more than she'd realized. If her mother were here, the woman would be crying. It wouldn't matter that Taryn wasn't her daughter. Nancy Owens loved a wedding.

Probably because she hadn't had a big one of her own, Larissa thought, feeling the familiar guilt. At least not the first time. Larissa's mother had gotten pregnant and then married in haste. Larissa had been born five months later.

She knew that she wasn't responsible for what had happened to her parents. That they'd made the decision to sleep together and then had suffered the consequences. But she also knew that if her mother hadn't gotten pregnant, her parents wouldn't have married each other. They wouldn't have suffered through a failing relationship for years before finally admitting what everyone else already knew. That they would be better off apart.

Their subsequent remarriages were happy ones. The extended family often spent holidays together. Some of Larissa's friends in high school had lamented how their own parents were so mean during their divorces. That Larissa was lucky with what she'd been through.

She understood how they'd meant the comments and had never admitted that in her heart, she felt responsible. She was the reason her parents had to get married. And although they never blamed her, she couldn't escape the sense of having messed up both of their lives.

PERCY STRUTTED INTO Jack's office. Jack took one look at him and groaned. Once Larissa saw what had happened, there would be hell to pay.

"Quit being so happy," he grumbled.

Percy grinned. "We won."

"Yeah, like that's going to matter when Larissa kills us both."

"She's only going to kill you. And maybe Consuelo."

Jack didn't think Larissa could take on Consuelo and win, but if Percy's words were true, he wouldn't be around to see it, anyway.

He studied the teen, taking in the swollen right eye and the growing bruise.

Their morning basketball sessions could be intense. Percy had been telling the truth—he had game. But he was also young and easily distracted. He'd made the mistake of watching Consuelo's ass instead of the rest of her and had ended up with an elbow in the face. Of course, each of them had suffered the same fate at one time or another in the past six or eight months, but that was little consolation when the pain exploded in your face. Still, Percy had reacted well and play had continued.

He stood and walked toward the door. "Come on," he told the kid.

"Where are we going?" Percy asked, following him.

"You'll see."

Jack led him to the side of the building where the actual campaign work was done. The graphics area had several offices, along with a big open layout room with massive printers that could handle poster-size paper. Behind that were a series of smaller offices.

Jack went to the end of the hall and pushed open a door. Inside was a small desk, a bookcase and not much else. There weren't any windows and the walls were bare. He was pretty sure this room was usually used by interns. He'd checked with Taryn before claiming it for Percy.

On the desk was a laptop. A small printer stand held an all-in-one, with plenty of paper and printer cartridges below. There was a desk chair and a second less-comfortable chair for visitors. Jack sat in that one and motioned for Percy to sit behind the desk.

The teen did so and looked at him.

"So here's the thing," Jack began. "You need to learn to read to succeed in life. So that's where we start." He pointed to the laptop. "You know how to work one of those?"

"Sure. We used them in school."

"Good. We're going to go online and you'll do a reading assessment. Then we'll download the appropriate software to get you to the next level. Once your reading skills are at a tenth-grade level, we'll move on to other topics. Kenny, Sam and I are going to divide up the subjects. You'll meet with us an hour or so a day for tutoring, then you'll be responsible for handling the study part on your own."

He held Percy's gaze. "I'm not going to kid you. This will be a lot of work. You'll get frustrated. You'll want to quit. None of us can make you do this. You have to want it. You have to be willing to do the work."

Percy's eyes filled with tears, but the teen didn't look away. "I don't understand. Why you doing this? You're some famous rich guy. I'm a kid from South Central L.A. You owe me nothing."

Jack leaned back in his chair. "Why aren't you in a gang?"

"I told you before. My mom would have killed me. She worked hard so that would never happen."

"Did you go to class?"

"Sure. But it was tough, you know. When I was little, I just couldn't get the letters and stuff. But they kept sending me to the next grade. When I was nine, I had this great teacher. She had me stay after and I was starting to get it. She said there was nothing wrong with my brain, that it had just taken longer for me to figure out what was what. Only she moved on and the next teacher didn't care as much."

Pushed through the system, Jack thought. He was sure it happened more than it should. Especially in inner-city schools where resources were limited.

"At some of the foster homes they cared about school and stuff. So I would learn a little. I got my reading back a few times, but then it was hard to keep up."

"How'd you find out about the summer camp?"

"There was a flier in my neighborhood. I went to see the guy who put it together and he got me enrolled."

Jack was sure there were thousands of kids who had lived a variation of Percy's story. While he and Larissa couldn't save them all, they could do something with this one.

"You up for this?" he asked.

"Getting my GED?" Percy nodded vigorously. "I'll do whatever it takes. You'll see. I can get my work done here, then do my schoolwork before we go home."

"Oh, you'll be working at home, too," Jack told him. Then he understood what the teen was missing. "Percy, this is your laptop to take back and forth with you."

Percy swallowed hard. He put his hands on the computer. "I'll take real good care of it. You'll see."

"I know you will." Jack tapped the laptop. "Start the assessment. We'll see where you are and move forward from there. It takes about an hour. Come get me when you're done."

His cell buzzed. He glanced at the screen and sighed. "Okay. I have to go help Taryn with something. If I'm not back by the time you're done, go see Kenny or Sam. They'll get the right software loaded."

"Sure thing." Percy was already booting up the laptop.

Jack got up and started out of the office. He paused, then glanced back. "Remember to eat lunch."

Percy grinned. "Promise."

JACK STARED AT the sign on the door. Closed for a Private Event. He thought about taking that as proof he should hightail it out of there but knew that running wasn't an option. Instead, he knocked.

A couple of seconds later Larissa opened the door of Paper Moon and grinned at him.

"I wondered if you'd come," she said by way of greeting. "I should have known better." She handed him a glass of champagne. "This is way more fun than I thought it would be."

She swayed just a little as she spoke. Her blue eyes were wide and a bit unfocused.

"Are you drunk?"

She smiled. "Maybe. Wow. I've never been drunk in the morning before."

"You've probably never had anything to drink before noon before."

"That's true."

He stepped into the store and put his free arm around her waist. To steady her, he told himself. The touching was purely medicinal. She rested her hand on top of his and leaned against him.

"Taryn is so beautiful," she said as they walked into the store. "She's going to make a lovely bride."

"I'm sure she is."

He led her to a small sofa facing a platform with several mirrors and got her seated. This was the viewing area, he would guess. Not that he'd ever been in a store like this before. He took in the fussy decorations, the feminine colors, the dresses and veils and other girlie stuff and told himself that, with luck, he would never have to be in one again.

Taryn stepped out of a dressing room. She wore a robe and had her hair up.

"You're here. Good. I need advice. I've narrowed my choices down to two." Taryn crossed to him, grabbed the glass from his hand and drained it. "I'm not cut out for this kind of crap." Her blue-violet eyes darkened with what he would guess was a lot of doubt, accompanied by a hint of fear. "Jack, is this insane?"

He took back the empty glass and kissed her cheek. "You're going to be a beautiful bride, Taryn. Angel won't know what hit him."

"You haven't seen me in either of the dresses."

"That doesn't matter."

She sighed. "Thank you." She put her free hand on his shoulder and pushed him onto the sofa. "Stay here. I'll be out in a second."

He sat next to Larissa, who poured him more champagne. He had a feeling this wasn't the first bottle of the morning.

"You ladies have made this into a party," he said.

Larissa giggled. "I know. At first it was kind of boring, but after a while, I got into it. Maybe I should have gone shopping with my sisters when they were buying their dresses."

"I doubt there was champagne involved," he pointed out. "That would have been a Taryn touch."

"You're right."

She set her glass on the small side table, leaned against him and sighed. "You're a good friend to help her. She's really freaked about finding the right dress."

"Being drunk will ease her pain."

Larissa looked up at him. "I think I might have had the most champagne."

Her blue eyes seemed to draw him closer. Despite the public setting and Kenny's recent warning, Jack felt himself start to lower his head. Because kissing Larissa would put everything else in perspective.

Her chin rose slightly, as if she were easing into position. Yeah, he thought, his mouth a whisper from hers. This was what they both—

"Percy has a black eye."

He knew he'd been the one to speak the words, but for the life of him he couldn't say why. Unexpected self-preservation?

Larissa scrambled to the other side of the small sofa and stared at him. "What?"

"It happened during the basketball game this morning."

"I'm going to kill Consuelo."

He raised his eyebrows.

She shrugged. "Okay, maybe not kill. But I'm going to talk to her. It's one thing when it's you guys, but Percy is a kid. She should be more careful around him."

He reached past her for her champagne and handed it to her. "Drink up. You'll feel better."

"How's Percy?"

"Proud as hell."

Isabel stepped out of the dressing room and walked to the platform. "Ladies and gentlemen, if I may have your attention, please… Taryn's first choice is a couture gown. It's a one-of-a-kind…"

Isabel kept talking, but Jack wasn't listening. Taryn had stepped out of the dressing room.

He didn't know much about wedding gowns. They were white and long and fussy. This one was all that, but somehow Taryn pulled it off. The top part was fitted and left her shoulders and arms bare. The skirt was full, falling in layers of some kind of frothy fabric. When she moved, the skirt swayed like a bell.

He remembered the first time he'd met her, nearly a decade before. She'd been packing up sandwiches left over from a meeting. Her determination, not to mention the collection of wrinkled plastic bags, had told him this was going to be her main meal of the day.

When they'd seen each other, he was sure he'd looked surprised. He knew she'd looked guilty, although she'd tried to pretend she wasn't hungry. At that time, he'd dated enough models and actresses to recognize good quality clothes when he saw them. Taryn had been dressed in a suit a couple sizes too big. Her shoes had been worn and she was using a tattered backpack for a handbag.

But she'd been pretty and she'd faced him defiantly. He'd admired her spirit and had asked her out to dinner.

One thing had led to another and they'd ended up at his place. He'd quickly discovered she was living out of her car while saving enough for a down payment on her own apartment. By the end of the week, she'd moved in with him.

It hadn't been love, he thought as she moved to the platform and stepped up in front of the mirrors. He'd liked her, had enjoyed being with her. Helping her out had made him feel as if he was doing something useful with his day. Lack of purpose was a chronic problem in the off-season.

A couple of months later, she'd turned up pregnant. He remembered Taryn's tears when she'd told him. Not tears of happiness or even regret. Instead, she'd been frustrated—mostly with herself for, as she'd put it, being so damned stupid.

"What do you think?" she now asked, her voice anxious.

He motioned for her to turn in a circle.

She did as he requested. The skirt moved with her, swaying like a bell. "You're beautiful," he told her honestly. "And the dress is good, too."

Taryn grinned. "Okay. Let me get into the other one and we'll decide."

Isabel helped her down from the platform and together they went into the dressing room.

Jack thought back to Taryn's first wedding, to him. They'd flown to Las Vegas the Friday after she'd discovered she was pregnant and had been married in the east chapel at the Bellagio hotel. They'd spent the weekend in a suite before flying home early Monday morning.

It hadn't been love for either of them. He'd been fine with that. Love wasn't in the cards for him. When you loved someone, they left and Jack had been left enough for three lifetimes. Maybe not in numbers but in how it had all played out. He wasn't risking that again.

With Taryn, he'd felt safe. They got along. They were friends who had sex. That had been plenty. The thought of a kid had terrified him at first. What if his child was like Lucas? But over the next few weeks, he'd told himself he would get through it, whatever happened.

Then Taryn had lost the baby. She'd started divorce proceedings the next day. Jack had wanted to tell her she didn't have to. He didn't mind being married to her, but she was determined. They'd stayed friends and had started Score together.

Looking back, he knew he had the best of all worlds. People he could care about, who cared about him. There weren't the highs, but there also weren't any risks.

"I'm feeling guilty," Larissa said, pulling him back to the present.

"Why?"

"Do you know how expensive these dresses are? Do you know how many people could be helped with that money?"

He took her hand in his and squeezed her fingers. "Taryn will not be moved by that argument."

"I know. But still."

He kissed her knuckles. "Pick a cause and we'll save something."

She looked at him. "But it's always with your money. What do I give back?"

"Your heart and that's enough."

"Are you sure?"

"Yes."

Because she was the most giving person he'd ever known and he liked how she dragged him along.

Without wanting to, he remembered the last time he'd offered all he had. He'd been nine.

It had been late. The hospital was as quiet as it could get. Both his parents were asleep and he'd been wandering the pediatric wing alone. He'd caught sight of his brother's cardiologist and had hurried over to speak to him. Because he'd finally figured out how to fix his brother.

"Dr. Madison."

The tall, weary man had smiled at him. "Jack. Why aren't you asleep?"

"I found a donor for Lucas. A heart donor. He's a good match, I'm sure of it." Jack knew all about transplants and matches. There had been talk of little else in his world for years.

Dr. Madison had shaken his head. "There's no donor, Jack."

"Yes, there is. Me." Jack remembered staring up at the doctor. "We're identical twins, so I'm the perfect match. Take my heart and make Lucas better."

Dr. Madison had smiled sadly. "We can't do that, Jack."

"But I want you to. Take my heart. Make Lucas better so he can live."

"It doesn't work that way, son."

The doctor had hugged him tight, then taken him back to where his parents slept in cots by Lucas's hospital bed. No mention had been made of Jack's offer. In the end, Lucas got a heart from someone else. He'd done well at first, and then he hadn't.

Larissa leaned against him again. He put his arm

around her. She knew that he'd lost a brother when a transplanted organ had failed. Nearly everyone knew that. But no one knew what it was like, day after day. To be the twin who hadn't gotten sick. To be the one who survived.

Six months after Lucas's death, his parents had left for a medical mission in Africa. There were children there who needed saving. They told Jack he would be fine on his own. He had his football scholarship and his strong, steady heart.

He remembered the shock that they would abandon him. Because somewhere in his head, he'd assumed that when Lucas was gone, they would still be a family. Only he'd been wrong.

He'd said all the right things—that of course he would be fine. And they'd believed him. At the time he hadn't known why, but over the years he'd figured it out. They'd believed him because it made their leaving easier. They could tell themselves he was okay and go without having to look back.

He understood what they'd done. And why. He was Lucas's identical twin. To look at him was to see what they had lost. Years of hoping and suffering and believing had taken their toll. The transplant had only bought a little time. It hadn't been the lifesaving operation it was supposed to be. Being with Jack had reminded them of everything bad. Leaving had been so much easier than staying.

They'd flown away and they'd never come back. He'd turned eighteen that summer with no family around to celebrate the day. He told himself it was because they knew he was completely capable of being on his own, even as he understood the truth was far less pretty. His parents hadn't cared enough about him. They'd lost Lucas and had abandoned him.

What he would guess they had never thought about was that he, too, had lost Lucas. And a few months later, he'd also lost his parents. Risking caring about anyone had become impossible. He knew the price of getting involved and he was never going to let that happen again.

He had the fame and the money to take on causes. And he did. From a distance. Larissa was the heart of their odd philanthropic partnership and he was the means. He believed it was a whole lot safer that way. For everyone, but mostly for him.

CHAPTER NINE

LARISSA SET OUT place mats and napkins. It was after five and dinner would be delivered within the half hour. She already had the wine open and breathing. It was a Washington State Cabernet—a favorite of everyone. Soft music played in the background.

Outside the conference rooms she could hear the other employees calling out as they left. Then it would be the five of them for dinner. The four partners and her.

She smiled as she continued to set the table. It had been far too long since they had a "family" dinner at work. Lately everyone was so busy with their personal lives. Taryn was rushing home to be with Angel. Sam was rushing home to be with Dellina. Kenny—well, Larissa wasn't sure where he rushed off to, but he was gone a lot. That left her and Jack, which was great, but every now and then she wanted the whole band back together.

Kenny strolled into the conference room. He'd taken off his tie and unbuttoned his shirt. The cuffs were already rolled up. He looked happy and relaxed, until he heard the music.

"Come on," he said, his tone complaining. "How about something good for a change?"

"These are all songs from this century," she pointed out.

"Not a great time for music."

"Do you want to know how many albums Taylor Swift has sold?"

He winced. "No, and I don't want to talk about her."

"Not every great song is from the 1960s."

"Want to bet?"

She laughed. Kenny was so predictable with his crazy love of oldies. "You weren't even born then."

"That doesn't mean the music wasn't great."

She opened the cabinet containing the dishes and glassware. Kenny joined her and reached for plates.

"Are your hands clean?" she asked, her voice teasing.

"Of course. You think I'd offer to help if they weren't?"

"You might."

"Not my style."

He set out the plates while she followed with the glasses. Kenny walked to the flatware drawer, but instead of opening it, he faced her.

"You doing okay?" he asked.

"Sure. Why?"

"Just checking."

"On me?"

He nodded.

She paused, wondering what all this was about.

Kenny was a good guy. Charming, easygoing. He was genuinely nice and kind. He called his mother regularly, paid his bills on time and rarely experienced the dark moods that Jack sometimes wrestled with.

He was also six feet four inches of pure speed. With his size, he could have played nearly anywhere on the football field, but Kenny loved to catch footballs and when they were around him, footballs loved to be caught.

All in all, the perfect man, she thought as he watched her carefully. Handsome, successful, rich. She was sure women everywhere wondered why he wasn't married. There must be a simple explanation, but it wasn't one he'd ever talked about to her.

So why was he worried about her?

"Jack," she said suddenly, feeling her cheeks heat up. "And my mother."

"Are they a thing? I didn't know."

Her mouth twisted. "Very funny. You know what I mean. He told you what my mom said."

Kenny nodded. "And about the kiss."

The heat grew until Larissa was sure she was bright red. This was when wearing makeup would be a good thing, she thought. Something to conceal her body's reaction to conflicting emotions.

"It didn't mean anything," she said.

"That's what Jack told me and I don't believe you, either."

She stared up into Kenny's blue eyes. "My mother said some stuff and now we're dealing. It'll pass."

"I want to believe that, but I'm not sure I can. La-rissa, you're one of us. We're family. Jack shouldn't mess with that. If you two get involved and then it goes badly..."

He didn't finish the sentence, but then he didn't have to. Larissa knew what would happen. Jack was an owner, she was an employee. It wasn't as if he would be the one to leave.

"We're not involved," she said firmly. "I promise."

"You're not in love with him?"

"What? No. I like Jack a lot. Just like I like you a lot. It's not more than that." At least she hoped it wasn't. Because as much as she adored Kenny, she had no desire to kiss him. Or Sam. In fact, there wasn't anyone she wanted to kiss except, of course, Jack.

"Kenny, I'm okay. This will get worked out and things will go back to normal."

He nodded slowly. "If you're sure. But if that changes and you get in trouble, let me know."

Because he would be there for her. "Thank you," she said, stepping forward and hugging him.

He held her for a second, then released her. "Did you get the extra-meat lasagna? Because if I have to eat pasta, it better have some protein on it."

She grinned. "Seriously? After all this time you're questioning my ordering skills?"

Thirty minutes later the five of them were sit-ting down to dinner. Angelo's had delivered football-player-size portions of double-meat lasagna for the guys, along with two normal servings for Taryn and

Larissa. There was salad, garlic bread and tiramisu for dessert. As they would all be walking home—except for Taryn, who would be picked up later by an adoring Angel—wine flowed freely.

"Where's Percy?" Taryn asked as she lightly sprinkled dressing on her salad. "Didn't he want to join us?"

"Have dinner with a bunch of old people?" Jack asked. "No way. I offered, but he said he'd rather eat by himself. And here I thought we were an interesting bunch."

"We are," Taryn assured him. "He's just too young to appreciate us."

Sam raised his glass of wine. "To old friends. The best kind."

Taryn winced. "I'm not fond of the *old* part of that statement, but I'll drink to the rest of it."

They clinked glasses, then drank.

Taryn sat at the head of the table. Larissa was to her right, next to Jack. Kenny and Sam were on the other side. She glanced at Kenny and he winked at her. A simple act that made her able to relax enough to enjoy the meal. Because she wanted things normal between them.

She didn't know what was happening with Jack. None of it made sense. Not the attraction, not the kissing. She only knew that he was a constant in her world and she never wanted that to change.

"The last thing we need is another alcohol-based client," Taryn was saying. "Isn't what we have enough?"

"There's a Polish vodka producer looking for a presence in America," Jack told her. "That would be good for us."

Taryn glared at him. "You're just saying that because you're hoping to plan a business meeting in mid-January. I know how you all love to torment me."

"Poland is relatively close to France," Sam said. "We could meet in Paris."

"Uh-huh. You're all in on this." She turned to Larissa. "You're the only one I can depend on."

"I wouldn't mind going to Poland," Larissa admitted. "In any month."

Kenny chuckled. "Imagine what you could rescue there."

As if listening to the conversation, Larissa's cell phone chirped. Everyone burst out laughing. Kenny pointed at Jack.

"Five bucks says you're screwed."

Jack rolled his eyes. "I'm not taking that bet."

"I have no idea what you're talking about," Larissa said primly as she pulled her phone out of her pocket and glanced at the text message on the screen.

It was from a wildlife organization. They needed a place to keep an injured wild Northern Spotted Owl. She turned to Jack.

"Can I keep a bird at your place?"

The table went silent as everyone waited.

Jack looked at her. "In a cage?"

"Yes."

"Just one bird?"

She nodded.

"For how long?"

"Less than a week."

"Okay, sure." He looked at Kenny. "It's a bird. I'm fine. You owe me five bucks."

"We'll see about that."

Larissa quickly texted back agreement to take the bird, then excused herself to get the rest of the information. When she was done with the call, she texted Percy to let him know what was going on, then returned to the conference room.

Jack and Kenny were arguing about a play from a game from who knew how many years ago. As she walked back in, Jack stood and walked to the microwave. He hit a couple of buttons while explaining to Kenny why he was wrong.

Because in the few minutes she'd been gone, he'd put her dinner in the microwave for her. So it wouldn't be cold. Taryn grabbed the open bottle of wine and topped off Larissa's glass while Sam put another slice of garlic bread on her side plate.

She smiled and took her place at the family table.

Two days later, Jack walked through Fool's Gold on his way to the library to pick up Percy. It was nearly seven on a weeknight, but people were still out. Families strolled together. Neighbors visited over fences. It was a good town, he thought. A place that welcomed strangers and made longtime residents not want to leave.

Taryn had hated the idea of moving here, but even she had come around. Sam was engaged to a local girl. It was just a matter of time until Kenny over-came his past and fell hard for some sweet young thing. Then they'd have roots here and Score would become a part of the Fool's Gold story.

He wanted that. A sense of belonging was nice—as long as he could keep his distance as it washed over him.

He turned the corner and headed for the library. As he got closer, he saw a tall skinny teen sitting on the front steps. Percy put his laptop away as Jack approached, then stood and walked toward him.

"When did the library close?" he asked.

"It's open a few more minutes, but I came out here to wait. I wanted to keep working on my reading." Percy grinned. "It's going good. Some of the stuff I know and I'm learning the rest of it."

"Good for you." Jack and the teen walked along the sidewalk. The sun had set about fifteen minutes before and now the sky darkened quickly.

Percy glanced at him. "There were a couple of guys in the library who were starting at Cal U Fool's Gold in a couple of weeks. They said they wished the school had a football team."

"Trying to influence my vote?" Jack asked.

"Maybe."

"You don't have to convince me, kid. I think having a football program will enrich the college. But I'm not the decision maker. Besides, starting a team from scratch…" He shook his head. That would be a tough one. "I'm not sure where they'll find a coach willing to take that on. It would be years before they were decent enough to play in any of the ranked leagues. You'd be giving up maybe a decade of your career to be in the shadows."

Percy brows drew together. "I thought coaches were in it for the love of the game and teaching their players."

"A lot are, but you also want to be seen as a winner. It's hard to win when you don't get to play." Jack wondered how long until the program could join the small leagues. Three years? Four? "Plus, it's going to take some real money to do it right. Scholarships have to be established, equipment bought, staff hired. A job like that would be consuming."

He knew what he was talking about. Football had consumed him for a couple of decades—but in the best way possible. He'd seen the sport change lives. Having a team on campus would be a good thing— he believed that. But he doubted the university was willing to make the commitment.

Football had saved him, he thought. Had given him a place to belong after his parents had left for Africa. It had been easier to survive that year after Lucas had died. The year of firsts. First Christmas without his brother. First birthday. In a way, the latter had been more difficult. Because he and Lucas were twins—they'd shared a birthday.

"At least they have a good name," Percy said. "They're the Warriors. That's from the town. The Máa-zib tribe that settled here. Larissa was telling me about it."

"Did she also tell you the Máa-zib are matriarchal?"

Percy looked blank.

Jack grinned. "That means the structure of the tribe was based on women having the power instead of men. A male-dominated society is patriarchal. Like if a boy is born, he'll be king, but women can't rule."

"There's a queen of England," Percy said.

"Right. But that's only because there weren't any male heirs. Prince Charles, her son, is her oldest child so her daughter will never rule."

"That sucks."

A generational comment, Jack thought humorously. He was pretty sure most men over the age of sixty would think nothing of that. But times had changed.

Percy grinned. "So you're saying the Cal U Fool's Gold Warriors should have a woman dressed up like a warrior instead of a guy?"

"Yup."

"Sweet. You gonna tell them?"

"Probably not."

"If you change your mind, I want to be there," Percy told him.

"On the fringe of making trouble, but not actually doing it yourself?"

The teen nodded. "All the show and none of the danger."

"My brother was like that," Jack said without thinking.

Percy glanced at him. "I didn't know you had a brother."

"I did. He died a long time ago."

Percy's humor faded. "I'm sorry."

"Thanks. He was..." Jack hesitated, then figured what the hell. "He was seventeen. We both were. Lucas was my identical twin." Although not completely identical, he thought. There was the matter of their very different hearts.

"That had to be hard."

"It was," Jack admitted. "He was a good guy. He saw the best in people. And he never complained." Not about all the treatments, the surgeries, the suffering. Not even about whatever twist of fate had landed him with the crappy heart.

"You still miss him." Percy wasn't asking a question.

"Every day," Jack admitted.

The kid nodded. "It's like that with my mom. Some days are easier, but I never forget her. I guess it's always like that when someone you love dies."

They continued to walk toward Jack's house. They were mostly silent, but it was companionable. He thought of his earlier conversation with Larissa. "So there's going to be a bird at the house."

Percy nodded. "Larissa said something about it coming to stay for a few days. It's nearly healed and they needed room for more injured birds."

Which was more than Jack knew. No doubt Larissa would have told him the details, but he liked to be as uninformed as possible. It made his life simpler.

"Did she mention how long it was staying?" he asked.

"Three days. By then it should be able to fly. Once it's ready, it'll be released in the wild." He sounded excited. "She's going to show me how to feed it and everything."

"I hope it's not a raptor."

"You mean like a dinosaur?"

"No. A raptor is a bird of prey. Like an eagle or a hawk." Because Jack was starting to have a bad feeling about the whole bird rescue-visit thing. No good deed, he reminded himself.

"She wouldn't do that," Percy said confidently.

"Uh-huh." Jack was less sure. After all, she'd left fighting dogs in his living room before.

They approached the house where they lived. From the outside, everything looked normal, but he knew better than to take any chances.

When they were on the front porch, he carefully inserted his key into the lock and turned it. The door opened slowly. He flipped on a couple of lights.

Immediately a loud squawking and hooting filled the house. The screeches were loud and angry. And whatever was making the sounds wasn't tiny.

Percy's eyes widened. "What do you think that is?"

"I have no idea."

They both stood on the porch. Jack motioned for Percy to go first.

"It's your house, man," the teen said. "The honor is yours."

Jack grimaced. "Maybe, but you're younger and faster. I say it's time for you to earn your keep."

"Chicken," Percy said.

"If it's a chicken, then you can mock me all you want."

Percy passed over his computer bag and then slowly, carefully, walked through the foyer and into the living room beyond.

"Oh, man, talk about a beauty."

The words were hard to understand because the mystery bird was throwing yet another hissy fit. Jack swore under his breath, then followed the kid into the living room where he found a cage that nearly filled the entire room.

All his furniture had been pushed back to the edges of the room. Protective tarps had been placed on the floor. The cage itself had to be at least ten feet high and inside of it was a massive owl.

"Oh, good, he's here."

Both Jack and Percy jumped. Larissa came in from behind them.

"What?" she demanded. "Are you frightened of her? Or him?" She tilted her head. "Now that you mention it, no one told me the gender. Maybe they didn't want to be rude and look." She smiled. "Either way, our owl is beautiful."

"It's a woman," Jack said flatly. "Look at how she's glaring at us."

Larissa laughed. "You might be right. Anyway, this is our guest. She's a Northern Spotted Owl. There are only five or six hundred breeding pairs in

California, so keeping her safe is important. She's nocturnal, she eats small rodents and she prefers old-growth forests. She'll be returned there in a few days, when she's fully healed."

The owl in question continued to glare, then she turned her head away.

"Her eyes are dark, unlike most owl species. They usually have light-colored eyes."

"Someone's been on Wikipedia," Jack murmured, wondering how loud the damn owl was going to be.

"The wilderness group sent me material. You can see why I couldn't take her home. I don't have room for the cage. Plus, Dyna would have been at risk."

Jack glanced at the owl and figured it could eat a whole cat with no problem. He returned his attention to Larissa. She beamed at the bird as if it were the most perfect creature ever invented. And to her, it probably was. Until the next rescue.

Her blue eyes were fixated on the bird. Her mouth was parted a tiny bit and color lightly stained her smooth skin.

She was lovely, he thought in surprise. Sure, she always looked good. Casual and easygoing. But there was something different about how she looked today, although he couldn't figure out what the change was.

"That owl is incredible," Percy said, moving a little closer. "Angry, but who wants to live in a cage?"

"She won't for long," Larissa assured him.

Jack stared at the floor of the cage. "What's that stuff?" he asked. There were odd-shaped things.

"A bird's gotta do what a bird's gotta do," Percy told him.

"I don't think so," Jack said as he inched closer to the cage.

"That's from her dinner," Larissa said cheerfully. "She eats her food whole then throws up the fur and bone."

"Of course she does," Jack said grimly while Percy started to laugh.

JACK TURNED IN close to eleven. But the second he clicked on the bedside light, he knew it was going to be a very long night.

Despite being an entire floor below, with at least one closed door between them, Jack could still clearly hear the owl protesting her confinement. Hoots and screeches were followed by just enough silence for him to get sleepy. Then she started up again.

He turned onto his side and punched his pillow. Not that it would help. Because the owl was only part of the problem. Larissa was the other part. Kissing her had been a mistake. Not because he hadn't liked it, but because it had changed things between them. Inevitable, he supposed. Now he had to figure out a way to put the genie back in the bottle.

With any other woman, he could simply end things. But there wasn't anything to end. Not technically. Besides, Larissa was an integral part of his life. Like air—he needed her to survive. She was the best part of him. Without her, he was nothing but an empty shell. Why would he want that when he could be—at least in her eyes—a perfect hero?

CHAPTER TEN

"Doesn't Jack care what you put on his calendar?" Percy asked. "You could write in anything. Like send him to Omaha for no reason."

Larissa grinned at the teen. "Technically that's true, but why would I? Jack's my boss and my friend. I don't want to torture him." No, what she had in mind for Jack had nothing to do with torture and everything to do with...

She cleared her throat and her mind. *Focus,* she told herself. No wayward sexual thoughts, especially not with Percy in the room. That would be too weird and icky.

Percy studied the calendar. They were in her office and she was explaining what her job entailed. Part of Percy's education was to understand the workings of Score.

"Still, he has to really trust you, right?" he asked.

"Uh-huh. That's part of the relationship." She pointed to the different events. "It's all color-coded. Speaking engagements, appearances for charity. Regular meetings."

"Golf is a charity event?" Percy asked.

"It can be. There's going to be a Pro-am here in a few weeks."

Percy frowned. "What's a Pro-am?"

"Professionals and amateurs playing together, only the amateurs are mostly celebrities."

"Jack plays professionally?"

She clicked on the square in the calendar, expanding it to show all the information. "This is golf where he's considered an amateur. It's a fund-raiser for a local charity. Professional golfers come play with people from TV and the movies, along with some other athletes."

"Like Jack."

"Exactly."

"Will you play?"

"I don't like golf. Plus, the amateurs are really kind of famous in their own right."

"Like Jack, Kenny and Sam."

"Uh-huh."

The teen leaned forward in his chair. "That makes sense. 'Cuz if people are going to pay to watch you play golf, you'd better be somebody they admire or something." He gave her a shy smile. "But you're prettier than Jack."

"Thank you, Percy."

He turned his attention back to the calendar. "You do a lot of massages."

They were in purple on the calendar. She clicked a tab, which shifted the screen to her weekly schedule. "I do less than I would if that was my full-time job," she told him. "But that's okay. I like the variety."

"Did you have to study to do massages?"

"I did. I had to learn about muscles and how the body works. Once I'd completed my instruction, I had to practice by giving massages. There are a certain number of hours required to be certified."

Which she wasn't, she reminded herself. She had the paperwork, the hours and the education. She really needed to get off her butt and send in the paperwork. Not that it would change her life at Score, but it would be nice to know she was employable anywhere.

Percy looked around at her office. "Even this is nice," he said, then cleared his throat. "I mean the other offices are really big."

"Tell me about it," she said with a grin. "You could practically go bowling in Jack's office. I'm fine with something a whole lot smaller." Besides, this was just for scheduling and making calls. Her real work was done in the massage room.

"I never knew businesses were like this," Percy told her. "All fancy and high-tech. It's nice."

"Maybe you'll get a job in a place like this," she told him. "After you go to college."

"I'd like that. Only college is a long way away. First I have to get my GED."

"And you will. Then you'll go to college."

His expression was doubtful. "Everyone here keeps talking about college, like everyone should go. But it's not like that. Where I'm from, you did what you had to so you could get by."

Life in the inner city. She had no frame of reference for that, Larissa thought. No moment to bond over.

"College gives you opportunities. Choices. You're right—not everyone has that in their future. But you do now. I hope you'll take advantage of the chance."

He shifted on his chair. "I don't know anyone who went to college. Not ever. My grandma didn't get past the seventh grade. None of my friends where I grew up were going to do much more than join a gang."

She'd been born and raised in Los Angeles, she thought. Probably not thirty miles from where Percy had spent most of his life. Yet they had very different world views.

"Change is hard," she admitted. "This is big change for you."

"But a good one," he said. "I know I got lucky when you found me in the park."

She smiled at him. "We're happy to have you here."

"You're nice. Everyone here is. Sam's kind of quiet, but he was explaining what he did. With the money and stuff. And Taryn's tough on the outside, but inside she's real soft. But she doesn't want anyone to know. Kenny's a good guy, but there's, like, a wall."

Larissa did her best not to react. Percy's assessments were more accurate than she'd expected. Impressively so. "What about Jack?" she asked.

Percy grinned. "You boss him around."

"I don't!"

"Yeah, you do, and he likes it."

THE NORTHERN SPOTTED Owl didn't look the least bit amused by the process of being moved. Wildlife sanctuary workers had maneuvered her into a smaller cage, which she hadn't liked at all. She screeched out her displeasure, her large wings flapping against the bars of the cage. Jack kept his distance and hoped the opening was secure because when that bird was finally free, she was so going to take out her bad temper on whoever was closest. He wanted to make sure that wasn't him.

The guys dismantled the larger cage, then carried it out to their truck. On their second trip into the house, Larissa followed them.

She was dressed as she always was. Yoga pants, a short-sleeved T-shirt and athletic shoes. Her long blond hair had been pulled back in a ponytail. Her face was clean and free of makeup. He happened to know she would smell like whatever scented body lotion she was currently using. For the past couple of days it had been a sweet kind of garden-y scent she said was verbena. Whatever the hell that was.

The week before it had been lemon and the previous month she'd gone on a vanilla binge. Regardless of the lotion, under the verbena, the lemon or the vanilla was the essence of Larissa herself. A warm, welcoming fragrance that had always been like home to him. Although these days it was home with an edge.

The taller of the two owl-retrieval guys—probably in his mid-twenties—dropped his gaze to Larissa's ass. His eyes widened appreciatively. Jack told himself it was okay for them to look and that his urge to put his fist through the guy's face wasn't an impulse he was going to act on. Still, he moved closer to her.

"Hey," he said, putting his arm around her.

She looked up at him. "Wendy's leaving already?"

"Wendy?"

"The owl."

"I got that, but why Wendy?"

"I don't know. She looked like a Wendy to me. They called a bit ago and said they were taking her back." She sighed. "I'm glad she's better, but I didn't get to spend as much time with her as I would have liked."

Jack normally would have teased her about the name and wanting to spend time with an owl whose idea of a party was eating small animals. But he was a little distracted by how good it felt to pull Larissa close. She was tall, but shorter than him. Slender— almost fragile. He knew she was strong and capable but at that moment, she seemed...delicate.

"There'll be another owl," he told her. "Or some other woodland creature you can bond with."

She laughed. "Did you just say 'woodland creature'?"

"I did."

The two guys carried the transport cage to the truck. Wendy glared as she squawked and threatened. Larissa sighed.

"She'll be released later today. That's good. I mean the purpose was to provide her with a place to stay and you did that."

He'd done nothing but provide housing, but if she wanted to make him a hero, he was willing to go with it.

Once Wendy and her escorts had driven away,

he closed the front door, then walked into the living room. All the furniture had been pushed to the outside walls. The tarps on the floors had protected the flooring from Wendy's need to spit up bones and fur.

Jack went to the largest sofa and reached down to shift it back into place. It moved easily, but as he shifted positions, he felt a familiar burning in his right shoulder. The one that told him all the scar tissue was tight and that it was going to be a very long night.

The cause was simple—too much football and not enough healing. He couldn't change the reality of either problem. He'd made his choice to play the game and he didn't regret one second of his time in the sport. As for the healing, well, there was only so much any one body could do.

While Larissa pushed the smaller chairs into place, he tackled the second sofa. They walked to the big, square coffee table at the same time.

"It's too heavy for you," he told her.

"I'm tough. Besides, I'm not the one who's hurting."

He wasn't surprised she'd noticed. Larissa knew his body as well as he did. Usually that wasn't a problem. Her familiarity with his aches and pains meant that when she worked him over, he was good for a couple of days. But lately he'd been avoiding her. Or rather her massages. Time on the table had become uncomfortable and it had nothing to do with his destroyed right shoulder.

They carried the coffee table into place. A couple

of lamps later, the room was back to normal. She headed for the kitchen.

"Come on," she called over her shoulder. "You know you need this."

He hesitated only a second, then trailed after her. While she went to the half bath to get a bottle of lotion, he unbuttoned his cuffs, then moved to the front of the shirt. By the time he sat down in the kitchen chair she'd pulled out, he had his shirt in his hands. She took it from him and tossed it onto the table. She moved to his right side and pressed her fingers into his shoulder.

The relief was nearly as powerful as the ache. She knew exactly how hard to press and where the scar tissue thickened. She was able to dig deeper, to find the places that bothered him the most, and release the buildup of acid and pain. Massages with her weren't gentle and they weren't pleasant, but when she was done, he was healed. At least for a couple of days.

He relaxed into the familiar burning, knowing he would sleep better because of it. At the same time, he half expected her to yell at him for avoiding their sessions. Or at least ask why he had. Only what was he supposed to say to that? The truth was impossible. No way he could admit he was terrified he would get turned on again. Talk about humiliating.

Twenty minutes later, she stepped back. "Better?"

"Much. Thanks." He reached for his shirt and shrugged it on. "Want to get lunch?"

"Sure. What do you have in the refrigerator?"

He had no idea. She was forever putting stuff in

there, then later, throwing it out if he didn't eat it. As he watched, she crossed the hardwood floor and opened the refrigerator.

"There's plenty. We'll have a bit of everything. How does that sound?"

"Good."

He rotated his arm, testing his shoulder. The ache had faded to a manageable level. When he went back to the office, he would spend some time in the steam room and be practically like new.

At her instruction, he collected plates and bowls, along with forks, knives and napkins. She heated containers in the microwave, then put food on the table.

There was an eclectic collection of leftover Chinese and Italian, a salad from a bag and couple of microwaveable burritos. He grabbed a diet cola for her and a bottle of water for himself, then joined her at the table.

"Quite the feast," he said as he sat across from her.

She grinned. "I really wanted to add Cheetos, but that seemed too much."

"There's always room for Cheetos."

"There is."

She took a serving spoonful of spicy cashew chicken and passed him the carton.

"I'm worried about Percy," she said as she licked her fingers.

Jack found himself more interested in what she was doing with her mouth than anything she might say. A dangerous state of affairs, he reminded himself, and forced his attention back to the topic at hand.

"Why?"

She took a small serving of lasagna. "We were talking about him going to college. He doesn't know anyone who's done that. I think he's nervous about having too many choices. For some people, dreaming can be dangerous."

A problem Jack understood. Lucas hadn't allowed himself to dream. He'd been careful to think in terms of days, not months or years. Later, when he'd had his heart transplant, the future had been his. There had been so much he'd wanted to see and do. The whole family had started to believe in possibilities. Only they'd been wrong about them.

"First Percy has to get his GED," Jack said, knowing he wasn't going to mention his brother.

"That's what he said."

"Once he has that, the next step will be more logical. We'll start small. Community college."

"He's going to need a job. A real one. Not just extra work at Score," she said. "Something where he feels really useful."

"You don't think he feels useful at Score? Taryn's a tough taskmaster."

"She is, but Percy knows he's only there because of you."

Jack took a bite of the burrito and chewed. Who knew that jalapeño-flavored beans went well with marinara sauce?

"He's not there because of me," he said when he'd swallowed. "You're the one who found him. I don't get any of the credit."

"He's living with you. You're the one he looks up to."

Jack shrugged. "Like I said, he'll figure it out. One step at a time."

She bit her lower lip. "I hope you're right."

"When am I wrong?"

The worry didn't leave her eyes. "What if the whole nurture-nature thing is right? What if Percy can't escape his environment?"

"He's young enough to learn a new way of doing things. He's a good kid. He wants more than he has. He was smart enough and determined enough to get to Fool's Gold. He knew it would be a better place for him. And thanks to you, it is. Now have a little faith."

Jack reached for his water and took a swallow.

"You'll talk to him about safe sex?" she asked.

He started to choke.

Larissa waited until he could breathe again. "I need you to say yes."

"I'm not talking about the birds and bees with Percy."

"I'm sure he knows where babies come from. He needs to practice safe sex. Having a child now would make things really hard on him. He needs a chance to fulfill his potential."

And things had been going so well for at least the past—Jack checked his watch—fifteen minutes.

"I don't get an entire day after Wendy leaves before you drop this particular bomb on me?"

She didn't smile. If anything, her mouth turned

down. "Jack, I'm serious. What if he got a girl pregnant?"

At least one of them would be getting some, he thought grimly. But that wasn't her point. Larissa's concern had a whole lot more to do with her past than with Percy. Not that she would admit it.

He stared into her blue eyes and saw the weariness of carrying around unreasonable guilt for years. It didn't matter that her mother getting pregnant twenty-nine years ago wasn't her fault. It didn't matter that her father had wanted to do the right thing and that two people who never should have gotten married had. It wasn't her responsibility that they'd been desperately unhappy until they'd finally divorced.

Larissa was the oldest child. She considered herself the reason her parents had been forced into an unhappy marriage. The fact that they were now happily married to other people didn't make her feel better at all.

Had she been nearly anyone else, he would have told her to get over it. But he couldn't. Because he carried the same type of guilt around, too. Not about his parents, but about his brother.

"Jack?"

"I'll talk to him," he said. "I promise."

"Soon, right?"

"Yes, soon. Right after I finish banging my head against the wall."

The worry faded as she smiled. "You always say that, but I've never seen you do it."

"Some things are best done in private. How's Dyna?"

"Beautiful. It's nice to have a warm, furry body in bed with me." She held up her hand. "Do *not* make any cracks about the guys I've dated."

"Would I do that?" he asked.

"In a heartbeat."

THE REST OF lunch passed in easy conversation. Larissa ate too much, but how was she supposed to choose just a couple of things when there were so many options?

She leaned back in her chair as Jack cleared the table. He was moving better now, she thought, noticing the lack of stiffness in his shoulder.

"You know there's surgery," she said before she could stop herself.

Jack scraped the plates into the sink, then ran water and turned on the garbage disposal. When he walked back to the table, he put both hands on her shoulders, then bent down and kissed the top of her head.

"No."

"They've made advances. It could help."

"I've had surgery. It didn't help."

"It helped a little."

"Not enough."

He released her and she scrambled to her feet, prepared to take him on. Because this was important. He was always in pain and what if she wasn't around to make him feel better?

"Taryn find her dress yet?" he asked in a very obvious attempt to change the subject. "Because I have to tell you, I don't think I can take another afternoon in a wedding-gown store."

"She's decided and she's going to look beautiful."

"Good. She and Angel are good together. They fit." He was relaxed as he spoke. There was no tension, no sense of hesitation. She knew in her heart that whatever had happened between them all those years ago had never grown into anything more than friendship. They hadn't been in love.

Because being in love would change everything. Being in love meant always thinking about the other person. It meant wanting to be close, having everything divided into Jack or not Jack. It meant being happier when he was around and needing his smile, his touch, like she needed air.

"Larissa?"

Jack's voice came from very far away. Like through water. Or over a distance. She could hear him but she couldn't react. She was too busy trying to stay standing as the truth slammed into her. That her mother had been right all along. She was in love with Jack.

"I have to go," she said as she raced for the front door.

"What's wrong?"

"Nothing." *Everything.* "I'm fine." She would never be fine again.

LARISSA DIDN'T REMEMBER much about getting from Jack's house to the Score offices. She was out of breath so she'd probably run more than she was used to. She hurried into the building and raced down the hall. She flung open the door to Taryn's office and stared at her friend.

Taryn was on the phone. She glanced up, took one look at Larissa and spoke into the receiver. "Jenny, I'm going to have to call you back…Uh-huh. This afternoon. I promise." She hung up and stood. "Who's dead?"

"No one. Everyone is fine."

Taryn's brows drew together. "You don't look like everyone is fine."

"They are. It's not that. It's me. It's my mother. She was right."

Larissa didn't want to say the words out loud, so she waited for the truth to sink in. Taryn's violet eyes widened.

Her friend swore. "Seriously? You're in love with Jack?"

"I think so. Maybe. I was having lunch with him and he mentioned how you and Angel fit. And then I started thinking what it means to be in love." She paused for breath. "Is it possible?"

Taryn sank back into her chair. "Dear God, I hope not."

Larissa settled across from her. "Because it will end badly."

"That's one way of putting it. Jack doesn't commit to anyone. He won't let himself get that involved." The worry returned. "You know that, right?"

Larissa nodded. "Of course. I've seen him with

his women. He's good for a few weeks and then he's gone." She was still trying to absorb the unexpected truth. In love with Jack? Seriously?

She didn't have to ask how it had happened. He was a great guy. Giving to her causes, always there for her. Funny, charming, sexy. Maybe loving him had been inevitable.

"I really hate that my mother was right," she admitted.

"That would be annoying."

"It could be a stage in my emotional development," she said slowly, thinking aloud. "Being around him like I have, maybe I didn't have a choice in the matter."

"I warned you about him when you first started."

"And that was supposed to be enough?"

Taryn sighed. "I suppose not. So now what?"

"I'm not sure. I guess I have to figure out a way to get over him."

"You're not going to try to get him to fall in love with you?"

"No way. That's not possible." Although it was nice to think about. "If Jack was going to see me as anything more than his friend, don't you think it would have happened by now?"

"Good point. So how exactly do you plan to get over Jack? He's kind of a great guy."

"How did you get over him?"

"I was never in love with him. We were friends and we still are."

Oh, right. "So how do women get over any guy?

You see him as he is, not as you want him to be. I need to focus on Jack's flaws. He doesn't commit, he's emotionally unavailable."

"Those would be the same thing," Taryn murmured.

"Okay, so there are others. He's not good boyfriend material. I know that. I've seen him with his other women. He's…" Larissa felt the pieces fall into place. "I have an unrealistic view of what a relationship with Jack would be like. I've only seen that part of his life from the outside."

"No," Taryn said firmly. "I'm not sure where this is going, but I don't like it."

"It's brilliant," Larissa told her. "Totally brilliant. I'm not going to convince Jack to fall in love with me, I'm going to convince him to have an affair with me. Then he won't be a romantic hero anymore. He'll just be this guy I used to date. And then I'll fall out of love with him."

Taryn's gaze was steady. "That is possibly the stupidest idea ever."

"No, it's brilliant. You'll see."

CHAPTER ELEVEN

"WHO ARE WE MEETING?" Larissa asked as she walked with Bailey to Brew-haha.

"Her name is Shelby Gilmore. She's Kipling Gilmore's sister." Bailey grinned. "You know Kipling Gilmore, right?"

"Not personally, but I might have caught one or two of his events on TV," Larissa admitted. Kipling had been a fantastic skier and had won two gold medals at the Olympic Games earlier that year. But right now she wasn't all that interested in him or any other man who wasn't Jack.

Not that she'd figured out what she was going to do about him, but she was mulling and eventually she would come up with a plan.

"I saw him, too," Bailey said. "He's totally hot."

"So there's an ulterior motive for helping his sister?"

Bailey laughed. "Not even close. Mayor Marsha asked that I help make Shelby feel at home. I'm still not sure how to do that myself, so I dragged you along. This has nothing to do with Kipling. He's just a frame of reference."

"Uh-huh. Like I buy that. So you're saying if he asked you out right now, you'd refuse?"

Bailey hesitated just long enough for Larissa to come to a stop and face her. "What?" she demanded.

"Or rather, who? There's somebody if you're not accepting a date with Kipling Gilmore. I've heard he's really nice. Why don't you want to go out with him?"

Bailey laughed. "Maybe because I've never met the man and he certainly hasn't asked me on a date. Besides, even if he were my type, which he's not, you forget. I'm a single mom. It's the best anti-date charm there is."

Larissa hadn't thought about that. Chloe, Bailey's daughter, was adorable. Funny and sweet. She showed up at Score from time to time to get help with various FWM projects. The FWM—Future Warriors of the Máa-zib—was kind of like a scouting organization. But local, and with a Fool's Gold twist.

"I thought guys were over worrying about women with kids," she said.

"Not as much as you might think. But it's fine. I'm not looking to get involved. Or date." Her tone was a little wistful.

"You don't sound convinced."

Bailey sighed. "Okay, one hot night with Kipling Gilmore would go a long way toward brightening up my week, but that's as much as I'm willing to commit to."

"It's enough."

"What about you?" Bailey asked. "Any interest in the hunky skier?"

"I'm around hunky athletes all day," Larissa reminded her as they crossed the street and approached the coffee shop. "I'm not looking for more."

Nope, what she was looking for was a way to get over Jack. As she'd told Taryn, having a romantic—i.e., sexual—relationship with the man seemed like the best way to get over him. The only stumbling block was how she was going to get him to figure out he wanted her. Assuming he did.

They walked into Brew-haha. The coffee place was well lit and welcoming with lots of primary colors and an exceptional display of tempting pastries. There were a dozen or so tables, most of them empty in the middle of the afternoon. But a lone woman sat at one of them.

"That's her," Bailey said in a low voice. "I saw a picture."

Shelby Gilmore was probably in her mid-twenties. She had gold-blond hair that fell past her shoulders and big blue eyes. She was petite, almost delicate. No, Larissa thought, suddenly feeling she had too long arms and legs and was way too tall. Not delicate. Ethereal. Like a fairy princess who had gotten caught in the wrong reality.

Talk about fanciful, she told herself. Where had that come from?

Shelby looked up as they approached the table. While she smiled, her gaze was wary.

"Hi," Bailey said as she took a seat opposite. "I'm Bailey Voss and this is Larissa Owens. Thanks for meeting us."

"You're welcome."

Bailey glanced at the small table between them. "We need coffee. I'm thinking a latte. What about you, Shelby?"

"Sure. A latte would be nice. Thank you."

Larissa nodded her agreement and Bailey went off to place the orders. There was no one else in line, so she was back in a matter of a minute or so.

She sat down and sighed. "Patience is bringing over pastries with the order. That will be fine for those of you who are annoyingly skinny, but I don't need the temptation."

Larissa shook her head. "Yeah, right. Who wouldn't want those curves of yours?" If she had Bailey's figure, she would have a much easier time of getting Jack's attention.

Bailey smiled. "If only that were true." She looked at Shelby. "So, you're wondering who we are and why we're here."

"A little," Shelby admitted.

"We want to welcome you to Fool's Gold. You're new here. I moved here only a few years ago, so I know what it's like to be a stranger in a small town where it seems like everyone knows everyone else."

"That would be tough," Larissa said, thinking when she'd moved to Fool's Gold in the spring, she'd been with her Score family. So she didn't have to feel by herself. But Shelby might not know anyone.

Shelby glanced between them. "I'm doing okay. I have a job at the bakery."

Patience, the owner of Brew-haha walked up with

a large tray. She put down three lattes and a plate of pastries. "You work for Amber, right? You're the new baker? That's great." She pointed at the pastries. "I've been eating too many of those. You're doing a really good job and you need to stop. I mean it."

Shelby smiled. "Thanks. I like my job. Amber is really easy to work for."

"She's just lovely," Patience said. "All right, I'll leave you three to your afternoon treats. Yell if you need anything."

Each of them took a latte. Shelby ignored the pastries, but Larissa reached for the cheese-and-blueberry one and took a bite.

"Heaven," she said when she'd chewed and swallowed. "One of yours?"

Shelby nodded.

Bailey eyed the high-calorie snack before pushing the plate away. "So, Shelby, how are you enjoying the town?"

"It's fine."

Larissa sensed the other woman wasn't comfortable with their meeting. "Have you been to any of the festivals? They're pretty fun. I loved the books festival. I met several of my favorite authors and got books signed as birthday and Christmas gifts for family. I grew up in Los Angeles. Killer weather, but there's not much of a small-town feel."

"Fool's Gold would be a change," Shelby said. "I'm from Colorado. I'm used to smaller towns but nothing like this."

"Fool's Gold is unique," Bailey said.

There was a moment of uncomfortable silence. Bailey glanced at Larissa, her expression desperate. Larissa struggled for something to say.

"Um, Bailey works for Mayor Marsha," she blurted. "She's the longest-serving mayor in California, by the way. She knows your brother."

Shelby turned her attention to Bailey. "When did she meet Kip?"

"Earlier this year. Right after his accident. She was in New Zealand." Bailey paused. "I'm not sure exactly how she met him, what with him being in a hospital and all."

Shelby's wariness faded. "Then it was her!"

"What was her?"

"The old lady my brother told me about. After…" She swallowed. "My mom died a couple of months ago. She had cancer and it wasn't unexpected, but it was still hard."

Larissa instinctively reached for Shelby's hand. Bailey was already touching her arm.

"I'm sorry," Bailey said. "About your mom. When you lose a family member, it's awful." She swallowed. "I lost my husband last year."

"Then you know," Shelby said quietly. "Thank you both for meeting me. I'm sorry if I seem a little stand-offish. It's just things were hard with my mom and my dad…well, there's no need to talk about him." She managed a slight smile. "Let's just say that right after Kip's accident, two men showed up out of nowhere and took care of me and my mom."

"Do you know their names?" Larissa asked, wondering if there was a town connection.

"Ford and Angel."

"Those are our guys," Bailey said. "They're both at the bodyguard school. Interesting that they came and found you." She looked at Larissa. "It has to be Mayor Marsha."

Larissa nodded. "Everyone says she knows things there's no way to know. It's kind of mystical. I like it."

Shelby nodded. "Me, too. I owe her." She glanced at her watch. "I have to get back to work, but it was great to meet you both. Maybe we could do this again."

"I'd like that," Larissa said.

Bailey nodded. "Very much."

They exchanged cell numbers and Shelby left. Bailey grabbed one of the pastries and took a bite.

"That was a challenge," she said when she'd swallowed. "I thought she was going to bolt when we first sat down."

"She was wary," Larissa said. "She's dealing with something and I think it's more than what happened to her mom." There had been something in her eyes. Something Larissa sometimes saw when she talked to parents of a child in need of a transplant that didn't look as if it was going to happen. Hopelessness.

Bailey finished the pastry and licked her fingers. "Thanks for coming with me. I would have totally blown it on my own."

"No, you wouldn't have. You would have done great."

"I wish. So what's new with you? Ready to admit you're in love with Jack?"

Larissa felt her mouth drop open. "How did you know?"

Bailey stared at her. "What? You are? I was kidding. You're in love with Jack? When did that happen? When did you two start dating? Why am I always the last to know?"

"We're not dating. We're friends."

Bailey sagged back in her seat. "What? You said you're in love with him. Start at the beginning and speak slowly. I need to catch up."

"When we talked about it before, I said my mother was insane. No way I was in love with him," Larissa said.

"Only you are."

"I didn't know it."

"Apparently not. So this revelation came over time?"

Larissa nodded. "I mean, it's Jack. He's good-looking and sweet. He's always there for me and he supports my causes. We hang out all the time. And he has a body."

"Which you've seen and touched." Bailey pressed her lips together. "I can see how it happened. You were minding your own business and the man sucked you in. Now what? Do you declare your undying devotion and beg to be taken?"

"Sort of."

"Wow. Impressive."

Larissa smiled. "Don't be impressed. What I mean

is I'm going to figure out how to fall out of love with Jack and that involves sex."

Bailey put down her latte. "I always thought I was one of the brighter bulbs in the chandelier. I guess that's not true. Where does the sex fit in?"

"Jack isn't going to fall for me. He's emotionally unavailable. So there's no happy ending with him. If I want a normal romantic life, it needs to be with someone else. Only how does a normal guy compete with Jack?"

"That would be tough. So how does having sex with Jack help?"

"It removes the mystery. I'll see him for who he is and let the fantasy go."

Bailey looked doubtful. "Or you'll bond with him and fall even deeper in love."

Something Larissa hadn't thought of. "I think if I focus on his flaws, I'll be fine."

"You do realize if you're wrong, you're digging a pit you'll never crawl out of."

Larissa brushed away the information. "I'll be fine."

"If you say so. I'm assuming there's a plan."

"There is."

Bailey raised her eyebrows expectantly. "And it is what?"

"I'm going to seduce him."

JACK CARRIED THE bags of takeout carefully. He had burritos, along with chips and salsa and guacamole from Margaritaville and he knew better than to risk anything spilling. The women in his life were serious about their chips and guacamole.

Larissa's call requesting he bring over dinner had come in the late afternoon. Percy was going to hang with Kenny for the evening. The former receiver was going to explain basic U.S. history using a couple of comic books he'd found on the subject. Percy's reading was improving every day but there was no way he was ready to tackle an actual high-school-level textbook on the subject.

Sam was already working with the teen on his math skills. Percy had a good grasp of basic concepts. Algebra came easy to him. Sam had actually looked gleeful when he'd mentioned taking Percy through introductory calculus. The man did love his numbers, which was good for the company and their individual financial portfolios.

Jack climbed the stairs to Larissa's second-floor apartment, knocked once and let himself inside.

"It's me," he called as he walked into the kitchen and set the food on the counter. Dyna strolled up to greet him.

"Hey, pretty girl." Jack picked up the cat. She instantly relaxed in his arms and began to purr. He rubbed her face. Big blue eyes stared back at him.

"Hi, Jack."

He turned, prepared to offer Larissa a greeting. But the words got stuck in his throat. Or maybe it was the fact that he couldn't breathe that made speaking impossible.

She stood in the center of her living room. That

was okay. People stood in living rooms all the time. He knew that. The difference wasn't the where, it was the what the hell. As in what the hell was she wearing?

Instead of her usual yoga pants and a T-shirt, or even jeans, she had on some kind of silky robe. The bottom barely covered her butt and just kissed her thighs. Her hair was long and a little curly and if he didn't know better he would say she was wearing makeup.

The combination was unbelievable sexy. Wanting hit him like a linebacker and nearly knocked him senseless. Or maybe it was the lack of air that killed the last few surviving brain cells. He wasn't sure.

He drew in a breath and carefully lowered Dyna to the floor. When he straightened, Larissa was still standing there in that damn robe.

"Am I, ah, early?" he asked, knowing it was just a matter of seconds before the blood pulsing through his body settled uncomfortably in his groin and his desire would be there for the world to see.

Dammit all to hell, why did she have to be so beautiful? And sexy?

Larissa stared at him coolly. "You're not early."

She tossed her hair over her shoulders. The movement caused the robe to shimmer around her and her breasts to move in such a way that he was reasonably confident she wasn't wearing a bra.

He swore silently and looked around desperately for a distraction. All he saw was the cat.

"I'll brush Dyna while you finish getting dressed,"

he mumbled, grabbing the unsuspecting feline and pulling her back into his arms. "I saw her brush in the kitchen."

With that, he stumbled away.

He hid in the tiny space, hoping Larissa would assume his moronic behavior was about low blood sugar or because of too many hits to the head. Anything but the truth, he thought desperately. He had to get a grip.

He held on to Dyna, petting her while she purred and thinking about baseball and the changes they were making in the Mercedes CLS and how global warming meant there would be vineyards in Alaska in the next ten years. Anything to distract him from his need to follow Larissa into her bedroom, peel that robe from her body and make love with her for the next five or six hours.

He wanted to touch her all over—first with his hands and then with his mouth. He wanted to explore every inch of her, he wanted to know what she sounded like when she got close and how her breathing changed when she came. He wanted—

Stop it! He sucked in a breath and reminded himself that he worked with Larissa. She was his friend. He wasn't going to screw that up by having sex with her. Talk about stupid. He wasn't some love-struck kid. He could control himself.

Slowly his heart rate returned to normal. He was breathing easier and the pounding need faded enough to be manageable. After a couple more minutes, he risked going back into the living room. Larissa was gone. He set down the cat before returning to the kitchen. He'd planned to have a beer with his dinner, but after what he'd just been through, he was going to need something a whole lot stronger.

LARISSA PUSHED THE beans and rice around on her plate. She'd managed to eat enough of her burrito to keep Jack from asking questions. It wasn't that she wasn't hungry, it was that swallowing past the lump of stupid in her throat made it difficult to get anything down.

Her attempt at seduction had been a total disaster. Instead of being overwhelmed by desire, Jack had simply assumed she wasn't dressed yet. Oh, right. Because she had a whole wardrobe of silk robes to pull on at a moment's notice. Jeez. Until today she hadn't owned even one.

She only half listened to Jack going on and on about how the guys were planning to get Percy ready for his GED. Not that she wasn't interested in all that. She was. But hadn't he noticed she was trying to get him into bed?

There was an obvious answer. No. He hadn't noticed. He didn't know she'd just spent ninety-eight dollars on a stupid robe she would never wear again. Nor had he noticed she'd curled her hair. That wasn't something she did very often. Jack was supposed to be so smooth with the ladies. Where was that smoothness now?

"You okay?" he asked.

She forced herself to smile. "Of course. So is there a lot of science on the test?"

Jack said something about downloading a sample test and getting information on what students were required to know. But what she was actually thinking was she probably shouldn't be blaming Jack for not getting what she was trying to do. The more likely culprit was herself.

What did she know about seducing men? In a word—*nothing.* Sure, she'd dated some, but she'd mostly avoided relationships. They were never what she wanted them to be. Never as fulfilling, never as exciting. She knew there were a lot of reasons. By holding herself back emotionally, she never had a real connection with the guy in question. Without the connection, she couldn't care enough to make the relationship worthwhile. Rooted in the middle of that mess was her guilt about being the reason her parents had had to get married. She probably needed intensive therapy, but she knew that was never going to happen.

"You're not seeing anyone," she said, interrupting Jack.

He put down his fork. "You mean like dating?"

"Uh-huh. You haven't had a woman in a while."

His shoulders tensed slightly as his gaze avoided hers. "We moved to a small town. Finding women to date is going to be challenging here."

"You'll have to import them."

"I guess I will. I have names."

Great. She'd been joking and he was serious. How was she supposed to get him into bed when he wouldn't even notice her as a woman? She'd been practically naked and he'd been more interested in brushing the cat than having his way with her. Maybe she needed to take some kind of remedial class.

She picked up her bottle of beer and took a sip. All right—she would accept that her plan had a big flaw and deal with it tomorrow. She'd already wasted enough of a perfectly good evening and meal. Time to return to normal.

She reached for a chip. "I met Shelby Gilmore today."

Jack looked confused. "Should I know the name?"

"She's Kipling Gilmore's sister."

"The skier."

"The Olympic gold medalist." She tilted her head and grinned. "So in the superstar athlete hierarchy, does a Super Bowl ring trump an Olympic gold medal? I'm thinking not."

"Your support is so heartening."

"But it's true. Kipling got those two gold medals on his own. You got your ring from being part of a team. And didn't Sam kick the winning field goal?"

"Making me practically the water boy?" Jack asked dryly.

"Something like that."

"Again, I revel in your awe of me."

"It's not about me," she said, digging her fork into the beans. "It's a town thing. I mean we have you and Raoul and Josh Golden. What if Kipling moves here? You guys can start a club. Once-famous athletes. OFA. You could have matching jackets and a secret handshake."

"Or I could find a new masseuse."

She chewed and swallowed the beans. "Cheap talk.
You would be lost without me and you know it. I'm
the one who keeps your fascia happy. And happy fas-
ciae mean a happy body."

"Truer words," he murmured, then took a bite.

The banter continued. Larissa took comfort in the
fact that even if Jack wasn't hot for her body, he was
still her friend. Which made him a nice guy. Which
meant being in love with him made even more sense.
He was sexy, he was smart and he was kind. How
could anyone resist him?

She sighed. At this rate, she was never going to get
over him. She needed a new plan. Maybe she would
talk to Taryn in the morning and get her input on
ways to seduce Jack.

They finished dinner and settled on the sofa to
watch a movie. Dyna curled up between them and did
a quick wash before falling asleep. At nearly eleven,
Larissa walked Jack to the door.

Had she been trying to do anything else but sleep
with him, she would have told him he was a blind
moron not to see what was right in front of him.
But given the subject matter, she wasn't feeling that
brave. So when he pulled her close and hugged her,
she wasn't expecting anything more than a quick
squeeze from a friend.

Only Jack didn't let go. Not for the longest time
and when he did, his expression was both intense
and almost angry.

"Larissa," he said, then stopped.

She stared into his dark eyes and tried to figure

out what was wrong. Was it his shoulder? His knees? Did he want to talk to her about—

"Ah, hell," he growled right before he grabbed her upper arms and kissed her.

Nothing about the contact was gentle or sweet or tentative. He pressed his mouth against her hungrily, as if he needed everything she had. The pressure aroused her quickly and left her straining toward him. Except at the same time his lips claimed hers, his arms held her away from his body.

She thought about struggling; only before she could figure out a way to break his grip on her, he touched her lower lip with his tongue and nothing else mattered. She parted for him. When he swept inside, she felt the tingles from the top of her head down to her toes. It was erotic electric shock therapy, with the result of full-body quivering and mind-emptying pleasure.

She met him stroke for stroke and lost herself in the feel of his deep kiss. Once again she struggled to get closer, but he held her firmly away from him. As if he wanted to make sure there was no other contact. Which made no sense. Not that she was going to think about it now, she thought.

Her body began to melt. Need pulsed and grew until she thought she might have to whimper. If he hadn't been holding her, she probably would have fallen right there.

He released her and she instinctively leaned against him. Their bodies touched everywhere. Chest to breast, thigh to thigh, erection to—

Erection?

The physical proof of his desire made her wrap her arms around him and start to laugh. Finally! They were going to do this. She would have glorious nights in Jack's bed, pleasing him and being pleased. She could lose herself in him.

In the back of her mind, a voice whispered there was supposed to be a plan. A reason that making love with him was a good idea, beyond how it would make her feel. But the voice was small and easily ignored.

Jack stared at her. "You're laughing."

"I know."

"This isn't going to happen, Larissa."

"Why not? We both want it to."

He shook his head and untangled her arms. "There are a thousand reasons and you know every one of them."

And with that cryptic statement, he was gone.

JACK HAD SPENT a lot of bad nights in his life. There had been all the times he'd worried about Lucas surviving to see another day. The emptiness after his twin had died. The confusion and hurt when his parents had left.

In college he'd gone through nights of physical pain from the game, the occasional tossing and turning because of how a relationship had gone and when Taryn had lost the baby, he'd spent hundreds of hours wondering how things would have been different if she hadn't.

But he couldn't remember the last time he'd stared

at the ceiling because of a damn hard-on for a woman he couldn't have.

Time had passed too slowly and he'd been up and in the shower by five. There wasn't a basketball game that morning, which put him in his suit and subsequently his office long before six.

He had to get this under control, he thought grimly as he waited for coffee to flow into his mug. There had to be a solution. Kenny had been right. Getting involved with Larissa would mess up everything. He liked her and he didn't want to lose that.

Last night had been a disaster. Worse, it wasn't her fault. It was seeing her in the robe, he thought grimly. Imagining her naked. Wanting to touch her. That was a slick road to hell. So what now? How did he make things better?

He lost himself in work and waited for the caffeine to do its thing. Sometime around seven-thirty other people began to arrive. At eight, Taryn strolled into his office.

"You look like crap," she announced.

"Thanks."

"What's wrong?"

"Nothing. I didn't sleep."

Taryn's violet-blue eyes always saw too much. "Larissa?" she asked.

"She told you?"

Taryn shook her head and muttered something under her breath. "Told me what?"

Now it was his turn to not get it. "You haven't talked to her?"

"I talk to her every day. I need context. Did she do something? Did you do something?"

The questions had easy answers, but he had a feeling they were talking in circles. "What do you know?" he asked.

"Nothing I'm telling you. You want answers, go see Larissa."

There were answers?

Jack was out of his chair and through the door. He walked to the end of the hall and entered Larissa's tiny office. She was already sitting at her computer.

"Hi," she said cheerily when he entered. "What's up? Oh, wow. You look tired. Didn't you sleep?"

He closed the door and leaned against it. "Talk."

"About?"

He raised one shoulder. "Whatever it is that has Taryn checking on me and asking what it is you've done. I'll stay for as long as it takes. I have a clear morning."

Larissa's smile drooped. "Taryn asked that?"

Jack crossed his arms over his chest and stared at her. On his side was the fact that she'd never been much of a liar and she couldn't handle pressure. He would give her two maybe three minutes before she cracked. Because if there was something going on, he wanted to know what.

"You won't like it," she said, staring at her desk. Her long, slim fingers twisted together.

"I'll deal. Now tell me, what's going on?"

She pressed her lips together and swallowed, then

stared up at him. Her cheeks flushed and her eyes were huge.

Jack felt the first slice of fear. It was bad, he thought suddenly. Real bad. Was she sick? Did she have cancer?

Okay, he told himself. He had resources. He would find her the best doctors in the country. Or in the world. They could fly anywhere. Switzerland. India. It didn't matter. He would make sure she got better.

"My mother was right. I'm in love with you."

The words were so unexpected, he didn't understand their meaning at first. Relief came first. Larissa wasn't sick. That was something. She would be fine.

"What did you say?"

The words burst out of him in a roar. She jumped a little, but didn't take them back.

"It's not my fault," she began. "Look at yourself, Jack. Is it any wonder it happened? I'm amazed I held on as long as I did. You're pretty irresistible."

"Lots of women resist. You should have tried harder." In love with him? He swore. If Kenny had been pissed before, he was going to blow a gasket now. In love with him? Why did that have to happen? Why couldn't she think of him as a brother?

"...getting over you. It's the only solution."

He shook his head as he tuned back in to what she was saying. "You want to get over being in love with me?"

"Of course. It's the only way things can work out between us. Don't take this wrong, but as a boyfriend, you're a disaster."

He told himself not to take offense at her words.
His ability to be a good boyfriend wasn't the issue
on the table.

"You have a plan?" he asked cautiously.

"I did. I was going to sleep with you. I figured
that would do it."

Jack stared at her. "Excuse me?"

She actually smiled. "I wanted us to have sex."

"Because it would be so awful that you wouldn't
be in love with me anymore?"

"No. I thought it would be pretty good. But if we
were that close, I'd see your flaws more clearly and
then I'd get over you." Her smile was triumphant.
"It's a good plan."

"What if I'm a god in bed?"

The smile widened. "Jack, I doubt you're all that.
Taryn says nice things, so I'm sure you're fine. Don't
get defensive. It wasn't about the sex, by the way. It
was about being in a relationship."

His head hurt. "So last night was on purpose?"

"Yes. I was trying to seduce you. It didn't go well."

It had gone just fine, but he wasn't going to tell
her that.

"Stop being in love with me," he told her.

"I agree, but telling me that isn't going to work."
She looked up, her expression hopeful. "Are you open
to the sex thing at all?"

Jack thought longingly of life on a deserted tropi-
cal island. One with a couple of coconut trees he could
use for food. Just him and the ocean. It would be a
good life. Lonely, but he would survive.

"No," he said firmly and opened the door to her office.

"Are you sure? Because we could do it right here."

He slammed the door behind him and started walking.

CHAPTER TWELVE

"You have to fix this," Jack said.

Taryn looked up from her computer. "No, I don't. It's your problem."

Technically the problem was Larissa's, he thought, but did that matter? He was stuck with the consequences.

"You created it," she continued. "You and Larissa are enmeshed in some pseudomarriage, anyway. Neither of you is moving forward. The difference is, she had the sense to recognize it."

"I have no idea what you're talking about."

Taryn stood and walked out from behind her desk. She'd already kicked off whatever ridiculous shoes she'd worn into the office and was barefoot. She'd painted her toes purple. Who did that?

"Jack, you're a good guy. A little too good. You don't have a lot of annoying flaws. But you also don't get involved."

"Love is for suckers."

"You don't mean that." She touched his chest. "Love is amazing."

"I don't want to hear about Angel."

"Then I won't say anything about him. My point is

falling in love is part of the human condition. You're trying to escape the inevitable and that's not going well."

"I don't need to fall in love. I have all the connection I need."

"No, you don't. You have friends who love you, but that's different. Don't you want one special person who will always be there for you?"

"No."

"Liar."

"I like being alone."

She shook her head. "That would be more believable if you were alone. But you're not. You have Larissa. She's the buffer who stands between you and the world. You get to play at things and not be involved on any level where you might get hurt. While that works for you, it's no longer working for her. She's in love with you and while she's in love with you, she can't find a man interested in forever and fall for him."

Nothing he wanted to hear. "So her mother was right."

"So it seems. Now this problem is yours. You're going to have to figure out a way to solve it."

BEING IN LOVE with Jack was less fun than Larissa had hoped. For one thing, now that he knew about her feelings, she rarely saw him. His ducking into offices and turning around and going the other way when he spotted her in the hall would have been funny— except it hurt too much for her to laugh.

She missed him, missed hanging out with him, talking to him. They hadn't had dinner together, although Percy had come over with takeout twice. Takeout she was sure Jack had paid for.

Even worse, Jack hadn't been in for any of his massages, which meant he had to be in pain. If he stood still long enough to listen, she was willing to explain that whatever her personal feelings, her work as his masseuse was separate from that. He needed help with his body.

She sat in her tiny office and tried to figure out how things had fallen apart so quickly. While she wanted to blame her mother, the other woman had only been speaking the truth. She'd seen what no one else had seen.

Which was great information but didn't solve the problem.

Taryn walked into her office. Her friend looked nervous and wary—two emotions Larissa didn't associate with her.

"What?" Larissa demanded. "Is someone hurt?"

"No," Taryn said slowly. "Look, don't shoot the messenger, okay? I'm telling you but I had no part in it. If he'd asked, I would have told him it was a disastrous idea."

Larissa blinked at her. "I have no idea what you're talking about."

"You will. Come on."

Larissa followed her friend down the long hallway. They made a turn and ended up at the massage room. Larissa was about to ask what they were doing there, when she heard noises from inside. Noises that sounded suspiciously like music and conversation.

"Which of you is playing around in my personal space?" she asked as she opened the door. Because what she expected to find was Sam or Kenny doing something ridiculous. What she saw instead was Jack on her massage table while another woman worked on his shoulder.

The sharp pain of betrayal cut through to her heart. It wasn't just that he'd gone to someone else, she thought frantically. It was that he'd violated what was theirs. He'd brought a stranger into a place that was supposed to be only for family.

The masseuse moved to cover Jack with the sheet. "Excuse me, we're in the middle of a treatment. Could you please leave?"

Larissa didn't recognize the woman. She must have come in from Sacramento. A long way to drive, she thought, still trying to process the ache filling her. Her whole body hurt and she had the strangest need to cry. Stupid tears, she told herself. Stupid man.

Larissa moved into the room. "You're using the wrong music," she said, her voice sounding like someone else was speaking. She wasn't moving right, either. It was as if she were physically disconnected from her body.

"That's Kenny's mix. And the oil is wrong, too. Jack's blend has anti-inflammatory properties."

Jack sat up. "Larissa, I'm sorry."

She couldn't look at him. "I can't believe you did this. You brought in someone else. How could you?

If you didn't want me to give you a massage, at least go to someone else. You're in my *room.*" She shook her head. "How am I supposed to let this go? You violated my trust, Jack."

He pulled the sheet across his body and stood. "Larissa, it wasn't like that."

She stared at the ground. "It was. You brought her here? How could you?"

Taryn stepped closer and put her hand on Larissa's shoulder. "I'm sorry," she murmured.

The masseuse looked between them. "What's going on here? Are you two married or something? I'm just here to do a job."

"Yes, you were," Taryn said soothingly. "Go ahead and get your things. When you're ready, come by my office and I'll have a check waiting."

JACK HAD SEEN Larissa cry before, but always because of someone she'd met through their charity work. Either a transplant was delayed or didn't take or a desperate family couldn't find someone to take care of their other children who would be staying back at home.

Those tears he could handle. Most of the problems were solved by him writing a check. When there wasn't an organ for transplant, he made phone calls or did a PSA. When he got visible, people checked the box on their driver's licenses. When he appeared on late-night TV to promote the cause, there was press. Whatever it took to stop her tears.

He'd never once been the cause. Now, watching

her blue eyes fill and her struggling not to let him see, he felt lower than slime.

The masseuse he'd hired through an agency gathered her things and left. Taryn shot him a glance that promised they would be discussing this later, and then he was alone with Larissa.

She walked over to the docking station and pushed a couple of buttons. The music changed to a contemporary mix that he always found so relaxing. She took away the oil the other woman had been using and pulled out another bottle. Then she washed her hands and moved next to the table.

"Lie back down," she said, her voice thick with tears.

"Larissa, no."

She sniffed. "You're in pain. You're my friend and my responsibility. I'm the reason you called in someone else. Because of the sex thing."

"I…" He honest to God didn't know what to say. Yes, that was the reason, but it still wasn't her fault. "I should have said something. I should have let you know that I was uncomfortable." He looked at the table. "We don't have to do this."

"We do. It's the only way to make things right between us."

He nodded once and stretched out facedown. She rearranged the sheet so he was covered from the waist down, then opened the bottle of oil. The familiar scent drifted to him and he closed his eyes.

Nothing made sense. Not her declaration of love nor her attempts to seduce him. He didn't want her to love him—that way lay disaster. Lovers were easy, but people he trusted, people he counted on, those were much harder to find.

She touched his back, lightly stroking at first, then reaching for the deeper muscles. His tension began to fade. She moved up toward his bad shoulder and began the familiar ritual of finding every inch of scar tissue and loosening it. She dug in deep, hurting him in the best way possible.

"I'm sorry," he said again.

"Shh. Don't talk."

"I have to talk. I'm sorry I hurt you, Larissa. I'm sorry I didn't come to you directly."

"I know."

"It's just, you shouldn't be in love with me. I'm not a good bet."

She gave a laugh that cracked in the middle, then sniffed. "It's okay, Jack. I get it."

He didn't know what to say to that. What did she get? And why did he know that the hell he found himself in wasn't over yet?

JACK'S BAD DAY got worse when he went into town for lunch. An innocent enough errand, just not that particular day. There was a food truck that had a place by the park. They served the best sandwiches and wraps he'd ever had. Now he made it a habit to stop by a couple of times a week.

He'd chosen today because getting out of the office had seemed like a good idea. No one had said anything about the incident with the masseuse, but he knew *they* knew. Worse, Larissa had gone home early, claiming she wasn't feeling well. He knew the truth. He knew he'd hurt her and that he was the lowest form of life there was.

The last thing he wanted was another warning conversation with Kenny, so he'd decided lunch out was a solution for all his ills. Only when he got in line, about six people back from the order window, he noticed a tall, lanky teen talking to a pretty girl. The girl was of average height, with auburn hair and green eyes. Pretty enough. Maybe too pretty.

Talking was fine, Jack thought, pleased Percy had made friends. Only then the girl put her hand on Percy's arm and dammit it all to hell if Percy didn't lightly kiss her.

Dating? Percy was dating? He'd only been in town, like, a month. How could he have found a girlfriend so quickly? This was something Jack didn't need. Because teenaged boys were one giant walking, breathing hormone. They had one thing on their minds and it wasn't how to study hard and better themselves. He'd ignored Larissa's request to talk to Percy about safe sex. Turned out he should have listened.

Worse, this was Fool's Gold. It was just a matter of time until everyone knew about Percy and the pretty redhead, and then there was going to be trouble. One of her parents would come calling to meet Percy's "guardians." What was Jack supposed to say? What did he really know about the kid?

The line moved. Percy and the girl placed their order. A few minutes later, Jack did the same. It was a testament to young love that they ate their entire lunch without noticing him only a couple of tables away. He waited until they'd said goodbye and Percy started back to the office to make his move. Jack walked behind him for a few feet, then increased his speed until they were level.

Percy grinned. "Hey, Jack. Were you in town for lunch, too? You should try the food truck, man. It's great. The lady who runs it—Ana Raquel—is Dellina's sister. Dellina is—"

"I know who Dellina is," he said curtly. "And I just had lunch there."

"You did? I didn't see you." Percy's smile faded. "Oh. You saw me with Melissa."

"I did."

Percy came to a stop and faced him. The teen's posture was defensive and combative at the same time. His shoulders were square and jaw thrust out.

"I know what you're thinking," he said defiantly.

"I doubt that."

"You think I don't belong with her. Is it because of the color of my skin?"

"What? Your skin? No. I think it's because you're eighteen years old and your head is run by your dick."

Percy's mouth twitched. "That's why you're upset? You thinking I'm banging her? I'm not. She's more important than that. We've only been seeing each other a couple of weeks."

Jack rubbed his temple. "Percy, Fool's Gold isn't like Los Angeles. It's a small town. People know things about each other. Melissa's parents know their daughter is dating some guy they know nothing about. So they're going to come looking for answers."

"She doesn't have parents. Not here. She lives with her aunt and uncle, when she's not at college." His mouth twitched again. "She's a year older than me."

"Oh, goodie." Jack pointed toward the office. "Start walking and start listening. Like I said, this is a small town. Sure it's nice to know a lot of people but that also means everybody gets to know your business. And in this case, your business is dating a hometown girl."

"Are you saying I shouldn't see her?"

"No. I'm saying I'm going to be bringing you a box of condoms. A big box. When that box gets close to empty, let me know and I'll buy another one."

Jack didn't look at Percy as they walked together and he really didn't want to be having this conversation. He wasn't the right guy for this. Surely that was clear to anyone who might be listening.

Percy chuckled. "You trying to tell me to have safe sex?"

"Yes," Jack growled. "That's exactly what I'm telling you. Put a hat on it, kid. Neither you nor Melissa want an unplanned pregnancy."

"I know where babies come from."

"Good. That will make it easier to keep it from happening without warning."

"Melissa and I are taking things slow. Keeping 'em casual. She heads back to school in a couple of weeks, so I don't think we're going to be doing anything like that. But I promise, if we do, I'll use a condom."

Jack nodded. "You know how?" he forced himself to ask, and prayed the answer was yes.

"I do. I've been putting a 'hat' on it for a while now." He chuckled. "Man, you are so old."

"Thanks."

Percy laughed harder. "You didn't like this one bit, did you?"

"No."

"But you got the job done. That's something."

If only it was enough.

LARISSA DREW THE brush across Dyna's back. The cat lay in a patch of sun, her eyes half-closed, her purring all rumbly.

"Is that nice?" she asked softly. "Do you like the attention?"

The rumble continued.

"I think I'd like being a cat," Larissa continued. "People to pet you and take care of you. And it's different in the cat world. Humans have to earn your trust, right? Like you and me. You were interested in living here, but cautious. Over time, I won you over. It's not like you were begging me to take you in and then I didn't love you back. Trust me, that sucks."

She paused mentally, if not with the petting, to consider that maybe she was anthropomorphizing the situation a little bit more than she should have. Dyna was a cat. She didn't fall in love—at least not romantically. She bonded with the person who took care of her. Larissa, on the other hand, had bonded where she wasn't welcome and was now suffering the consequences.

Someone knocked on her door. She looked over her shoulder before scrambling to her feet. She was pretty sure she knew who would be there. Someone from Score. Odds were on Taryn or Jack. She knew who her heart wanted her visitor to be.

She drew in a breath, then turned the knob. Jack stood on the small landing. He looked at her with a steady gaze.

"We have to talk," he told her.

A few weeks ago she would have teased him about turning into a woman, saying something like that. He would have teased her back. Things had been easy. Before, she thought sadly. Before she'd realized she'd fallen in love with him.

Ignorance really was bliss, she admitted to herself as she stepped back to allow him in. Right now she was battling an uncomfortable combination of hurt, humiliation and, the real kicker—happiness to bask in his presence. How ridiculous was that?

Jack stepped into her small apartment. He bent down and scooped Dyna up in his arms. The long-haired feline relaxed completely and continued to purr.

"Hey, gorgeous," he said as he rubbed the side of her face. Dyna snuggled closer.

Larissa had to admit that the sight of a big tough guy holding a fluffy cat was pretty hard to resist. Not that she was interested in resisting all that much.

Which was part of the problem. Her lack of will-power.

Jack set Dyna on the sofa and then drew in a breath. "I'm sorry about the masseuse," he said. "That was wrong on a lot of different levels. I shouldn't have called her at all, but having called, I should have gone to see her somewhere else. I violated your personal space. I apologize for that."

She nodded, knowing he wasn't responsible for all the blame.

"I changed the rules," she admitted, not quite meeting his gaze.

"You did and you scared the hell out of me."

That made her look at him. "How do you figure?"

"Larissa, you're important to me. You and I are close and I like that. I like everything about our relationship. I trust you and there aren't a whole lot of people I can say that about. What we have…" He paused. "I saw Percy in town today."

"Okay, and that's relevant how?"

"He was with a girl. Her name is Melissa and they're seeing each other."

"Percy has a girlfriend? Why didn't I know about this? Who is she and do I approve?"

Jack smiled gently. "Not my point. When I freaked out, he told me not to worry. That he wasn't, ah, sleeping with her. She was too important for that. Now, I used to be an eighteen-year-old guy so I know exactly how much sex matters. What I think he meant is hooking up is easy. Relationships are a whole other thing. That's what I mean about you. I don't want to date you because my romantic relationships always end badly. If we don't go down that path, we can stay together forever."

Maybe, but the way things were, she was stuck being in love with him. "What if I want more?"

"I can't give you that."

"You mean you don't want to."

"Isn't it the same thing?" he asked.

"Not really. I just wish you were interested in me in that way." She wanted to ask if he could try a little harder, but that seemed too much like begging. And a girl either had to have Dyna's looks or a little pride.

He closed the space between them and took her hands in his. "We're a great team. Look at all we get done. Your causes, my causes. We laugh a lot. Isn't that better than being in love with me?"

She pulled her hands free. "I don't like this any more than you do. It's humiliating to think you don't want me or think of me as other than a friend. Why can't you be begging me for something I don't want to give?"

"I'll beg for things to go back the way they were before, if that helps."

She crossed her arms over her chest. "I just want to be a part of something. I want…" She paused as yet another uncomfortable truth rose to the surface. "I want what my sisters have. A conventional, normal marriage with a couple of kids and a great husband."

A muscle twitched in Jack's jaw, but what he said was, "I want that for you, too."

"With another guy?"

"Unless you're playing for the other team these days. If so, I know a really cute girl who might be your type."

"Ha ha." She sighed. "I'm so boring."

"You're not. You're lovely."

"I'm nearly thirty, single and desperately in love with a man who has no interest in me. The only thing that would make me more of a cliché was if you were married. Honestly, how did this happen?"

He shrugged. "You couldn't help yourself, Larissa. You never had a chance. I mean, come on. It's me."

Which was both funny and completely the truth, she thought as she smiled at him. "You're not all that."

"I would agree with you, except for this situation between us. It kind of proves my point."

"You're so annoying."

He held out his arms.

She hesitated for a second, then stepped into his embrace. It wasn't like the one from a few nights ago. There was no erection, no kissing. Just the familiar feel of Jack's arms around her.

"Friends?" he asked.

She nodded. "I wonder if Kenny would like to go out with me."

"Aren't you the funny one? Want to go get dinner?"

"Sure. I'm going to order the most expensive item on the menu."

"That's my girl."

ORDER WAS RESTORED to the Score family, at least on the surface. Larissa was grateful to have something close to normal in her relationship with Jack. They hung out together, she gave him massages—without him getting aroused—and together she and Percy teased him mercilessly about his somewhat pathetic attempt to have the birds-and-bees talk with a streetwise teen.

But in her quiet moments, when she was alone, she wondered how she was supposed to move on with her life. How was she supposed to fall out of love with Jack and in love with someone else? Score sucked up all her time. While she hung out with her friends a lot, she rarely saw any man who didn't work at Score, and the ones she did were engaged or married to her friends. While it seemed Fool's Gold had a few good men around, she wasn't meeting them. If only she'd been more excited about cowboy Zane.

Larissa confirmed Jack's foursome for the Pro-am, answered a couple of emails from previous recipients of Jack's largess on the transplant front and was about to start on putting away the clean linens that had been delivered when her cell phone rang.

"Hello?"

"Larissa? It's Dan. We have an emergency. Remember the lady in Stockton with the chiweenies? We finally got in and it's as we feared. We have a hoarding situation. It seems like she started out with the best of intentions and then it all got out of hand. We're heading down within the hour."

Larissa closed the linen cabinet and walked into the hallway. "What do you need?"

"Help with the dogs. We're going to take the rescue

van with us. That should hold most of the dogs. Two other people are bringing SUVs so we have enough cargo space. What we need is help walking, feeding and watering the dogs. It's only going to be a day or so. We'll meet in north Sacramento tomorrow morning at seven and then drive down. Her place is east of Modesto by about thirty miles. We'll collect the dogs and drive them back here. Once they're evaluated, we'll get them into foster homes. We're going to need help with that, too."

She nodded. "I can be there at seven, no problem. As for fostering, just tell me how many dogs we're talking about and I'll find temporary homes." She'd had great luck a couple of months ago with placing cats.

"You're a lifesaver."

Nothing that dramatic, she thought, but it was nice to be needed.

THE NEXT MORNING, Larissa was on the road by six, heading to Sacramento. She met up with the small caravan that would make its way down to Modesto to rescue forty chiweenies and they started south. She was a little tired from not having slept that well, but she must not have been the only one who was lagging a little. Halfway to their destination, they all pulled into a Starbucks for a pick-me-up.

"It's always the same," one of the women was saying as Larissa joined the group. "Somebody thinks he or she can start breeding dogs, with absolutely no experience, of course. They get overwhelmed and suddenly they have fifty animals running around."

"Are they charging her with something?" a man asked.

Dan shook his head. "No. She's surrendering all the animals voluntarily, so she won't be charged. The court will insist she not have more than two pets at any given time. If she has more, she can be charged with contempt."

"If you ask me they should stick her in a too-small cage for a few months," another woman said, her expression fierce. "Then we'll see how she likes it."

Larissa understood someone being overwhelmed. She just wished the woman in question had asked for help sooner.

The small caravan got back on the road. Larissa was the last car in the group. Radio reception wasn't great but she managed to find an oldies station. The songs made her think of Kenny, who loved that kind of music. He would be in heaven.

Twenty miles from Stockton, her car started to make a strange knocking sound. She made it through Stockton and down to Modesto where everyone turned east onto a very narrow two-lane road. According to what she'd been told, they still had about twenty-five miles to go. She glanced down at her temperature gauge and saw the needle all the way in the red band. Seconds later steam or smoke or something equally upsetting started to pour from the hood of her car. She pulled over as best she could on the tiny road and watched the caravan drive away. Before she could turn off the engine, it stopped on its own and everything was ominously silent.

She couldn't believe it. Really? This had to happen now? Not when she was driving in Fool's Gold where she knew she could easily get her car fixed? She thought she was done messing up when she tried to help. After the whole incident with the snake and Angel, she'd vowed to be more careful with the type of creatures she got involved with. She was helping with chiweenies, for heaven's sake. How could they hurt anyone? And her reward was a car breakdown?

But that was all distraction and she knew it. If her car wasn't working right it was because she hadn't bothered to keep up with servicing.

Her cell rang. She answered it.

"Hey, you okay?" Dan asked.

"I'm having car trouble," she said. "Just go on without me. I'll get back to Fool's Gold somehow."

"Will do. You still up for taking in dogs to foster? They won't be ready for about two days."

"No problem. Call when they are. I can place about eight with no problem." There were plenty of people in town who had helped with her last cat rescue. She suspected they would be willing to foster cute chiweenies. She also thought Shelby might enjoy a temporary pet to make her feel at home. And Jack's house was huge, so he could take several, especially with Percy to help her with the care.

Dan said he would be in touch and hung up. Larissa sat alone in the quiet of the Modesto wilderness and knew there was only one way out of her predicament.

CHAPTER THIRTEEN

JACK LOOKED OVER the weekly report that listed ad buys for various clients. Mostly he left this sort of thing to Taryn, but there were a couple of accounts that he monitored more closely. Mostly because the connection with Score was personal. Each of them had brought in clients who were also friends. It was part of how they did business—making sure the personal touch never went away.

He made a few notes on the report, then wrote a couple of emails to update the clients in question. Just as he pushed Send, his cell rang.

He glanced at the screen and saw Larissa's picture. Taryn had mentioned something about Larissa not coming in today because of an animal rescue. He hadn't stayed to hear any of the details. There was no reason. Whatever she was doing would manifest itself later, most likely in his living room.

Now he took the call as a nibble of worry took up residence in his gut.

"What's wrong?" he asked.

On the other end of the phone there was a second of silence. "I want to say nothing," Larissa said quietly.

"But?"

"My car died. I'm east of Modesto with a group that's rescuing chiweenies. A lady was breeding them and the situation got out of control and now she's going to surrender them. I was one of the volunteers who would walk the dogs on the trip back."

"They're not being driven?"

"Of course they're being driven. But it's several hours. They're going to need a chance to go to the bathroom." She sighed. "It wasn't supposed to be like this," she said softly. "I'm trying to do a good thing."

"You are doing a good thing. The weak link is your car. It's what? Thirty years old?"

"Fifteen and I guess it needs servicing."

"If you'd let me buy you a new car," he began, only to realize that wasn't the point. At least not now. Larissa needed him. "Is your location finder on your phone turned on?"

"Uh-huh."

"Good. I'll be there within the hour."

"Not even the way you drive. Jack, you don't have to come get me. I just wanted you to call a tow truck."

"Not happening. I'll be there in person." He wrote down the route she'd taken that morning and told her to stay with her car. "Lock the doors."

"I'm perfectly safe," she assured him.

"Lock your doors."

"I promise."

He hung up and headed out the door.

"SHE SHOULD BE right around here," the helicopter pilot said, pointing to the ground.

Jack nodded. He glanced at his cell phone and saw the blinking red dot that was Larissa was nearly under them. He looked through the trees and saw her aging import pulled off the side of a two-lane road. The knot of worry that had been growing since he got her call finally eased. He was here. Whatever was wrong, he would fix it.

The helicopter set down on a dirt road only a few yards away from her car. Jack pulled off his headset and climbed out as the dust swirled around the whirling blades.

Larissa got out of her car and shook her head. He knew what she was thinking. He couldn't take a car like a normal person? Sure, he could have, but then the trip would have been much longer. She needed to be rescued and he was the man to do it.

They walked toward each other. She had on jeans and T-shirt under a hoodie. Her hair was pulled back into a ponytail and she wasn't wearing any makeup. But when her gaze met his, he felt the pull all the way down to his soul. Whatever they were going through now, this was Larissa and she would always be a part of him. As much as she needed him, he needed her more.

He held open his arms and she ran to him. When he drew her against him, he knew that he was done fighting the inevitable. How could he resist a woman who wanted to rescue chiweenies—whatever the hell they were? A woman who claimed to love him and wanted to use sex to get over him?

Hunger burned inside of him. Hunger and need and desire, but they were all second to what he really ached for. He didn't have an itch to be scratched. He had a bad feeling that if he gave in to what they both wanted, the trouble to follow would be cataclysmic. Yet there was an inevitability in the moment. He could run but he couldn't hide. So maybe it was time to stop running.

She buried her face in his chest and trembled slightly. When she finally raised her head, he saw tears in her eyes. "Everything I touch turns to crap," she murmured.

"That's not true."

"It is. I just wanted to help walk some dogs."

"They're still going to be rescued and if I know you, you'll be arranging for a dozen or so to be fostered in Fool's Gold." Possibly half that number in his house, but so what? "You care, Larissa. That's rare. Treasure your compassion. I do."

"I just feel stupid. I do this to myself. I'm so busy running from crisis to crisis, I don't take care of the important things like getting my car serviced. What if I'd been the only one going to get those dogs?"

"I would have brought a bigger helicopter."

He hoped she would smile, but she didn't. She stepped back. "I'm serious, Jack. Look at me. I'm twenty-eight years old and you're still rescuing me. How can I save the world if I can't keep my car running?"

"I don't agree they're related problems."

"They're symbolic." She shook her head. "Sorry.
I'll beat myself up later. Thank you for rescuing me.
I really appreciate it. Now what happens? We can't
leave my car here."

He pointed and she turned. A woman was collect-
ing a big tool box from inside the helicopter.

"That's Donna. She's going to get your car running
and then drive it back to Fool's Gold."

"What if it can't be fixed?"

"She'll call for a tow truck." Jack put his arm
around her. "Come on. Let's get your stuff and we'll
get out of here."

"We can't just leave that woman alone with my
car."

"She'll be fine." Jack wasn't going to mention the
outrageous sum he'd offered to get Donna to go with
him. That would only make Larissa feel worse.

Larissa got her purse and cell phone, then explained what had happened with her car. Donna
grinned. "No problem. I'll have her running like
new."

Jack doubted that, but at least functional would
be good. Larissa thanked the other woman, then followed Jack to the helicopter.

"I've never been in one of these before."

He grinned. "Then it's about time you were."

LARISSA HAD FLOWN lots of times, so she was expecting the slow ramp-up to takeoff speed. The helicopter
wasn't like that. The sound of the engine got louder
and louder as, she would guess, the blades whirled

faster and faster. But there was no warning it was time. One second they were safely on land, the next they were airborne and climbing higher.

She and Jack were sitting side by side in the bird's rear seats. They both had on headsets so they could hear each other and the pilot. Before they'd taken off, Jack had made several phone calls. Larissa hoped none of them were to tell everyone at Score how stupid she'd been. But as soon as the thought formed, she pushed it away. Jack wouldn't do that to her. The only one beating up on her was herself.

She watched out the window as the ground disappeared below, then they were moving fast through the sky. She tried to calculate how far they were from Fool's Gold. She'd had the trip to just north of Sacramento to join the group, then they'd all gone south maybe eighty or ninety miles. But the helicopter could fly straight. She would guess their trip would last about an hour.

Forty minutes later she looked out the window to find they weren't anywhere near Fool's Gold. Out in front of them was the Pacific Ocean. And up ahead…

"San Francisco?" she asked, speaking into the microphone.

Jack nodded.

She wanted to ask why but knew the pilot could hear everything they said. She waited until they were on the ground, which came only a few minutes later. They didn't land at the international airport, but instead settled on a tarmac very near the center of the city.

When they stepped out, she saw a limo was waiting for them. She turned to Jack. "I don't get it. What are we doing here?"

He stared at her. "I'm going to help you get over me."

She felt her mouth drop open and consciously closed it. "You're here to sleep with me?"

He raised one shoulder. "There's more to it than that. We're going to stay the night here. Whatever happens is up to you."

She had more questions, but realized she didn't actually want to know. The city beckoned and the man next to her was irresistible and she was in love with him. A night away was exactly what she wanted. Why would she want to spoil the mood with a bunch of questions?

Anticipation bubbled inside of her. Whatever the outcome, this was going to be a great day.

She followed him to the limo. The driver stepped out and opened the rear door.

"Fisherman's Wharf," Jack said before sliding in next to her.

"I already talked to Percy," he said. "He's going to feed Dyna tonight and spend some time with her. Taryn knows you won't be back until tomorrow."

"What did she say when you told her where we were going to be?"

He took her hand and laced his fingers with hers. "She said I was going to get into more trouble than I could handle."

"Did you believe her?"

"Sure. Taryn's never wrong."

Larissa laughed.

They drove into the city and the driver dropped them off at the wharf. She and Jack walked around for a couple of hours before getting lunch in a waterfront restaurant. After they'd eaten, he excused himself to make a few more calls. Larissa sat at the table, content to stare out the window and enjoy the warm sunny day in the beautiful city.

Tomorrow she would return to her regularly scheduled life. Tomorrow she would have to face the consequences of what she'd done today. But that was okay—the price would be worth it. She loved Jack—of course she wanted to spend time with him.

He returned to the table and paid the bill, then they walked out of the restaurant and he hailed a cab.

"Where are we going?" she asked.

"To the hotel."

Already? Her toes curled in her athletic shoes.

"The Ritz," Jack told the driver.

The Ritz? As in the Ritz-Carlton? "I'm not dressed for a fancy hotel," she said, aware that while she'd brushed her teeth that morning, she hadn't showered. And that her jeans were a little frayed at the hems and her T-shirt had seen better days. She'd been planning to rescue dogs, not go to the Ritz.

"Don't worry," he said and took her hand in his.

Good advice she couldn't follow. Not only did she look as if she didn't belong, they weren't checking in with luggage. That couldn't be good.

"I'm going to need a toothbrush," she told him. "And shampoo. And something to wear tonight."

"Not to worry. It's all taken care of."

They pulled up in front of the magnificent hotel. An elegantly dressed middle-aged woman was waiting and smiled at Larissa. "Ms. Owens?" she asked.

Larissa nodded.

"I'm Francine. If you'll come with me, please?"

Larissa looked at Jack. "What are you doing?"

"You're going to have to go with her to find out." He leaned in and lightly kissed her. "You'll like it. I promise."

She wasn't sure but decided to go along with whatever had been planned. She was in the Ritz-Carlton. It wasn't as if anything bad could happen here.

Francine led her through the luxury hotel to the spa. Once she was there, she was checked in for an afternoon of relaxation and pampering, according to the very perky attendant. There would be a facial followed by a manicure and pedicure. After that she would get her hair done.

"It sounds wonderful," Larissa said, grateful Jack hadn't booked her for a massage. There were only a few people she trusted to do that.

She spent the next couple of hours relaxing in a treatment chair while her face was steamed and wrapped and smothered in various concoctions. Later she had a wonderful manicure and pedicure. By the time she was led into the salon, she was feeling relaxed and pampered.

José, a charming young man with a big smile, played with her hair for a few minutes before declaring the color "perfection" and the length "a disaster."

"How much do you want to cut off?" she asked warily.

"Trust me," he said.

"That so isn't going to happen."

"It's hair. It will grow back." He fingered the ends. "Maybe a few inches. It will still be long, but you'll have layers and style."

She'd never been much for style, she thought humorously. Taryn had enough for all her friends. Still, it would be nice to be glamorous for once.

"Okay, do what you think is best, but not short."

José nodded. "You'll see."

He whipped up a mysterious brew and gave her a few highlights. When her hair was wet, he went to work with a razor. Strands went flying. When he was done with the cut, he used a big round brush to blow out her hair, then put in a few hot rollers. During the entire session, she wasn't allowed to see herself in the mirror.

After José, a woman came over and applied makeup. Larissa listened carefully as she gave advice. The last time she'd tried to conquer the smoky eye, Sam had asked if she'd gotten in an accident.

When the makeup artist was done, José reappeared. He pulled out curlers, teased, finger-combed then applied enough hair spray to turn her into a plastic doll. At last he spun the chair so she was facing the mirror.

She almost didn't recognize herself. She was still a blue-eyed blonde, but instead of looking like the fresh-faced girl next door, she'd been transformed into a sexy, elegant stranger.

Her hair tumbled in big soft curls that shifted every time she moved. José had given her long bangs that softened her features and made her eyes look huge. Or maybe it was the expertly applied makeup that made her eyes so large. She couldn't decide. Either way, she loved it.

"Wow," she said. "Just wow."

José patted her shoulder. "You're a swan now. A beautiful swan."

Francine was waiting when she left the spa. "Ms. Owens, did you enjoy your time with us?"

"I did. It was magical."

The older woman smiled. "I'm glad. Now just one more stop."

They went into what looked like a conference room. Only instead of long tables and plenty of chairs, there was a rack of fancy dresses, boxes filled with shoes and a makeshift dressing room.

"I'll be right outside," Francine said. "Come out when you're done."

Larissa stared at all the clothes. They were in her size and from designers she'd only ever seen Taryn wear. She reached for one, then pulled back her hand. No way she could wear any of these.

"Oh, good. You're here."

A petite brunette walked into the room and smiled at her. "I'm Holly. I've brought cocktail attire, along with everything you'll need to wear with it." Holly was beautiful and wearing a simple red dress that looked custom-made for her. "Your guy said the trip was impulsive and you didn't even have a toothbrush." Holly winked. "He sounds like my kind of man. So what do you like?"

Larissa felt overwhelmed by too much input. "I'm not sure."

"Reach for one and let's see what it is."

Larissa started to bite her lower lip and remembered the lipstick. So she settled on just feeling nervous. She reached for the rack of clothes and chose a simple black dress.

It had a scooped neck, front and back, with a fuller skirt that looked to be about knee length. The fabric was interesting, with a texture, but not too thick.

"Nice," Holly said. "Oscar de la Renta. A silk cloque cocktail dress. You have good taste. Try it on. Oh, you'll need these."

She held out several black bras along with matching pairs of low-cut panties, also in black. Larissa took everything with her and went into the dressing area.

She found the right bra immediately. It added a little something to her modest assets. The dress slipped over her head and when she zipped it, the fit felt perfect. She stepped out and Holly grinned.

"You go, girl. Now try these."

She held a pair of lace peep-toe pumps with a bow. The heel was only a couple of inches—a good thing considering she didn't have Taryn's ability to walk in anything higher.

After slipping on the shoes, she walked to the mirror and stared at herself.

The woman looking back was vaguely familiar. Same face shape, same eyes. But the hair, the clothes, the makeup were all different. While it wasn't something she would do every day, she was starting to see the value in making a little effort.

"You like?" Holly asked with a grin.

"I do. It's amazing."

"Good. I'll have your clothes delivered to your room. Come on. Francine is waiting."

Larissa and Francine went to the elevator bank and rode up. Larissa pressed her hand to her stomach and tried to hold in nerves. Because with everything that had been happening, she hadn't had time to think about what Jack had said. *I'm going to help you get over me.*

Did that mean what she thought it meant? It had to. She had told him she wanted to have sex with him in her effort to get over being in love with him. At the time the words had probably made sense, but she was less sure now. He was everything she wanted. The possibility of not loving him seemed impossible.

But that was a problem for another time. Tonight she was going to enjoy everything as it came. She had a fabulous new look and she was going to have dinner with the man of her dreams. That was enough for now.

Francine led her down an elegant hallway. They stopped in front of wide double doors and Francine let her inside.

"Enjoy your stay," she said.

"Thank you."

She went inside.

Her first impression was of space. There were sofas and chairs, all done in taupes and beiges. On one side of the room was a baby grand piano, which was so over-the-top, she started to laugh. Through glass doors was a terrace about three times the size of her apartment back home. She could see a private dining room and at the other end of the room was the bedroom.

It was too much, she thought, dazed by all she was seeing. And it was exactly what Jack would do to seduce her.

She heard a sound and turned. The man of the hour stood just outside the bedroom. He wore a dark suit with a white shirt and red tie. He looked good. Better than good. The laughter faded, replaced by a sense of her world being made right. Even nicer was his wide-eyed appreciation as he stared at her.

"Larissa," he breathed. "You look beautiful."

"Thank you."

He started toward her, so tall and strong. Her heart fluttered just a little.

"Great dress," he told her. "You make it shine."

He took her hand and lightly kissed her knuckles, then led her into the dining room where a bottle of champagne waited in an ice bucket. Next to it were two Tiffany boxes.

"Don't get too excited," he told her. "These are on loan."

"You can do that?"

"I know people."

She'd bought his goodbye gifts to his various girl-friends for years now and, per his request, always shopped at Tiffany. She knew the beauty of the se-lection and loved how her favorite associate always made her feel special. She was used to the sparkle, the elegance, the perfect presentation. What she wasn't used to was seeing a diamond necklace that nearly blinded and was probably worth as much as the GDP of California.

"Oh, my."

He put it on her, then handed her the matching earrings. The style was simple. A single row of dia-monds with a diamond-studded X-shaped clasp. But the size, the clarity, the sheer brilliance was enough to make her rethink her philosophy that she wasn't the least bit interested in jewelry.

"You're allowed a night off," Jack said, turning her so she could see herself in the mirror. His gaze met hers. "There is a second bedroom attached to this suite," he told her. "I want you to have a good time. But at the end of the night, if you've changed your mind, that's where I'll sleep."

"I'll never change my mind," she told him as she turned and faced him. A statement that was also a challenge, she thought.

Ever smooth Jack simply smiled. "My kind of woman," he told her as he handed her a glass of cham-pagne.

They settled on the sofa. Jack pulled out a remote and started the music, then they toasted each other.

"Impressive," she said after she'd taken a sip. "No wonder you have women lining up to date you."

He chuckled. "This isn't what I usually do for a date. I'm more the dinner-and-a-movie type."

Which meant this was especially for her? She hoped so.

She smoothed the front of her dress. "When we get home, I want to talk to Taryn about her castoffs. I never got the whole designer clothes thing before, but I'm starting to see the appeal. This feels really nice."

"It looks better than it feels."

"You can't know that."

His smile was slow and sexy. "Yeah, I can. So tell me about the chiweenies."

The change in topic caught her off guard. "What do you want to know?"

"What are they?"

"A Chihuahua-dachshund mix. So not purebreds. They're cute and have good characteristics of both breeds. I guess that's what makes them popular."

"And a breeding program had gotten out of hand?"

She nodded. "I can see how it would happen. Someone who doesn't have the experience thinks it might be fun and moves forward. Then a couple of years later, there are too many dogs and not enough buyers."

"Like the people who think a baby alligator would be fun and then it grows?"

"Right, but I don't think chiweenies endanger as many chickens."

"We're all against chicken death."

She laughed, then picked up her champagne. "I checked my phone while I was getting my hair done. The dogs are safely in Sacramento. They'll be evaluated by veterinary staff. The ones that are okay will be treated for parasites, vaccinated, then put out to foster."

"Which is where you come in."

She nodded. "I have already checked with a few people to see if they'll take in a dog or two temporarily."

"How many am I getting?"

She studied the lines of his face, the way his suit jacket emphasized his broad shoulders.

"Does it bother you that I do that?" she asked. "Do you mind about the owls and dogs and everything else I bring into your life?"

He took the champagne glass from her hand and set it on the coffee table, then leaned in, cupped her face in his large hands and kissed her.

The touch of his mouth against hers was soft and caring, with the slight hint of restrained passion. Tenderness ripped her apart from the inside until she was nothing but a beating heart filled with love.

He drew back and stared into her eyes. "I need you to be exactly who you are, Larissa. Chiweenies and all."

She thought about how easily her dress undid from

the back. The single long zipper would make it easy for anyone to help her out of the dress.

She slipped out of her shoes, then stood. "Come on," she said quietly as she started for the bedroom.

Jack stayed on the sofa. "Larissa, you need to be sure."

She smiled at him. "I'm leaving on the diamonds."

He laughed, then got to his feet and followed her.

The bedroom was large, dominated by the big bed. She got as far as the middle of the room before suddenly losing her courage. It was one thing for Jack to seduce her but quite another for her to take charge. She'd had boyfriends before and it wasn't as if she was a virgin, but Jack was, well, Jack.

She was sure there was more self-doubt on the way, but before she could form it into coherent thought, he walked up to her and pulled her close. She went into his embrace, reveling in the feel of his body against hers.

She reached up as he lowered his head and they met in an openmouthed kiss that started her body humming. His tongue tangled with hers, his hands roamed her from shoulders to hips. She wrapped her arms around him and hung on for all she was worth.

This was what she'd wanted for so long, she thought. Him and them. At last.

He moved his mouth over hers, even as he kissed her deeply. She found herself wanting to move in the same rhythm as the kisses, rubbing her body against him. But there were too many layers, too many clothes. She'd seen Jack naked a thousand times, but never like this. Never in an intimate setting. She wanted to be free to study and touch and explore without the constraints of work or professional conduct.

She tugged at his suit jacket. He drew back and smiled at her. "Impatient?"

"You have no idea."

"Then let me help."

He shrugged out of his jacket and tossed it onto a chair. While he toed off his shoes, he unfastened his tie and slid it through the collar.

She'd planned on undoing her dress so it could be out of the way, but found herself mesmerized by what he was doing. Because while she regularly saw Jack without clothes, she'd never once seen him take them off.

There was something erotic about watching his big hands move gracefully on the buttons at his cuffs and then down the front of his shirt. When he pulled away the white cotton, she saw strong muscles and the scars from his various surgeries.

He pulled off his socks, then reached for the buckle of his belt. She felt both shy and eager.

Seconds later he was naked and standing in front of her. Six feet two inches of honed, aroused male. Passion darkened his eyes. His breathing was a little fast, and when he reached for her, she knew that for the rest of her life, there was nowhere else she wanted to be.

"Now it's your turn," he said as he tugged on the zipper. "This is going to be good."

The dress drifted to the ground. She stood in front

of him wearing a black push-up bra and ridiculously tiny panties. His breathing hitched slightly.

"Damn."

She smiled. "Oh, please. You've been with some of the most beautiful women in the world."

"Not one of them is anything like you."

Exactly the right thing to say, she thought happily. She stepped closer and he wrapped his arms around her. They kissed again. She leaned into him, letting him take her weight, wanting to surrender as much as possible. He stroked her arms, then her back. His fingers were warm and sure as he unfastened her bra.

The scrap of lace dropped away and then his hands were cupping her breasts. As his fingers moved against her tight nipples, he kissed his way from her mouth to her jaw. He nibbled and licked until he reached her ear. He sucked on the lobe before biting down.

Shivers rippled through her. There were too many sensations. She didn't know what to focus on. The way he rubbed her breasts or the feel of his fingers dancing against her nipples? The hot breath on her neck or the pattern traced by his tongue? The heat of his body or the surge of his erection against her belly?

He shifted slightly, then sat on the bed. He pulled her between his parted legs and settled his mouth on her right breast. The hot, wet heat caressed her sensitive skin. He sucked her in, then flicked her nipple with his tongue. At the same time, he drew her panties down and she stepped out of them.

He shifted to her other breast, giving it the same attention. Something heavy and delicious connected her breasts to the very core of her and with each stroke, each suck, each second that passed, she felt herself readying for him more and more.

She stroked his hair and his shoulders. The ache between her thighs intensified. He needed to touch her there, she thought. Only what he was doing with her breasts was too good. She didn't want that to stop, either.

He put his hands on her thighs and slid them up slowly. His thumbs moved closer and closer to the very core of her but didn't touch. He moved against her labia, the very outside, lightly touching. Playing, she thought, arching her hips toward him in what she hoped was an unmistakable invitation. He ignored her.

He ran his fingers along the outside, just touching the seam, but not parting her or going deeper. He explored the crease where her thighs met her body and lightly stroked her butt. Fingers slipped between her thighs again, but still didn't go deep enough to get to anything good—all the while he sucked and licked and caressed her breasts.

Arousal grew until it was nearly painful. Her clit was swollen and aching. Hunger burned. She held in a whimper.

With lightning speed, he put his hands on her waist. He shifted her, lifting and turning until she was flat on her back in the center of the bed with no idea how she'd gotten there. Before she could catch her breath, Jack was between her bent legs, parting her sensitive flesh and pressing his mouth to the very center of her body.

The feel of his tongue against her core nearly made her scream with pleasure. She was wet and more than halfway there. A couple of strokes later, she was gasping and digging her heels into the bed. When he sucked on her swollen clit, she thought she was going to lose it and when he flicked his tongue over her again, she did.

She came in a rush of shuddering pleasure that claimed every cell of her body. She writhed and gasped, wanting it to never end. He stayed with her, his pace steady, until she was able to breathe again. Only then did he slow, drawing it out until she had nothing left.

He moved next to her on the bed and drew her against him. She snuggled close, feeling the aftereffects of her release rippling through her. He kissed her forehead, then her cheeks. She opened her eyes and saw him watching her.

The need still darkened his eyes but there was something else there, as well. Smugness. That damned male swagger that came from having a well-pleased woman in his bed.

She smiled. "Yes, you were all that."

He grinned.

She sat up. "Now it's your turn."

"I like it when you're fair."

He opened the nightstand drawer and pulled out a box of condoms. She shifted onto her knees and took the box from him. He raised an eyebrow.

"You're doing all the work?" he asked.

"You just did."

She opened the package and slid the condom over his impressive erection, then straddled him. Jack's eyes widened.

"On top?"

"Don't you like it that way?"

"It's a personal favorite."

"For me, too."

While it never had been before, she found herself wanting to be able to see what they were doing. Maybe it was silly, but she wanted to watch him as he got close. She wanted to see him come.

She straddled him. He put his hands on her hips and guided her into place. Her long hair hung down, nearly brushing his chest.

"This is going to be good," he said and lowered her onto his arousal.

She felt him slide inside. He stretched and filled her. She shifted so she was more upright, able to take all of him. When he was completely inside of her, she squeezed and they both groaned. She bent forward and braced her hands on the bed, then began to move.

Their eyes locked. His hands cupped her breasts and he stroked her sensitized skin. In and out and in and out. He filled her again and again. She increased the pace, watching his face tighten.

Their breathing increased. The friction deep inside made her push harder, faster. She was getting close again. Just being with Jack was enough to make her want to climax a second time. With him, she thought. That was what she wanted.

"Larissa," he breathed, her name nearly a groan. He swore and tensed. She could feel his muscles pushing him forward. She was close, but not there, she thought frantically, and rode him harder.

Need burned. Tension filled her. She strained to find the last bit of magic needed to push her over the edge.

He slipped a hand between them and pressed his thumb against her and circled the swollen knot of nerves.

It was all she needed. She felt her release begin deep inside of her before spiraling out to claim all of her. She cried out and shuddered, still moving up and down. Jack put his hands on her hips and kept her steady. He half rose and groaned deeply as his release overtook him.

Their eyes locked in that moment of perfect pleasure, and for the first time in her life, she saw down to her lover's soul.

CHAPTER FOURTEEN

THE DRIVE FROM San Francisco to Fool's Gold took about three hours. Larissa was content to sit quietly in the rental car while Jack drove. The miles passed quickly. Too quickly, she thought. She wasn't ready to return to the real world.

The past twenty-four hours had been amazing. The previous night, after they'd made love, they'd dressed and gone downstairs for dinner. Later, they'd filled the huge bathtub and had touched each other with the thrill that comes with exploration. They'd made love with the water sloshing onto the floor.

She'd slept in Jack's arms. Larissa turned to look out the window so he wouldn't see her smile as she explored that nearly unbelievable thought. She'd awakened to find him holding her tight—as if he never wanted to let go.

The concept might be wishful thinking on her part, but she was going to go with it for now.

She glanced back at him. "Thank you for all that."

"You're welcome. I had a good time." He glanced at her and smiled before returning his attention to the road.

She sighed with contentment. "This could make your massages really interesting."

He laughed. "You're right. I'm going to have even more trouble not getting a hard-on."

She thought about the massage table. "Oh, I think we could use that to our advantage."

"Intriguing. I look forward to what you have in mind."

JACK WALKED INTO his house to find Percy on the living room floor playing with what looked like a dozen small dogs. They were tumbling together in a mass of dogs and teen. When Percy saw him, he sat up and grinned.

"We've got dogs."

"I see that."

Jack put the garment bag he'd purchased in San Francisco over the stair railing. Now that they weren't moving, he could see there were five. All small with big ears. Some looked more like Chihuahuas and others favored their dachshund blood.

"The guy who dropped them off said these ones were healthy. Probably all under three years old. They should be easy to adopt."

"Good. I don't want five dogs."

Jack started toward the living room. All the chiweenies rushed toward him and began sniffing his shoes and jeans, jumping in front of him and yipping. He bent down to offer pats. One of the little girls flipped onto her back and offered her tummy for a quick rub.

"At least they're socialized," he said. "That's something."

He sat on the floor across from Percy and picked up a knotted rope toy. Two of the dogs dived for it and started a game of tug-of-war. The little girl climbed into his lap while the remaining two walked over to harass Percy.

"When did they get here?" Jack asked.

"A couple of hours ago. They're fun."

"Yeah, but are they housebroken?"

Percy looked blank.

Jack sighed. "Have you taken them outside?"

"No. But we should do that right now." The teen scrambled to his feet. "I did give them water."

Water without access to a bathroom could be a bad combination, Jack thought as he stood. Together they herded the dogs out the back.

The five of them ran onto the grass and started chasing each other.

"Keep watch," Jack instructed. "I want to make sure everyone goes."

When they were all back inside, Percy showed him the food that had been delivered along with a couple of big dog beds.

"The guy says they're used to sleeping together in a pack. So we should keep them in the same room."

"How about your room?" Jack asked.

Percy laughed. "Works for me. I like the little guys."

The dogs played for another hour or so, then as a group headed for the beds. They went around and around, moving from one bed to the other until they'd found where they wanted to be and flopped down. Seconds later, they were out.

"You're right about the schedule," Jack told the teen. "For walking and everything else." He glanced around at his house. "I don't think we should be leaving five active dogs home alone." Another complication, compliments of Larissa. Yet he wasn't the least bit upset. How could he be after yesterday?

There would be hell to pay later for all that. He was sure of it. But whatever the price, his twenty-four hours with her had been worth it. He'd enjoyed every second of his time with her. The sex had been incredible, but it had been more than that. It had been about connecting with her in a way they hadn't before. About being with her.

For a second he allowed himself to wonder *what if.* What if he could be like everyone else? What if he was willing to believe? Foolish questions. Because he wasn't. He'd lost Lucas and on the heels of that, his parents had gone away. They'd told him he would be fine, but that had been about them assuaging their own consciences. They hadn't wanted to know their only living son needed them. Their need to escape the pain of what they'd been through had been stronger than their love for him. He got that. He even understood the logic. But he couldn't forgive and he sure as hell couldn't forget.

He'd vowed never to care that deeply again, and he hadn't. With Taryn, he'd liked her a lot, but there hadn't been love. Not beyond friendship. When she'd turned up pregnant, he'd known he was going to have to suck it up and give his heart to their baby. He'd been willing to take the risk. But then she'd miscarried and the moment had been lost.

He had a good life, he reminded himself. People he cared about and who cared about him. The relationships he had these days were safe. They would last. There wasn't anything on the line so there wasn't anything to lose.

Percy got up. "I'll be right back," he said and headed up the stairs. Two of the dogs opened their eyes and watched him go, but they didn't move.

Percy returned with a book in his hand. He gave it to Jack and sat on the sofa.

"I read it," he said, both proud and shy. "The whole thing. Kenny's been working with me and that software program really helped. I wasn't as bad as I thought. I think I can do it. I want to get my GED."

Jack patted him on the back. "Good for you. I'm glad. Congratulations on finishing the book. Let me know when you want some more. We'll go get them."

"Sam already took me. I'm going to work real hard, Jack. You've given me a great opportunity and I'm going to take advantage of it."

"I'm glad."

"I want to go to college. And I know what I want to do while I'm there." He paused for effect.

Jack held in a groan. Percy looked eager as he spoke. Excited. Jack had a bad idea he knew where this was going. It made sense. He was around the three of them all day. He saw the glamorous side of the sport. But to play football professionally?

He studied the kid impersonally. Percy wasn't big enough and he hadn't been working on his skill set. With a lot of coaching maybe he could make a team at the community college, but his odds of going pro were about zero. That required a gift from the gods and Percy hadn't been chosen. At least not as far as Jack could tell.

He would let him down gently, Jack told himself. Maybe run him through some drills so he could see how much work was ahead. Maybe if they went to a Pac-12 game with UCLA or Stanford, Percy could see what was expected of a—

"I want to study to be a teacher. I want to help kids like me. Kids who slip through the cracks and are sent on to the next grade, even though they're not ready."

Jack stared at him. "A teacher?"

"Uh-huh."

Jack started to smile. If Larissa were here, she would take this moment to point out that despite his best efforts, he wasn't at the center of the universe every single minute.

"That's great," he told Percy. "I think you'll be a terrific teacher." There was more to discuss. Like the fact that he should start at a community college to build up his study habits in a less competitive environment. And that Jack wanted to make sure they found the best four-year for him to transfer to. But that was for later.

"You've got a goal," he told Percy. "That's how all greatness begins."

"Kenny says it's all about fundamentals."

"Kenny would say that," Jack murmured, feeling kind of good about himself and what was happening with Percy. Was this why Larissa did it? For the sense of accomplishment and knowing she'd made a real difference? He had to admit, he liked it.

The front door opened and Kenny walked in.

Percy grinned. "We were just talking about you. I was telling Jack what you said about fundamentals."

Jack watched his friend approach and saw the blood in the other man's eyes. As he stood, prepared for what was coming, he had the brief thought that word traveled fast. Then a fist flew into his face and the world went dark.

"NOTHING'S BROKEN," KENNY grumbled as he put ice into a dish towel.

Jack sat at the kitchen table and carefully felt his face. His friend was right. All the bones felt as they had before. There was swelling, but that would go down with time. On the bright side, Kenny was holding his right hand as if it hurt him. One fact the movies never mentioned when they showed those fight scenes—it hurt as much to hit as be hit.

Percy hovered in the entrance to the kitchen. "I don't understand," he said for fourth time. "You're not mad at each other."

"I was mad," Kenny said. "I made my point and now it's over."

"Fighting doesn't accomplish anything," Percy told him.

Jack took the offered ice and put it on his jaw. "There wasn't a fight. I was hit. There's a difference."

Five chiweenies danced in the kitchen, trying hard to trip anyone standing. Jack was grateful to be in the chair. His face hurt and he knew it was going to get worse before it got better.

Percy looked between the two men. "You're not going to tell me what that was about, are you?"

"Nope," Kenny said.

"So I should go upstairs?"

"Probably a good idea," Jack told him.

"Whatever," Percy muttered and left.

The chiweenies went with him. Jack had a feeling all five of them would end up on the bed, rocking out to music he was too old to understand.

When they were alone, Kenny took the chair opposite Jack's and sat down.

"You had to sleep with her. I warned you to leave her alone, that she was family. But you did it, anyway."

Jack was torn. On the one hand, he was glad Larissa had someone looking out for her. On the other, he didn't want to get hit in the face again.

"We're both adults."

"She's like a sister to me. Sister trumps being an adult." Kenny's mouth twisted. "You're going to break her heart."

"She wants to get over me. This is her way of doing that."

Kenny glared at him. "Don't try that bullshit on me. She's crazy about you. Has been forever. Now you're making it worse. This is going to end badly for all of us. Have you thought about that? The consequences? You could destroy what we have."

Jack hadn't thought about that, nor did he want to. "I care about her. I won't hurt her." But even as he said the words, he wondered if he was lying. Because he couldn't give Larissa what she wanted. Or if he could, he wouldn't. Because he wouldn't take the risk.

"She'll figure out I'm not the one for her," he said at last. "She'll find someone else. You'll see."

Kenny shook his head. "I can't believe you're that stupid, but sure. Go ahead. I can't stop you. But when this all hits the fan, I'll be on her side."

Something for which Jack could be grateful.

"I STILL DON'T understand," Larissa said. She was snuggled in Jack's huge bed. Percy was in his room and the chiweenies were curled up asleep on their beds in the corner of the master bedroom.

Ever since she'd arrived earlier that evening, Jack hadn't answered any of her questions about why Kenny had come over and hit him.

"There's nothing much *to* understand," Jack told her. "Kenny's afraid I'm going to hurt you."

"Did you tell him this was my plan? That I'm doing my best to get over you?"

"He didn't seem to appreciate the argument."

At this moment, Kenny's concern made sense. Naked and satiated from Jack's lovemaking, she couldn't imagine wanting to be anywhere else. But she had to give it time. Eventually Jack would start to get on her nerves and then she would be free of him.

Jack pulled her close and kissed her. "Just let it go and be grateful he's looking out for you."

She studied the bruise on Jack's jaw. "He could have hurt you. Percy said you didn't try to defend yourself."

"I knew I had it coming."

Which was so like Jack, she thought with a sigh. Yup, getting over him was getting further away by the minute.

"THIS IS DANGEROUS," Bailey said as she held on to both leashes. "You knew that and asked us to help you, anyway."

Larissa laughed. "They're small dogs. I think you're safe."

Her friend glared at her. "You know that's not what I'm talking about. Look at her."

Up ahead, Chloe held the leash of one of the chi-weenies. The eight-year-old girl and the little dog looked adorable together.

"I see a happy child and a cute dog."

"Exactly. I'm just thinking about buying my first house. Why on earth would I take on the responsibility of a dog right now?"

"It's not like she's going to eat much. And having a dog will teach Chloe responsibility."

Bailey rolled her eyes. "You're no help. I work all day and Chloe's in school. Is that fair to the dog?"

She had Larissa there. "You could ask Mayor Marsha how she would feel if you brought your dog to work with you."

"That's professional," Bailey grumbled. "She'll be so impressed. We're not getting a dog. Not right now."

"If you say so." Larissa wasn't concerned. There was plenty of interest in the chiweenies. "I'm not trying to push you into taking a dog."

Bailey looked at her daughter and sighed. "You don't have to. It's going to happen, anyway."

They reached the park and started along the path. The morning was warm and clear. Larissa was spending her days doing work she loved and her nights in Jack's bed. Percy was excited about studying for his GED, and she'd helped rescue dogs in need. How could anything be better?

"Tell me about the house you're buying," Larissa said. "You'd said you were thinking about it but I didn't know it had gone further."

Bailey smiled. "It's so cool. There's a program in town where people can apply for a grant that gives them the money for a down payment. I had to fill out a bunch of paperwork and then be interviewed by this lady at the bank. The amount of the down payment depends on my salary and credit history. Chloe and I qualified."

"That's great," Larissa told her. "So you've found a house you like?"

"Maybe. There's a cute little Craftsman in the older part of town. It needs fixing up, but I'm okay with that. There's a darling upstairs bedroom that Chloe completely loves, and there's a small study for us to share as an office."

"Congratulations."

"Don't congratulate me yet. I'm still thinking about it. A mortgage is a big thing to take on by myself. It's scary to think about."

"It's a lot of responsibility," Larissa said, impressed by her friend's willingness to handle so much on her own. For a second Larissa wondered when she'd been inclined to take on anything close. Her involvements tended to be fleeting. She gave intensely, then moved on. Dyna was her first ever pet. She certainly didn't have a child to care for and her family's needs were minimal. The only person she really had to worry about was herself.

The realization took a little joy from the day.

"Ladies."

She turned and saw Kenny jogging toward them. Her pleasure at seeing him was tempered by the memory of what he'd done to Jack. Of course, he'd done it for her, so could she really be mad at him?

"Hi, Kenny," Chloe called and hurried toward him. "I haven't seen you in a long time."

"Hey, munchkin. How's your knot tying?"

"Excellent. I have my bead. I can show you."

He stopped and squatted down to pat the dog. "I'd like to see it."

Bailey cleared her throat. "Hi. Chloe told me you helped her last spring. With the knots. Thanks for that."

He waved away her words. "No problem. So who's this pretty girl?"

"She's one of Larissa's chiweenies. We're walking them today. They don't have homes." Chloe stared at her mother. "It's sad when puppies don't have a home."

Larissa winced. "Sorry," she muttered.

Bailey shrugged. "I'll deal."

Kenny stood. "I'll leave you to it, then."

"Are you going to help with the walking?" Larissa asked, thinking that Bailey and Kenny looked good together. And he was great around children. Now that she thought about it, he'd never been married. Maybe it was time for that to change.

Kenny glanced at the little dogs sniffing his running shoes. "Not if I don't have to. They're not exactly my size."

"They'd be a chick magnet," Bailey said, then flushed. "Not that you need help with that sort of thing, I'm sure."

Was that flirting? Interest? Larissa was frustrated to realize she was much better at finding stray animals a home than figuring out random boy-girl attraction.

"Bailey's thinking of buying a house," she blurted.

Both Bailey and Kenny stared at her.

"Okay," he said slowly. "Congratulations."

"She's worried about all the responsibility, what with being a single mom and all. You could help."

Bailey frowned. "Larissa, I'm fine. You don't need to get him involved."

"Kenny's bought a lot of property. You could ask him questions."

"Our situations couldn't be more different."

"Still—"

Bailey shook her head and faced Kenny. "There's nothing for you to do. I'm fine. It was nice to see you. Run while you can."

Kenny glanced between them, nodded once and took off. Larissa watched him go. The man really did have some speed on him.

She turned to Bailey. "Sorry. Was I meddling too much?"

"Yes, but I know it comes from love so I forgive you."

They started walking again. Chloe and her dog ran ahead.

"So Kenny," Larissa began.

"No," Bailey said firmly.

"But he's—"

"No. He's gorgeous—I'll admit that. But so out of my league. Trust me on this. I have a beautiful daughter and maybe a new house, not to mention the possibility of a dog. The last thing I need is a man."

LARISSA WROTE DOWN item numbers for some new oils she wanted to try. She'd been doing some reading about their healing properties and thought the guys would like them. She closed the browser window just as Kenny walked into her office.

He'd showered after his run and dressed in work clothes. He crossed to her desk and stared at her. As

Kenny was well over six feet, it was a long way to look down.

"Don't do that," he said firmly. "Don't set me up. Don't try to get involved in my personal life."

She blinked at him. "Okay," she said slowly. "I thought—"

"No."

"But Bailey is—"

He raised a single eyebrow. "Larissa." His voice was a warning growl. Not a tone he usually took with her.

The message was really clear, she thought. Back off.

"Okay, I won't set you up and I won't throw you at Bailey anymore, even though she's really nice and pretty and better than you deserve."

One corner of his mouth twitched, as if he were holding in a smile. That made her feel a little better.

"Thanks," he said, and then he was gone.

She was still staring at where he'd been when Taryn walked in.

"What?" the other woman asked. "You have the strangest look on your face."

"I feel strange. Kenny just warned me off setting him up with Bailey."

Taryn took the chair in front of the desk. "He's right about that. Bailey's not for him."

"How can you know that? I thought you were her friend."

"I am. I'm also Kenny's friend. Trust me, they're not right for each other."

Larissa started to protest, but Taryn leaned toward her and shook her head.

"You're going to have to trust me on this," her friend said softly. "I know on the surface they seem well matched, but the truth is Bailey is the last woman Kenny should be with."

Larissa started to ask why, then reminded herself there were things from his past she didn't know. While Jack and Taryn had talked about their previous relationships, Kenny and Sam weren't so forthcoming.

"Okay," she said slowly. "I won't try to get them together."

"Good." Taryn crossed her legs and smiled. "So, you had sex with Jack. How was that?"

The casual question had Larissa nearly choking. "How did you... Did Jack..." She cleared her throat. "It was nice."

Taryn didn't smile. "No one told me. No one had to. I figured it out the second I saw you after you got back from San Francisco." She hesitated.

"You think it's a bad idea."

Taryn raised one shoulder. "I'm not sure. I think it's great that you're focusing on your own life instead of always distracting yourself with your causes. But I worry about how all this is going to end. You know Jack isn't looking for the same things you are, right?"

Larissa nodded. "He's been very clear and it's not like I haven't seen him go through hordes of women over the years."

"But?"

"I want to get over him. What's that old saying? The only way over is through?"

"You need to go through a relationship with Jack to move on." Taryn sighed. "I hope you're right. That you're going to be able to move on and not just get more involved."

"I'm open to suggestions," Larissa told her. "If you can think of another way to deal with this."

"Sorry, no."

"Then I'm going to move forward with the plan and hope for the best."

CHAPTER FIFTEEN

LARISSA SAT UP and stared at the clock beside her bed. The numbers weren't very different from the last time she'd looked. Instead of 3:15 it now read 3:18. At this rate, she was in for an extra shot of espresso come morning.

She flopped back on her mattress and tried to clear her brain. Turning the same thoughts over and over wasn't helping her get sleep. Yet she couldn't get Taryn's words out of her head.

Nor could she forget her conversation with Bailey. Sure Larissa made sure the latest tree moth or chiweenie was rescued, but that was all short-term. Bailey was dealing with so much more. She was raising a kid on her own. Talk about having to pull it all together. Larissa wondered if her own personal resources and character would rise to the occasion.

Dyna jumped onto the bed and walked toward her.

"Hey, pretty girl," Larissa said as she rolled onto her side and stroked the cat. "Am I keeping you awake? Sorry. I have too much on my mind."

Dyna sank down next to her and purred while Larissa continued to stroke her. She rested her head on her arm and wondered when everything had gotten so complicated.

She'd always had a desire to take care of animals in need. But once she got to know Jack and had access to his resources, the sphere had grown. She liked being able to make a difference. She liked coordinating with families who were waiting for a transplant and helping them find temporary housing. She liked knowing that she'd found homes for cats or chiweenies or even owls. Helping wasn't bad.

Except when it was something to hide behind, she thought slowly. Except when it offered a way to hide from her real life.

Had she done that? Had she be so busy rescuing everything in her path that she'd forgotten about herself? She wanted to say no but the fact that it took her mother to point out that she was in love with Jack sort of said she very well might have lost her way.

So what was she going to do about it? How was she going to reclaim her life?

"What do you think I should do?" she asked aloud.

Dyna turned to gaze at her. The cat's blue eyes closed slowly.

"You're right," Larissa told her. "It's my problem and therefore the solution is in me. But maybe you could give me a hint?"

Dyna continued to purr. Larissa closed her own eyes and felt herself start to relax. The answer would be there, she told herself. All she had to do was keep looking for it.

"I CAN'T TASTE anymore truffles," Taryn said. "If I do, I won't fit in my dress. You and Angel can decide. But I do want the larger sprays of flowers for the ceremony."

She paused, then groaned. "Is that right? Are they too big?"

Dellina took notes as Taryn spoke. "Either size will be beautiful."

Her voice was calm, almost soothing. Jack figured it was a trick she'd picked up, given her line of business. Psycho brides would go with the territory. He'd heard rumors about them but until recently, he'd thought they were an urban myth. Now he knew better. He would never have guessed he would hear Taryn worrying about flower arrangements for any reason. Or tuxedo truffles or tulle, whatever the hell that was.

Accompanying their very female conversation was the steady beat from Percy's speakers. Despite the fact that the kid was upstairs, the throbbing of his music's bass vibrated through the house. The front door opened and the two chiweenies Larissa hadn't taken with her to walk started barking. Jack looked around his living room and thought longingly of escape.

"We come carrying beer," Sam said as he walked into the living room. "It's nearly time."

Kenny held up two giant bags of takeout. "I don't know if I got enough."

"You're fine," Taryn said before Jack could speak. "Angel will be by shortly with chips, dip and nuts." She bent down and scooped up one of the dogs. The other one ran to Jack and began scratching at his knee, trying to get Jack to pick him up.

Sam and Kenny disappeared into the kitchen with the food and the beer, Angel walked in with more shopping bags. Taryn called to him while Dellina went to sort through all the food. Kenny stuck his head back into the living room.

"Hey," he said. "It's starting. We need the TV on."

Jack stood in the middle of the chaos and wondered why he'd thought this was a good idea. Sure watching the first game of the season together was a tradition, but it wasn't as if it was a good one. He would prefer a little peace and quiet. Right now his house felt like a war zone.

The front door opened again and both dogs started barking. The sound intensified when Larissa came in with the three dogs she'd taken out. There were barks and yips and calls for quiet and the theme music for the NFL game. Jack was about to grab his car keys and run when his gaze locked on Larissa.

She was bent over, releasing the three chiweenies from their leashes. Nothing about the moment was all that special, yet seeing her allowed him to breathe again. He scooped up a couple of the dogs and told them to be quiet. Everyone found their way to the sofas to watch the game and he went in the other direction. Toward Larissa.

"They're all walked," she told him, absently taking one of the dogs he held. "They should be good for the rest of the day. They can use the backyard for their potty breaks."

He drew her into the kitchen. There was an open twelve-pack of beer, several covered dishes that probably needed to be put in the refrigerator. Chips and nuts had to be put into bowls. But he didn't care about that.

He set his dog down, took hers from her and did the same, then pulled her close and kissed her.

Her mouth was soft and warm. She moved against him, her tongue tangling with his until all he could think about was taking her upstairs and having his way with her. Only they had a house full of company and there was a teenager awake and dogs to worry about. When had his life gotten so complicated?

She drew back and smiled at him. "Nice greeting. So I should leave more often?"

"Not really. I just missed you."

She looked at the mess in the kitchen. "Too many people going in too many directions?"

"Taryn and Dellina were discussing tulle."

She laughed. "Do you know what that is?"

"It's something to do with the wedding, so no."

She hugged him. "You're such a guy."

"That should make you happy."

"It does."

THE L.A. STALLIONS won their season opener, which put everyone in a good mood. Larissa enjoyed watching football with the guys. Not because she cared about the sport, but because they did. Plus, when they complained about a bad call or sloppy play, they knew exactly what they were talking about. She'd worked with them for so long she sometimes forgot that expertise was fun.

After everyone had left and the kitchen was clean, Percy returned to his room. She let out the chiweenies one last time, then herded them all upstairs where they collapsed together on a huge dog bed in the corner. She gave each of them a quick pat, then followed the sound of running water into the giant master bath.

Jack had water flowing into the tub. The scent of jasmine and vanilla drifted through the steam. He had already kicked off his shoes and removed his socks. She leaned against the door frame to watch him remove the rest of his clothing.

It was a good show. No matter how many times she saw Jack naked, she never got tired of looking. Maybe it was the way his muscles moved. Muscles she knew intimately. Maybe it was because she was in love with him and therefore couldn't get enough of him. Maybe it was a combination. But whatever the reason, she stood and watched as Jack undressed, then walked into his embrace.

He pulled her close, then touched her face. His hands cupped her cheeks as he pressed his mouth to hers. His lips claimed with heady passion. She parted for him and welcomed the erotic feel of his tongue against hers.

With the first stroke, she felt electric tingles moving through her torso. With the second, those tingles settled in her breasts and between her legs. He hadn't even touched her anywhere and she was already squirming to get closer, to be taken and to take. But first there would be the journey.

He dropped his hands to her waist and began to tug on her T-shirt. She reluctantly drew back so he could pull off the shirt. Her bra followed and then his hands were on her breasts.

He cupped her curves before bending over and sucking on her left nipple. She arched against him, wanting him to take her in deeper. She touched his hair, his bare shoulders. As his teeth lightly rubbed against her sensitive nipple, his hands reached for her jeans.

She fumbled in her attempts to help him undress her. Jeans and panties were pushed to the ground, then his mouth was on her other breast and she was having a little trouble keeping her breathing steady.

He broke away and turned off the faucets, then dimmed the lights. "Come on," he said. "Let's see how big a mess we can make."

She laughed and reached for a clip. After securing her hair on top of her head, she stepped into the hot water. He got in, as well, then sat down in the tub and held out his arms. She got in, her back to his front. His erection poked her in the small of her back. She tried to turn, but he wouldn't let her.

"We're going to play first," he told her. "You'll like it."

"I'm pretty sure you're right," she said, relaxing against him. The water was exactly the right temperature and the sensual fragrance surrounded them.

Jack wrapped both arms around her. He rested one

hand across her breasts and the other on her belly. At the same time he began to lick and kiss the back of her neck.

Shivers rippled through her. Her nipples tightened and he squeezed first one, then the other. She waited for the other hand to move lower. Instead, he raised his arm and flipped a switch. Seconds later the motor started and the tub jets began to spray hot water.

She laughed. "Seriously? You're turning on the Jacuzzi?"

"Trust me," he said and slipped his hand between her thighs.

He found her core right away. She was already swollen. When he rubbed her, she let her legs fall open and relaxed into the pleasure.

He'd already learned how she liked it. The speed, the pressure. He used that knowledge now to take her from interested to aroused in only a couple of minutes—aided by his magical stroking of her breasts. But just when she thought he was going to turn her toward him and make things really fun, he instead shifted her closer to one of the jets.

She started to sit up. "Wait," she said. "You can't expect me to do that."

"Why not? It'll be fun."

She looked at him, at the face of the man she loved, then nodded tentatively. "I don't think it's going to work."

"It's going to work great."

He helped her slide forward, moving with her so she could lean against him and stay above water. She planted her feet on the edge of the tub and bent her legs so the jet blew directly on her swollen center. At the same time Jack put both his hands on her breasts and rubbed them.

The bubbling water felt good, she thought, shifting to find the right position, but not as good as him. She liked the feel of his hands on her breasts, she thought, pulsing her hips slightly. When he rubbed and squeezed, she began to breathe more quickly. She could feel herself getting close, but realized it wasn't going to happen.

"It's too weird," she told him as she turned toward him.

"No problem."

He lifted her onto the flat side of the tub. He knelt between her thighs and pressed his mouth directly against her aroused center.

Apparently the jets had done more than she'd thought because the second time he ran his tongue over her clitoris, she began to come.

The orgasm was unexpected and she gasped out her pleasure. Jack immediately plunged two fingers inside of her, which made her tremble. She had to hang on to him to keep from slipping back into the tub. She drew her legs apart wider and pressed into him as her release rippled through her over and over.

When she was finished, she opened her eyes and saw him smiling at her.

"So, about the jets," he began.

She laughed. "Maybe they're not so weird."

She slipped back into the water. He pulled her close

and gently touched her between her legs. She shuddered at the feel of him.

"Your turn," she whispered and patted the edge of the tub.

He sat where she had. He was already hard and when she bent to take him in her mouth, he groaned.

She shifted to brace herself on the tub, anchoring her knees and her feet, then drew him into her mouth again. At that moment, Jack shifted her so that one of the jets was pointed directly at the apex of her thighs. The bubbling water caressed her exactly where she was most swollen.

"This way it's good for both of us," Jack told her.

And it was.

THE LAST THING Jack was looking for was another meeting, but here he was, back at Cal U Fool's Gold for another go-round with Tad, the athletic director, on the subject of the university starting a football program. Normally he would have been looking for an excuse to cancel. He could claim a last-minute meeting with a client. But he didn't—for two reasons. First, he was kind of excited about the thought of watching a team being built from the ground up. Second, these days he was nice and mellow most of the time. He knew the cause and was looking forward to having his way with her later that night.

He walked into the conference room three minutes before the start of the meeting and nodded at everyone. University president Newham was there, across from Tad. There was also a guy Jack didn't recognize. He was tall enough and built, but if Jack had to guess, he would say the other man worked hard for a living. His muscles were more from labor than sports.

The man in question nodded at him, then reached across the table to shake hands.

"Zane Nicholson."

"Jack McGarry."

Zane sat down. "So you're the football player. I've been hearing about you."

"I can't say the same. You're alumni?"

Zane's expression tightened. "No. I went to Texas A&M."

"You play ball?"

"No. I worked to put myself through school."

Jack had, too. His job had been on the field. But he knew what the other man meant. A lot of people assumed that an athletic scholarship was a free ride to education. What they didn't understand was that there were pitfalls along the way. An injury could knock an athlete out of the program in an instant. Bad performance was nearly as quick. There was also training time, practices, appearances, the games themselves. All of which kept the student athlete from his or her classes.

Worse, the star athletes often passed classes they rarely attended, which meant at the end of four or five years of college, the student had a degree but little actual education. And the odds of going pro were incredibly small.

Jack had insisted on getting his grades the old-fashioned way. Which meant his GPA wasn't impressive, but he had graduated on his own terms. He'd had plenty of friends who had injured themselves in their junior or senior year and then had lost the scholarship along with any chance at staying in college.

But there was no point in explaining that to anyone. No one had a whole lot of sympathy.

"The Aggies have a good team this year," Jack said, then grinned. "You know, for Texans."

Zane smiled. "Don't expect me to defend the state. I was a California boy in the middle of all that. I took my share of ribbing. But it was where I wanted to study."

"Mr. Nicholson has a large ranch north of town," President Newham said. "He's here at the request of the mayor. He's our second citizen liaison."

A muscle in Zane's jaw tightened. "Something I will be taking up with the mayor."

Jack relaxed back in his chair. "She has a way of getting people to do things they don't want to do."

"Tell me about it," Zane growled. "First the town annexed my land, now this."

"What do you mean 'annexed'? They took it from you?"

"No. Most of my ranch is on unincorporated land. They moved the boundaries of the city to include the house and barn area." He scowled. "Mayor Marsha swears they'll be bringing in city water and sewer in the next few years."

"You'd rather not have the city at all," Jack said, guessing the other man preferred to do things his way.

"The ranch has been there over a hundred years

without Fool's Gold getting involved. We can survive another hundred just as well."

Two more people joined them. President Newham glanced at the paperwork in front of her. "I believe that's everyone. Thank you all for coming today. At our last meeting we had a spirited discussion on whether or not to begin a football program at the university. It's a complex and expensive decision to make. As Jack reminded us, there is a long-term financial implication to consider. Tad felt our programs were complete as they were and nothing else was required. I've met privately with Zane to bring him up to speed. Today I'd like to see if we can get consensus from this committee so I can report back to the regents and we can come up with a final decision."

"Why don't we call a vote now?" Jack asked conversationally. "To see where we stand. After all, no one's going to change Tad's mind."

The athletic director glared at him. "We also know where you stand, Jack."

Jack nodded. "Using the 'you are, too' argument, Tad?"

President Newham sighed heavily. "Gentlemen, if we could stay on the subject at hand, please. A vote isn't a bad idea. This will be nonbinding, of course, until after the discussion. All those in favor of moving forward with starting a football team, raise your hands."

Jack was gratified to see that everyone except Tad voted with him. Even the Aggie.

"You surprise me," he told Zane.

"I have a kid brother in high school. If I can get him to go to Cal U Fool's Gold instead of MIT, my life will be a lot easier. A football team would help."

Done in by self-interest, Jack thought humorously. Still, it was good when a plan came together.

CHAPTER SIXTEEN

"YOU WERE GONE," Larissa told Sam the following Friday. "You were gone for two days and no one knew where you were."

She didn't mean the statement to come out like an accusation, but she didn't like it when the guys traveled. Score felt empty without the whole team there.

"You have my cell number," Sam told her. "You could have called if there was a problem."

"I know. But still." She looked at him and waited. "Well?"

"Well, what?"

"Where were you?"

"I'm not going to tell."

"Were you with Dellina?"

"None of your business."

She sighed. "Your need for privacy is annoying. You were gone two days. You could have been anywhere."

"Good to know. How about you, Jack and Percy join me for dinner tonight at Jo's Bar and I'll answer all your questions."

"Really?"

Sam being Sam paused for a second. "Almost all of them."

"Good enough for me. We'll see you tonight."

His dark gaze settled on her face. "No chiweenies."

"Oh, Sam, I wouldn't bring a dog into a restaurant."

"No chiweenies."

"I heard you the first time. Besides, one of the five at Jack's has already been adopted. Only four more to go."

She was smiling as she spoke, but Sam didn't look happy or relieved.

"What?" she asked.

He lightly touched her shoulder. "Have you ever wondered why you keep doing this?" he asked.

"Rescuing animals? I care about their welfare."

He didn't look convinced.

"You don't agree?"

"I don't disagree. I find it curious. You respond in the moment instead of having a place to put your energy on a regular basis."

"You mean like joining a local organization?"

"Wouldn't you find that more satisfying? Being able to see a project through?"

"Maybe." She always enjoyed working with the transplant families and a lot of that was because she got to stay close with them for a while. Often they became friends.

"I want you to be happy," he told her, his voice gentle.

She hugged him. "Thanks, Sam."

"You're welcome." He kissed her forehead. "No chiweenies."

She laughed.

Larissa, Jack and Percy got to Jo's right on time. There was a sign on the door that read Closed for a Private Event.

"Does that mean we can go in?" Larissa asked. "Did Sam know about this?"

"Sam knows," Jack told her.

She looked at him. "What aren't you telling me?"

"That you look especially beautiful tonight."

"Hey," Percy said as he walked in with them. "It's still early in the evening. Don't gross me out with your old-people lovey-dovey talk."

Larissa laughed. "Hey, we're not that old."

The teen's grin was unrepentant. "You are to me. I'm a man in my prime."

The bar was filled with forty or fifty people all standing around and talking. Servers circulated with appetizers. Jo and a couple of other bartenders manned the bar.

One of the servers approached and offered them crab puffs. "Dinner will be served upstairs in about an hour," she said as she held the tray steady.

Larissa took a crab puff. "Thanks." She turned to Jack. "Do you know what this is about? Sam isn't leaving Score, is he?"

"No. He wouldn't make that kind of announcement in public."

Percy pointed across the room. "Melissa's here. I gotta go."

He took off before either of them could say anything.

"Ah, young love," Larissa said. "Better than old love."

Jack put his arm around her. "You're not so old."

She shoved at him but he didn't budge. "Gee, thanks."

"Anytime."

They went to the bar. While all drinks were offered, most people chose champagne. Larissa took a sip and enjoyed the bubbles bouncing off her tongue. She recognized everyone at the party. There were the Score folks, of course, along with the bodyguard-school folks. Noelle and her husband, Felicia and Gideon. Even Mayor Marsha seemed to be making the rounds.

The older woman spotted them, then headed in their direction.

"Jack, Larissa. Nice to see you both," the mayor said. "Jack, I understand you made quite an impression on the university committee."

Jack shrugged modestly. "They're interested in the possibility of starting a football program. I think it's a good move."

"You impressed President Newham very much."

"Thanks."

"It's going to be an ambitious project. Finding a coach will be difficult." The mayor smiled. "Not my problem, fortunately. If you'll excuse me, I have a few announcements to make."

"There are announcements," Larissa murmured. "At a party?"

"It's a town thing," Jack told her and tucked his arm more firmly around her.

Sure enough the mayor walked to the bar where she took a microphone from Jo. Larissa hadn't known there was a microphone in Jo's Bar.

"Thank you all for coming," the mayor said. The room went quiet as everyone turned to her. "I have the most wonderful job. I get to live here and know all of you. I also have presided over a number of weddings and I do try to be in the hospital for every birth I can." She smiled. "After the messy work is done, of course."

Several people laughed.

"So it is with great pleasure that I continue the tradition of making wonderful and happy announcements like this one. Ladies and gentlemen, I present to you Fool's Gold's most recently married couple. Dellina and Sam Ridge."

It took a few seconds for the words to sink in. Sam and Dellina walked toward the mayor just as Larissa realized what she'd said. She shrieked and raced toward her friends.

"You're married?" she asked, hugging them both.

Taryn joined in, as did Dellina's sisters and several of her friends.

Larissa grabbed Sam. "That's what you were doing when you were gone?"

He smiled, looking both happy and content. "I don't need a big ceremony and the last thing Dellina wanted to do was plan another wedding. This is our reception."

Kenny and Jack joined the crowd. They hugged their friend and kissed the bride. Everyone looked at the diamond eternity band Dellina wore on her ring finger.

Larissa let the happy feelings wash over her. This was how it was supposed to be, she thought. People in love getting married. Because that's what people in love did. She wanted that.

Her gaze drifted to Jack. He had his arm around Taryn and Dellina, and Kenny was taking pictures. Sam pushed his friend away and claimed his wife with a kiss that had people hooting. Jack laughed.

Would he ever do this? Would he ever give his heart? She wanted to say he would. She wanted to believe, but she'd known Jack a long time and he always kept himself at a distance. Not getting too involved worked for him. There was no reason to think that was going to change, no matter how much she loved him.

Eddie Carberry, wearing one of her infamous brightly colored tracksuits, walked up to her. "So I heard about those chiweenies," the old lady said. "I might come by and take a look at them. I could use a little companionship and a small dog would be better for me. I could take him or her to work." She smiled slyly. "I already have a cat named Marilyn. After Marilyn Monroe. I could name my dog JFK."

Odd, but okay, Larissa thought. Whatever it took to find the chiweenies homes. "That would be great," she said. "Let me know when you want to come see them."

"I will." Eddie cackled. "Unless you're feeding them to that owl of yours."

Larissa took a step back. "I'd never do that. The owl is gone. Released back in the wild."

"Good to know. I wonder what you'll rescue next." Eddie patted her arm. "I'll call about the chiweenies."

Larissa nodded. As the older woman moved away, she told herself she should be happy about finding another dog a home. Only she couldn't seem to find the joy. While Eddie had been kidding, her comment had still hurt a little.

Larissa knew that she might take the rescue thing a little far, but she'd never considered herself a joke. Was that how the rest of the world saw her? And did the opinions of other people really matter?

Or maybe the real question was deeper and more significant. Maybe it went to what her friends had been talking about lately. That much like Jack used distance to keep from truly getting involved, she used her causes to hold the world at bay. Was that what was keeping her from her heart's desire? And if so, how on earth was she going to figure out how to change?

A problem for another time, she told herself, as she returned to Jack's side. He was talking to Dellina's sister Fayrene. She held out some kind of tickets.

"It's an auction," Fayrene was saying. "To raise money for the high-school track team."

"You run track in the spring," Jack said, eyeing the tickets mistrustfully.

"They're getting an early start. It's an evening event with a buffet and it's not until March."

Jack sighed heavily. "Sure. I'll take two."

Fayrene raised her eyebrows.

"Six," he amended.

Larissa leaned against him. "You're such a softy. Besides, the event might be fun. We can dress up."

Jack shot her a confused glanced. "Why would we—" He paused. "Sure. Dressy would be great."

She kept smiling and nodded, even grabbed a glass of champagne from a passing server. But on the inside, she felt cold and alone.

Jack's reaction couldn't have been more clear. While she was blithely planning their future together, he was assuming she was going to do as she'd promised. Get over him. That by March they would no longer be together. Because while Jack meant the world to her, to him, she was just a friend he was helping out.

He didn't love her. For him, nothing had changed. And it was never going to.

SAM AND DELLINA'S party stretched on for hours. Everyone was having a good time and no one seemed to want to be the first one to leave. Jack circulated through the main level of the bar. About an hour earlier, Larissa had dragged him upstairs to try the buffet. Now he watched her talk with Bailey and Dellina, along with several other women from town.

For a while he'd thought something was wrong. She'd gotten quiet. But she seemed fine now.

Conversation and laughter surrounded him. Everyone was having a good time and all he could think about was getting home. He wanted the quiet. He wanted to be alone with Larissa. Everything else was just noise.

"Hey."

He turned and saw Taryn walking toward him. She wobbled a little as she approached. Which could have been her ridiculous shoes, but he doubted it. He raised an eyebrow.

"Feeling our champagne, are we?" he asked.

She smiled. "Maybe. Why not? Sam finally found someone normal. Who would have thought that could happen? I'm thrilled for him." She leaned against him. "You know it's this damn town, right? It's sucking us all in against our will. I blame you."

He put his arm around her. "I'm sure you do. However, I'll remind you there was a legal vote."

She dismissed that with a flick of her wrist. "It was three against one. And none of you cared that I didn't want to move here."

"If we hadn't moved here, you wouldn't have met Angel."

"An interesting point. I do love that man. But you're trying to distract me. We're here because of you. You're the one who suggested moving to Sam and Kenny." She looked at him. "I think you knew you needed Fool's Gold."

As always Taryn found the exact core of truth. Not

that he would admit it to her. "Why would I need a place like this?"

"Because it allows you to belong, at least in theory." She sighed. "I love you, Jack, but you have got to stop protecting yourself. You obviously *want* to be a part of something bigger, something real, but you're fighting it at the same time. I just don't want you to die alone."

"Sam says I can live over his garage."

"So he told me. It's cute now, but will be less of a good story when you're sixty." She sipped her champagne. "I'm marrying Angel."

"I know. I saw the dress."

Her gaze locked with his. "I want you to be my maid of honor." Her brows drew together. "I guess you'd be the man of honor. Whatever. I want you to be the one next to me."

Which was just like her. "As long as I don't have to wear a dress."

"I was thinking a nice tux would work."

"Then I'm in."

She tilted her head. "You're sure. It won't bother you?"

He knew what she meant. They'd been married before. They had an unusual past that could have made things awkward, but didn't.

"If Angel's good with it, I'm all in."

She leaned her head against his shoulder. "You know I'll always love you."

"I do. The same way I'll always love you."

Like family. Not exactly exes and not exactly siblings. They were connected. And he would happily stand next to her while she married Angel. Whatever romantic feelings he'd once had for Taryn were long gone.

She hugged him, then wobbled off to find her fiancé. Jack watched her go, then shifted so he could search for Larissa.

AFTER WEEKS OF prep work, Larissa woke up three days before the Pro-am event to find she had nothing left to prepare. She'd confirmed Jack's team, had double-checked on the sponsors, had coordinated every detail with the people in charge and now there was nothing to do.

She showered and dressed, then fed Dyna and looked at her email. Not much was going on today at all. She had a woman coming by to look at a chiweenie. That appointment was at ten. Eddie had come through and taken one a few days ago. Now there were only two left at Jack's place.

Work was good, Percy was continuing to study for the GED and, according to Kenny and Sam, making great progress. Larissa decided to reward herself for a calm and organized life by going for a run.

She went down the stairs of her apartment building and decided to head for the park. She would take the trail there. It was a beautiful late-summer morning. There was the slightest hint of crispness to the air. Fall wasn't that far away.

Larissa started with a fast walk as her warm-up. She crossed the street and wondered what all the trees would look like as they changed colors. She imagined children playing in piles of leaves.

This would be her first year with the full change of seasons, she thought happily. In Los Angeles, the passing months were marked by different clothing in the stores, but the actual temperatures didn't vary that much. It was in the sixties in winter and near a hundred in the summer. But it wasn't as if they ever got super cold or had snow. Some years it barely rained.

She picked up her pace to a slow jog. She was looking forward to snow and all the fall and winter festivals. Christmas was going to be great, she thought happily. Beautiful and fun. She'd heard rumors of a giving tree, where you could pick a tag from a child and get them a gift. That would be fun.

She reached the park and started along the jogging path. Her pace increased, as did her breathing. Would she be spending Christmas with Jack this year? Of course, they were frequently together around the holidays, but things were different now. They were together. She spent a few nights a week at his place.

A week or so ago, she would have said yes, of course they would be together for the holidays, but now she wasn't so sure. While she was supposed to be getting over Jack, she was actually falling for him more each day. He, on the other hand, didn't seem to have the same problem. He'd been unable to plan for six or seven months in the future.

Obviously her "get over Jack" plan had flaws. Like the fact that spending time with him only made her want to be with him more. And the thought of being with anyone else was horrifying. Which didn't bode well for her future. She wanted...

She wanted what Dellina had, she admitted to herself. A happy relationship with a future. She wanted what Taryn had. A gleam in her eye when she talked about the man she loved. She wanted to be the most important person in someone's life. She wanted to matter.

She wanted to be more than her causes.

Larissa came to a stop in the middle of the path and blinked against unexpected tears. That was it, she realized. She wanted to be more than the woman who rescued owls and snakes and chiweenies. She wanted to be a part of something that lasted longer than a temporary rescue. She wanted a family of her own. She wanted love and happiness and forever.

Maybe it was her fault that her parents had had to get married and maybe it wasn't. The guilt had been with her so long, she couldn't imagine what it would feel like not to have it. But however she'd come to exist in the world, she deserved more than the half life she was living. Her happiness or lack thereof didn't change the past. It only affected her future.

"YOU SURE ABOUT THIS?" Percy asked, sounding doubtful.

Jack laughed. "Kid, it's no big deal. I mean come on. It's golf."

Percy didn't look convinced. Jack guessed that from his perspective, the scene was a little chaotic. The charity event had begun with a breakfast with the pros and the celebrities were introduced. Percy had gone a little wide-eyed when he'd realized that a couple of basketball greats were part of the lineup, along with baseball players, a few guys from the car-racing world and several actors.

Adding to the noise were the paparazzi and the spectators milling around.

"I don't know anything about golf," Percy admitted. "Larissa gave me a couple of articles to read last week. I got through them okay, and I understand the basics. But you have to pick clubs and stuff. I can't help with that."

Jack put his hand on the teen's shoulder. "You want to be my caddy?"

"Yes, but—"

"No buts. You'll have a great time." He paused. "Melissa will be impressed."

That had Percy grinning. "Anything I can do to impress her works for me."

"Yeah? Why did I think you were going to say that?"

They were by the clubhouse at the Fool's Gold golf course. The Pro-am was being played on a public course, which added to the logistics involved. Raoul Moreno was one of the key sponsors and a large portion of the proceeds would go to his organization, End Zone for Kids.

Jack thought it was interesting that he'd agreed to the event long before Percy had shown up. And that Percy had been brought to town by End Zone. Life was nothing if not coincidental.

He'd already met the other men in his foursome. There were two professional golfers, Jack and an action movie star named Jonny Blaze.

Jack watched as Jonny stood in a crowd of women. He signed autographs on paper, pictures of himself and—Jack cringed—one young woman's cleavage.

Kenny walked up and saw the crowd.

"Don't judge," his friend told him. "He's still in his twenties. It'll get better as he gets older."

"Not everyone matures," Jack said.

"True enough. Sam and I are wagering on the game. We wondered if you wanted in on the bet."

"Sure. A hundred bucks a stroke?"

"Done." Kenny offered a fist for Jack to bump.

Jack knew that regardless of who won, the money would go to charity. Still, he wanted to be the one to walk away with the bragging rights.

Larissa hurried toward them. She had a large tote over one shoulder. She pointed at Kenny. "I've already seen you," she said.

"You have and it was memorable."

Larissa laughed, then turned to Jack and Percy. She set her tote on the grass and started pulling out the contents.

"Event hats," she said, handing them each one. "Very stylish."

"Nice," Percy said, trying his on, then adjusting the sizing band for the baseball cap.

She straightened again and held out a tube of sunscreen. "Both of you," she said firmly. "It's a warm sunny day."

Percy frowned. "You do know I'm black, right?"

"You can still get burned and sun damage. Don't you want to still look hot when you're forty?"

He grinned. "I'll always look hot."

"There's the attitude. Now put on the sunscreen, young man."

Jack was already applying his. He knew better than to argue.

"Stay hydrated," Larissa added. "When the drink cart comes around, take water." She pointed at Percy. "You can have soda when you've had two waters. Promise?"

The teen signed heavily. "Yes, ma'am."

"Good." She looked at Jack. "You, on the other hand, know the importance of hydration. Have you met the other guys in your foursome?"

"We have," Percy told her. "We have Jonny Blaze."

Larissa wrinkled her nose. "He was signing breasts earlier. Women were actually pulling down their shirts and having him sign their cleavage. Don't you think that's a little skanky?"

"I don't know," Kenny began, then stopped talking when Larissa glared at him. The former receiver cleared his throat. "Yes, it's very skanky. They should be ashamed."

Jack nodded. "Appalling."

"I don't care that you're humoring me," Larissa told them both. "I appreciate it."

She stood on her tiptoes and kissed Jack, then hugged Percy and Kenny.

"All right. Everyone do good. I'll be cheering from the sidelines."

With that, she waved and hurried off. No doubt to hunt down Sam, Jack thought, watching her go.

Her ponytail bounced with each step. She moved with purpose and grace. She was quite a woman, he thought happily. And later that night, he would have her naked in his bed. Life, he decided, was very, very good.

LIFE WENT TO HELL later that afternoon, Jack thought as he faced President Newham at the end of his first round. His team had done pretty well, considering Jonny Blaze was more interested in posing for pictures than playing golf. But when the action star focused, he had a decent swing and could get the ball on the green. But the women constantly lifting up their shirts and flashing their boobs was making it difficult for them all to keep their heads in the game.

With the eighteen holes finished, all he wanted was to have a beer, grab Larissa, eat dinner, then go to bed. He would take things in the opposite order, except he had Percy along with him.

But all that was put on hold when the university president asked if she could have a word.

"Now?" he asked.

"Yes." She sounded very certain. "This will only take a minute."

Percy didn't know who President Newham was, but obviously recognized her innate authority. The teen took possession of Jack's clubs and announced, "I'll wait for you here."

Jack's sense of foreboding only got worse when he followed President Newham into a small meeting room in the clubhouse and found Mayor Marsha waiting for them. No good ever came from an unscheduled meeting with her.

"You played well today, Jack," the mayor said by way of greeting.

He nodded cautiously. The small windowless conference room only had one exit. And right now, it looked very far away.

He tried to distract himself from his sense of dread by paying attention to details. The mayor, for example, wore a suit, like she always did. With pearls. They were at a golf course. Couldn't she lighten up? Put on some jeans and maybe a T-shirt?

Trying to generate the image required more imagination than he had, but the effort was enough to allow him to relax a little.

"Jonny Blaze seems nice enough," the mayor added. "Although he needs a little maturing."

Jack held up both hands. "If you're asking me to take him—"

"Not why we're here," President Newham said. "Jack, we wanted you to be the first to know that we're moving ahead with reactivating the football program at Cal U Fool's Gold. The regents have approved preliminary funding."

He stared at her. "That's great. I'm surprised they came through. It's going to take a lot of work, but in the end, you'll add to the prestige of the school and the bottom line." He started to add it would be a win-win, but something about the way both women were looking at him made his mouth go dry.

"What?" he asked, his voice a little higher than he would like.

"There's a condition," Mayor Marsha said. "For the funding." She and the university president exchanged a look.

"They're very specific about who they want running the program," President Newham added. "And that person, Jack, is you."

THE NEXT MORNING, Jack was still randomly telling people no. He'd said it to the mayor, the university president and neither of them had listened. Percy had thought the news was cool and Larissa had stared at him as if he'd just solved every animal welfare problem on the planet. Even Taryn had nodded sagely and said she could see him taking on something like that.

What no one seemed to remember was that he didn't get involved. Ever. He wasn't that guy. He was the one who wrote the check. Other people did the work. Other people got involved. Other people cared. He was heartless Jack and he liked it that way.

He joined the other players on the course. Jonny Blaze looked as if he'd been at it all night. Jack knew he'd slept just as little, but for far less fun reasons. He'd tried, but he'd been unable to relax. Him start a football team? He wasn't a coach. He didn't know the first thing about coaching. He wasn't the guy the university should depend on to get the program up and running.

He had to explain that. Yesterday he'd said no. They'd pressed him. Unfortunately he'd been too shocked to do more than promise to think about it. But now...

The guys and their caddies headed toward the tee. The two pros went first. Jack carried his iron in his hands. Jonny Blaze stepped close to him.

"You're doing good," the action star said. "Only five strokes behind the pros. My last two holes yesterday really blew." He yawned. "I'm feeling more on my game today."

Jack wondered how that was possible. "Good luck with that."

"Thanks." Jonny nodded toward Percy. "You must have been about twelve when you had him. You have the same eyes. His mother must have been hot as hell."

It took a second for the meaning of the words to sink in.

Jonny thought Percy was his? Jack felt the noose of responsibility tightening around his throat. He didn't need one more thing right now. He was already getting in too deep with Larissa and now the college coming after him to be the coach?

"He's not mine," he said quickly. "He's a responsibility that won't go away."

As soon as the words were out, Jack regretted them. None of this was Percy's fault. Besides, he liked the teen a lot. Sometimes helping Percy was the best part of his day.

But before he could say any of that, he heard a crash. He turned and saw the teen had dropped his bag of clubs onto the grass and was running in the opposite direction.

CHAPTER SEVENTEEN

LARISSA STOOD ON the porch of the large house and waited for someone to answer the door. Taryn had found the address for her, although it had taken nearly a day and a half. Apparently halfway house locations weren't heavily advertised.

The front door opened and a woman in her mid-thirties stepped out. She was pretty, dressed in jeans and a T-shirt. "Yes? Can I help you?"

"I'm looking for Percy," Larissa said. "I heard he was here."

The woman hesitated for a second, then nodded. "Sure. What's your name?"

"Larissa."

"I'll tell him you're here."

With that she stepped back into the house and closed the door. Larissa didn't check, but she was pretty sure the door had locked automatically. She had a feeling that was a lot more about keeping people out than keeping the residents in.

She paced the width of the porch while she waited. The last day had been awful. Percy had disappeared during the tournament and she couldn't figure out why. Jack had said it was his fault, but he wouldn't tell her what had happened. No one had seen or heard anything. She thought Percy was happy in his new life. She thought he was excited about his future. So what had gone wrong?

The door opened and Percy stepped out onto the porch. Until that second, she hadn't realized that she'd half expected him to refuse to see her.

She rushed toward him and wrapped her arms around him. He was still for a second, before hugging her back.

"I've missed you," she told him, moving back so she could see his face. "Are you okay?"

One corner of his mouth turned up. "Larissa, it's been a *day*. I'm fine."

"You're not fine. Fine people don't leave. You just left."

His gaze shifted from her to something over her shoulder. "I had to go. I can't mooch off you forever."

"Who said anything about mooching? You're a part of the Score family." She stared into his dark eyes. "Why did you leave? What happened?"

Percy raised one shoulder and looked past her again. "Nothing. It was time. Look, I have to live my own life. It's time for me to be a man."

"You're already a man. Percy, come on. What about finishing your GED and going to college?"

"I'm still going to do that. I'm going to be a teacher and help kids like me." His gaze returned to hers. "This is better. Jack doesn't need me crowding him. I'm looking for a job. I'll be fine. The people here are decent. Don't worry about me."

There was so much information in that short speech, she thought. She didn't know where to start.

"Why would you think you crowd Jack? He likes you. He likes having you around. You're like family."

Percy's expression tightened. "I'm not family, Larissa. I'm a project. You think I don't know that?"

"No," she said stubbornly. "It's not like that. It's never been like that."

He looked at her then and for a moment, he seemed much older than his years. "Don't worry about me. I'm not going to change my mind about college or being a teacher. I'm going to get it done. I've talked to the people here and they're going to help me get a job."

"You already have a job at Score."

His mouth twisted. "I have a made-up position. I want a job I got because of who I am, not who I know."

"It's not like that," she said again. "Percy, this is all wrong. Come home. If you don't want to stay with Jack, stay with me."

The smile returned. "I've seen your apartment. You don't have room for Dyna, let alone me. It's better this way."

"It's not." She felt her eyes fill with tears. "What happened? Just tell me that. Something happened to make everything different."

He wrapped his arms around her and kissed the top of her head. The action was so much like what Jack would have done.

"I was trying to rescue you," she admitted. "And now you've gone and grown up."

He chuckled. "I had to eventually."

"We could have put it off a while longer."

He released her. "I'm okay, Larissa. Thank you for all your help. You really did save me. I'm staying in town, so we'll still see each other. But I gotta make my own way. I hope you understand that."

She nodded, even though she didn't. She didn't understand at all.

TARYN WALKED INTO Jack's office without knocking. Unfortunately he wasn't on the phone, so he couldn't pretend to be busy. Because when Taryn had fire in her eyes, it was always best to be somewhere she was not.

Still, he wasn't going to let her know she had him worried, so he gave her a smile and then leaned back in his chair.

"What's up?" he asked, even though he already had a good idea of the problem.

She put her hands on her hips and glared at him. "What the hell is wrong with you? You hurt that kid and that means you hurt Larissa, too."

The smile faded and he brought himself into an upright position. An unfamiliar crawling sensation coiled in his belly and it took him a second to realize it was shame. Not that he would admit to it.

"We all took Percy in," she continued. "We were there for him. You've got Sam and Kenny tutoring him so he can get his GED. We all care and now he's gone. Worse, he won't say what happened."

"Then how do you know it was me?"

She rolled her eyes. "Seriously? That's your defense? Dammit, Jack, you can't act like this."

"Why not?" He rose and glared at her, fighting an anger that surprised him with its intensity. "You care. Kenny cares. Sam cares. Great. I don't. Percy was one more problem Larissa dumped at my feet. I did what I could and now he's gone."

"I don't accept that," she snapped. "You can tell the rest of the world you don't give a shit, but I know differently."

"You don't know as much as you think you know. Too many people want too much. You're all dragging me down. Percy was dead weight."

He had no idea where the words were coming from, but he couldn't stop them. He narrowed his gaze.

"You may not like the truth," he continued, "but that doesn't change it. I'm the guy who writes a check."

"There's more to you than that," she said firmly.

"You think? I can prove it. I don't care that Percy's gone. As for you, I'm not interested in being in your wedding. You have enough people helping you play princess."

Taryn's face went white. She sucked in a breath, but didn't speak. Just as well, because he was already walking out the door.

LARISSA PAUSED IN the center of town. The decorations were up for the Fall Festival the following weekend. Normally she loved seeing the process of "dressing" the storefronts and streetlights. But today seeing it all didn't seem to be helping. Everything was wrong and she didn't know how to make it right. In a matter of a couple of days, her whole world was upside down.

Percy was still gone. He'd gotten a job working for Josh Golden at the cycling school. He was learning how to repair the bikes and keep them ready for the rental side of the business. He said the halfway house was a good place to be and Kenny and Sam swore he was still coming in for his tutoring sessions.

But it wasn't the same, she thought sadly. Percy wasn't a part of her day-to-day life. She didn't see him as much. Which, she realized, made it all about her. What was far more important was what had happened between Percy and Jack. Because that had been the beginning of the trouble.

She hadn't seen Jack since Tuesday. He hadn't been in the office and Taryn wasn't talking and from what she could tell, Kenny and Sam were genuinely clueless.

The two remaining chiweenies with Jack were still being walked by volunteers and none of them claimed to have seen him. What really had her worried was he wasn't taking her calls. Jack always took her calls. Two years ago, he'd answered her call while having sex with one of his bimbos. But now he wouldn't talk to her? What was going on?

Her cell phone rang. She grabbed it and pushed the button.

"Hello? Jack?"

"Uh, no. This is Martin Guley. I got your name from a mutual friend. I work for an animal shelter in Sacramento and we have an unusual situation. A family took in a mountain lion as a cub. Now she's grown to the point where they can't keep her and I was told you might be able to help. We only need a home for her until we can figure out what to do. So a few weeks at best. She's friendly, but she can be a little rough on the furniture."

Larissa's first instinct was to say of course she could help with the mountain lion. Jack's place was plenty big. Only she'd been forced to admit that maybe she was guilty of hiding behind her causes. She couldn't rescue the world. Her time would be far better spent trying to make her little piece of it better.

"Martin, I'm afraid I can't take in a mountain lion right now. However, I do have the names of several large-cat rescue facilities. They'll have the space and the resources to help. I'm on my way home right now. I'll email you the contact info within the hour."

"Thanks so much," Martin said gratefully. "I'm new to the shelter and I didn't know what to do."

"Not a problem."

She hung up and started walking toward her apartment. She would get Martin the information he needed, then get a couple of cat cuddles from Dyna to heal her restless heart. But after that, she didn't have a plan...except maybe to confront Jack and get to the bottom of what on earth was going on.

LARISSA LET HERSELF into Jack's house around four that afternoon. "It's me," she called as she closed the front door behind her.

The last two chiweenies came running to greet her. She petted them both, then walked into the large living room.

"Jack?"

"I'm here."

He was sitting on the sofa. His hair was a mess and he hadn't shaved in a couple of days, which made her wonder if he'd showered. He wore a worn T-shirt over jeans. His feet were bare. One of his dress shirts lay in tatters on the carpet by the coffee table. It had obviously been sacrificed to the chiweenies. More troubling was the bottle of Scotch in front of him and the half-empty glass next to it.

She bit her lower lip. Jack wasn't one to drink alone and certainly not in the middle of the day. Something was very, very wrong.

She crossed to the sofa and sat angled toward him. He didn't bother looking at her. Instead, he stared straight ahead, but with purpose. As if there was something going on that only he could see.

"Jack," she said softly. "What's going on? You're scaring me. You just disappeared the other day. You're not taking my calls. Taryn's upset so I know something happened with her. Plus, Percy's gone."

He picked up the glass and swallowed the contents. "Damn fool kid."

He turned to look at her. His eyes were bloodshot and he looked as if he hadn't slept in days. She wanted to pull him close and let her love heal him. Instead, she stayed where she was and let him tell her whatever it was he had to say.

"Where is he?" Jack asked.

"A halfway house. He got a job with Josh Golden, at the cycling school, and he's still studying with Kenny and Sam."

"They're good men. They won't screw up."

"You didn't screw up."

One eyebrow rose. "You can't defend me because you don't know what happened." He poured another drink. "Because it's all my fault, Larissa. I destroyed it all." He picked up the glass. "You know what? I turned down the job."

Was he drunk? He sure wasn't making any sense. "What job?"

"For the football program. Like I know anything about how to do it."

She clasped her hands together. "Jack, you would have been so good with the players."

"Would I?" His dark gaze settled on her face. "Yeah, I don't think so. Because I'm the reason Percy left. At the tournament Jonny Blaze asked if he was my kid. He said we had the same eyes."

"You're pretty young to be his father," she said.

"That's not the point." Jack's voice was angry. "I

don't want that kid. Any kid. I would be a lousy father."

"No, you wouldn't. You would do a great job."

"You're blind. I told him that Percy wasn't mine. That he was a problem that wouldn't go away."

Larissa felt her eyes widen. "Jack," she began.

He cut her off with a shake of his head. "I didn't mean it, or maybe I did. Hell if I know anything anymore. Percy heard. That's why he left. Nobody wants to be charity, Larissa. People don't want to be saved, they want to believe they can save themselves."

She considered what he'd just said. "Have you talked to him? If you explain it was an accident and you're sorry, then he'll come back."

"He's not coming back," Jack told her. "And I don't want him to. He needed too much. I'm not getting involved. I write the checks, you do the rest of it."

"Jack, no."

"Face it. I'm the sales guy. I'm into flash. I tell the customers what they want and Taryn takes care of the rest. It's better that way. That's what I told President Newham and the mayor. Thanks but no thanks. I'm not your guy."

This was a side of Jack she hadn't seen before. Coldly cynical and almost mean.

"No," she said firmly. "You're wrong. You're more than a sales guy. You love what you do. As for coaching, you should really think about it. It would fill your soul."

He laughed and took a drink. "My soul is plenty full."

"You have to give back," she persisted. "It's the law of the jungle. You have more so you have to give more."

He gave her a withering look. "That's not the law of the jungle. I believe what you're searching for is kill or be killed. I'm taking the easy way out, Larissa. I always have. Why can't you see that?"

What she saw was how much he hated himself right now. He felt pressured by the job offer and he'd reacted badly. She knew all the reasons why. She understood him, she always had. He—

She looked at him and got it. He was pushing them all away because it made it easier for him to deal with what was happening. After years of not getting involved, he was being sucked in. By her, by the town, by Percy and the university. The need to connect overwhelmed him. The lashing out was simply a symptom.

She slid toward him and put her hand on his arm. "Jack, it's okay. We'll get through this together."

"I doubt that."

"You don't understand. You can't scare me away. I love you." She paused as the truth sank in. "I'm not trying to get over you. I don't think I ever was. I'm in love with you and I'm going to love you for the rest of my life."

JACK HAD ENJOYED his English classes in college. Writing papers had come easy to him, mostly because he knew how to spread about the bullshit with the best of them. He could read a book and then answer essay questions with ease.

He remembered some book about a guy who had no purpose and how that was its own brand of hell. He hadn't understood it at the time, but he got it now. Because he was that guy. At one time he'd had a goal— to win. And before that, well, no reason to go there. Now, however, there was nothing. He'd already destroyed his relationship with Percy and Taryn, why not go for gold?

He stood up, careful to carry his glass with him. He turned to face Larissa, taking in her blue eyes, the fullness of her mouth. He knew everything about her, so he knew exactly where to slide the knife.

"Don't love me," he told her. "I'm not interested in your love. Or you. I can't save you and if I could, I wouldn't."

She stared at him without flinching. "I don't need saving."

"Sure you do. Without me, you have no causes. And without your causes, you're nothing."

Her shoulders squared and her chin came up. "You're wrong. I have value. We all do. You're a whole lot more than just the guy who writes the checks."

"But I don't want to be. I'm not interested in the work involved."

He'd already offered all he had to save his brother and he'd been turned down. He knew what it was like to beg to save the person he loved most in the world. And he knew what it was like to watch him die.

But he'd gotten through Lucas's funeral and the days that followed. He'd hung on. Until his parents had come to him and explained they were leaving the country. They were going to some village in Africa to help poor children. Jack wasn't sure what they would do there—he'd stopped listening. Because the real message had mattered more. They were leaving because there was nothing left for them here. Having a son who was living, having him around, wasn't important enough.

That was the moment that had truly changed him. He'd said all the right things—that he was heading off to college and of course, he would be fine on his own. He had his friends and football. He didn't need his parents. At that moment, watching them leave, he'd vowed never to give his heart again. He'd vowed never to get involved again, and he'd kept that promise. For a while he'd gotten soft. He'd allowed himself to care about Taryn, about Larissa. But all that was over now. Taryn was gone and he was about to get rid of Larissa.

"Jack, you have to believe in yourself."

"I do," he told her, then took a drink. "It's you I don't believe in. You're fired."

She stared at him. "What?"

"You're fired. I'm your boss at Score and I'm firing you. Go get your things out of the building, turn in your key and never come back. I want nothing to do with you."

For a second she didn't move. In that heartbeat, he found himself hoping she would call him on his asshole behavior. That she would force him to see that he was making a mistake and doing things he would regret. He wanted her to be the one to show him the error of his ways. Because somewhere inside there was still enough humanity to know that one day soon he was going to have regrets.

But he'd placed the knife too perfectly and she didn't have the strength. He saw the way her hands trembled. He saw the tears fill her eyes. She swallowed, then nodded and stood.

As she walked past him, she paused.

He'd always had the gift of timing in the game and apparently it followed him into life. Now he was able to sigh with the right combination of long suffering and boredom before shaking his head.

"Don't bother telling me you love me," he said. "I can't stand to hear it again."

A single tear slipped down her cheek. Jack watched it and felt that knife he'd placed so deliberately turn and cut through him. It made its way to the aching part of his own heart—the part that had never healed—and found a home there. The pain made it impossible to move, impossible to breathe. He could only stand there bleeding from the inside out and watch the very essence of who he had always wanted to be walk out without once looking back.

CHAPTER EIGHTEEN

LARISSA LAY STRETCHED on her sofa with Dyna sprawled across her. The fluffy cat purred loudly and stared into Larissa's eyes, as if offering all the feline support she had.

"Thank you," Larissa murmured, her voice muffled because her throat hurt. It was all the crying, she thought with a sniff. The horror of what had happened with Jack yesterday hadn't gotten any better with the passage of a night and most of a morning. Her heart was still as shattered, her spirit crushed. Right now all that kept her going was the purring devotion of her cat.

"I'm glad we've bonded," she told Dyna, tears slipping from the outer corners of her eyes and down her temples to get lost in her hair. "It really helps to know you're here for me."

Dyna's gaze never wavered.

"It's just I don't understand," she continued. "Jack is a lot of things. He can be stubborn and when he's tired he can be a little snappish. He resists getting involved. But he's also giving and fair. He's been there for everyone he cares about. He's never once been mean."

But he'd been plenty mean yesterday. He'd broken her heart and left her feeling small. As if the gift of her love was both annoying and a burden.

She'd spent a long night trying to figure out what had gone wrong. Because something had. Something big. Something that had made him lash out.

She cradled Dyna and sat up, then wiped her face. She really had to get moving on her day. For one thing, she had to clear out her stuff from Score. Although just thinking about that was enough to get her crying again.

She set her cat on the warm sofa cushion and walked into her tiny kitchen. Once there she boiled water for tea and then sniffed through waiting for the bag to steep. Once the tea was ready, she carried it back to the living room and set it on the coffee table.

She stared at the pad of paper she'd dug out sometime in the long night. She needed to start making lists. If she didn't work at Score, what was she going to do with her life? Should she stay in Fool's Gold or move back to L.A.? The former meant seeing Jack, which added a whole new level of salt in the wound, while leaving was a lot like giving up. More important, she really *liked* living in Fool's Gold. She liked her friends and the community. She wanted to see it at Christmas and in the spring.

Just as pressing was how she was going to make her living. She'd never been much of a saver. All her extra money had gone to various causes. She looked around the apartment and consoled herself with the fact that the rent was cheap. So she could stay and get a job.

She heard footsteps on the stairs outside her door, followed by a knock. Her heart knew better than to hope, so she figured her visitor had to be one of her friends.

She opened the front door and found both Taryn and Bailey waiting for her. An unusual pairing, she thought, fighting more tears. At some point, wasn't she going to run out of fluids?

Taryn didn't say anything. Instead, she reached for Larissa and held her close.

"That man is a total jackass. I don't know what's going on, but it's something. And I'm willing to bet it's all about him and not us. Even so, I'm sorry he hurt you."

Larissa accepted the comforting and told herself that having good friends was going to get her through this. Bailey hugged her, as well, then they all went into the apartment.

"How did you find out?" Larissa asked when she'd gotten her guests tea and they'd settled on the sofa and single chair. Dyna remained loyal and curled up on Larissa's lap.

Taryn groaned. "He called me this morning. He said he wouldn't be in and you wouldn't, either. I figured that was good news until he said he'd fired you." She reached across the couch and took Larissa's hand. "So what happened?"

"I don't know," Larissa admitted. "He was upset and we were talking. I wanted to know what had gone on between him and Percy." She thought about what Jack had told her and still had trouble believing it.

"Jonny Blaze asked if he was Percy's father. Jack took the question badly. He said he would be a lousy father, which I don't think is true. He holds himself back a lot emotionally but I know he cares. If he had a child—"

Taryn squeezed her fingers. "Honey, stay on topic please."

"What? Oh. Sorry. He said that Percy was a problem that wouldn't go away."

Bailey winced. "And Percy heard? No wonder he left. I feel so awful for him. That would have been devastating."

"Jack's on a roll," Taryn muttered. "He blew me off and he was a real jerk about it."

"He's overwhelmed by everything that's happening," Larissa said quickly. "He was offered the job of rebuilding the university's football team. I think he wants to take it but he won't let himself. Because he can't do it without connecting with the players. And he doesn't want to risk himself by caring. You know, because of everything that happened to him with his brother."

Taryn swore. "You are way too nice. Stop defending him. Jack ripped out your heart and did a touchdown dance on the pieces."

Larissa swallowed against the lump in her throat. "I know what he did."

Taryn groaned, then leaned toward her. "I'm sorry.

I didn't mean to be insensitive. It's just you're still taking his side in all this."

"I can't help it. I understand what he went through as a kid—always having to be the good one, the quiet one, because Lucas was sick. Then his brother got the transplant and for a little while Jack believed he was going to have a normal life."

Taryn sighed. "You're making me crazy. You know that, right?"

"I do."

Taryn looked at Bailey. "Jack's brother had a heart condition that required a transplant. Only it didn't go well and he died. Then Jack's parents took off, leaving him on his own." She turned back to Larissa. "Okay, he had it rough. That doesn't excuse what he's doing now."

"No, it doesn't, but it explains it." She thought about what it was like to be with Jack and knew that bad with him was better than great with anyone else. "I love him. I don't want to get over him and find someone else. I want him to love me back. I want us to be together always." The tears returned and filled her eyes. "He doesn't want me. What if I love him forever?"

Bailey moved to the sofa and wrapped her arms around Larissa. "Just keep breathing. I know it doesn't feel like it now, but you'll heal in time. Clichés work for a reason."

Larissa wanted to scream at them both, saying she would never be able to get over Jack. Only she didn't. Not only because she loved her friends, but because Bailey had lost a husband. If anyone knew about overcoming pain, she did.

So she swallowed the words and let herself breathe in their concern. Right now friends were a good thing to have around.

She wiped her cheeks and drew in a breath. "I'm okay," she whispered. "Or I will be. One day at a time, right? While we're riding the cliché wagon?"

Bailey smiled. "Exactly. Keep moving forward."

Except forward how? Larissa turned to Taryn. "I'm really fired, aren't I?"

Taryn shrugged her shoulders. "You can't work for Jack anymore, so you're not his assistant. But the guys and I want you to stay on."

"No," Larissa said, accepting the truth for the first time since Jack had said those painful words. "I can't. I need to figure out what I want to do with my life."

"As long as it's here," Bailey said, returning to the chair. "You're staying in Fool's Gold, aren't you?"

"You have to," Taryn told her. "Please don't go." She pressed her lips together. "I'm sorry. I'm being selfish. I don't want you to go, but if it's what you think is best, then I'll help you find a place in L.A. and pack up your stuff."

Larissa managed a wobbly smile. "You're a good person."

"Yeah? Don't tell anyone."

What to do? Stay or go? Even as she asked the question, she already knew the answer.

"I want to stay," she said firmly. "I like the town and I want to be near you guys."

"Good." Bailey pulled a piece of paper from her bag. "There's a room for rent at the local day spa." She handed over the flyer. "I've seen the space and I like it, but you're the actual professional. Just call and say who you are. You can see it anytime."

"I don't have my license," Larissa said. "I have the forms and I'm certainly qualified with the hours of education and practice, but I'll have to take care of that before I can get any customers."

Bailey's green eyes brightened. "Yes, well, it turns out there are advantages to working with California's longest serving mayor. She knows everyone. In fact, she's already spoken to the licensing board and your paperwork will be expedited. You can be in business within a couple of weeks."

Larissa found herself fighting more tears, but for a very different reason.

"I've spoken to Kenny and Sam," Taryn said. "We had a feeling you wouldn't stay with us after what happened." She pulled an envelope out of her designer tote and handed it over.

"Six months' pay as severance. We'll keep you on the company insurance until your business is up and running." Taryn gave her a smile. "As you know, I've taken on a couple of silent partnerships. I want to do the same with you. I'll front you the money you need to get your business started and you can buy me out over time."

Larissa hugged her. "Thank you," she said. "For everything." She knew that Taryn had helped Isabel buy Paper Moon and expand the business. There were probably other dealings Taryn kept to herself.

She released Taryn and smiled at her. "And while I appreciate the offer to be my silent partner, I want you as my friend. Money has a way of changing that." She waved the envelope. "This will go a long way to getting me going. The table will be the biggest expense. If I need more than this, I'll talk to my mom. She'll be so happy I'm not working for Jack anymore that she'll be thrilled to help me."

Just saying his name was enough to make her feel broken again. She fought against the emotions and struggled to find another smile.

"It's so annoying that she was right about my feelings for him."

Taryn touched her hand. "I know it is."

Bailey looked at her. "Let us know if you want to do a painting party or anything like that. I'm so there."

"Thank you." Larissa sipped her tea, then looked at Taryn. "Have you seen him?"

Something flashed in Taryn's eyes. Hurt maybe. Or betrayal. "No, and right now I don't want to."

Larissa nodded, because it was expected. Unfortunately what she was thinking on the inside was that she would do anything to see Jack again. Would give anything to be in his arms. Which only told her how far she had to go.

As soon as Taryn and Bailey left, Larissa went to work on the paperwork required for her massage therapist certification. She had most of it filled out, along with transcripts from her massage therapy school and proof of the continuing education classes she'd taken. She included a copy of her driver's license and the required passport-size photos, then put everything into a large envelope. After calling and talking to the owner of the day spa and setting up an appointment to see the room for rent, Larissa walked over to the express mail center and sent it overnight, addressed to the name on the business card Bailey had given her. Then she walked home.

When she got there, she found Kenny and Sam waiting for her. At the sight of them, she started crying again, which was totally ridiculous. They both pulled her close, then Kenny handed her a grocery bag filled with every flavor of Ben & Jerry's.

"Because, you know, girls eat ice cream," he told her sheepishly.

"You're a very nice man," she said as she let them both into her apartment.

She put away the ice cream, got them each a beer from her Jack stash, then settled across from them. Dyna looked up from her perch in the south-facing window as if to ask why there were so many humans around today.

"Have you seen Percy?" Larissa asked.

"Today," Kenny told her. "You know he's working for Josh Golden."

She nodded. "He mentioned that."

"I tried to get him to come back to Score," Sam

said. "He wouldn't. But he's showing up for his tutoring sessions."

"I've taken over Jack's part of his studies," Kenny added. "We're not going to let him disappear on us. He'll get his GED and then he'll start at Fool's Gold community college."

"We're all chipping in." Sam raised his beer. "Even Taryn."

The two men looked at each other, as if searching for something else to say. Larissa finally understood why they were so concerned about keeping the conversation going.

"I'm okay," she told them. "Still crying, but surviving."

Sam looked relieved. "Taryn called and said you were staying in town."

"I'm going to open a massage practice in a day spa."

"Count me in," Kenny said quickly. "Three times a week."

"Me, too," Sam added.

"It'll take me a couple of weeks to get my license. Until then, if you want to set up a table in one of your places, I can take care of you there."

Kenny sighed. "You're really not coming back to Score, are you?"

"Jack fired me."

"So be my assistant."

She managed a smile. "You don't have any work for me. Besides, I don't want to see Jack every day. It would be too hard."

"You really do love him?" Sam asked.

She nodded. "I really do. And he's not interested."

She managed to get out the words without crying, although her voice shook a little as she spoke. It was going to be hard for a while, she reminded herself. But then it would get easier.

"I brought my checkbook," Kenny said. "How much do you need to start your business? Whatever I have, it's yours."

"You're killing me," she said lightly. "It's a great offer, but I'm fine. Taryn gave me a severance check that should cover most of what I need."

"Let me buy the massage table," Kenny said. "That'll be the biggest expense."

"We'll share the cost," Sam added. "I want in, too. We'll get the super-charged one."

"I want to do this on my own."

"And we want to help someone we care about," Kenny told her. "Hey, we learned from the best. When it comes to what we care about, we have to be all in. We're all in with you, Larissa."

She nodded because she couldn't speak. They were so sweet. She sighed, wishing she could have fallen for one of them instead of Jack. That would have made things a whole lot easier. "I'll send you a link," she said. "It'll be after I make arrangements to rent the room."

"What else?" Sam asked. "We're going to hunt down Jack next and beat the shit out of him. Want to watch?"

"No. But could you get the last two chiweenies? I

have homes for them. I was going to go by later and get them, but it would be easier if I didn't have to."

"Sure thing, kid."

Sam rose and pulled Larissa to her feet, then dragged her against him. He was tall and strong and warm as he held her. She closed her eyes and let the comfort wash over her. Maybe it wasn't romantic love, but she had love all the same. From so many sources. And maybe, just maybe, that would eventually be enough.

JACK SAT ALONE in his living room. He'd thought that he would have a steady stream of people stopping by to tell him off, but so far there hadn't even been one. He'd taken the last two damned chiweenies for a walk earlier that morning, hoping someone somewhere would yell at him, but they hadn't. He'd marched through the center of town with dogs happily trotting along with him and hadn't heard a word.

What was wrong with this place? Why weren't they outside his house with torches and pitchforks?

His front door opened. He sat up straighter wondering if Larissa had...

Sam and Kenny walked into the living room. Jack told himself it was for the better. He couldn't be around Larissa anymore. Not only had he hurt her—and that was in itself inexcusable—but he didn't deserve her. She was light and good and he was nothing but a useless shell. She gave and he took up space.

He stood and waited for his friends to approach. They both looked determined. With luck, they would beat him into unconsciousness. Right now not being able to think was worth any price.

"You look like shit," Kenny said conversationally.

"I haven't been sleeping."

"Good," Sam told him. "Dammit, Jack, what the hell? Is there anyone you haven't tried to hurt in the past couple of days? Percy is just a kid and Taryn is your best friend. I won't even mention Larissa whose biggest crime is caring about your sorry ass. You're a piss-poor excuse for a man."

The words fell like rain on parched soil. They were a balm. At last, he thought with relief. Someone was going to call him on all his crap. Someone was going to tell him to his face what a useless piece of shit he was. Someone was going to speak the truth.

No one had in such a long time. Not since his brother had died.

"Sam's right," Kenny said. "Hasn't Percy been through enough already? He's homeless, Jack. He's got nothing and you're making him feel worse. Taryn's looking at the happiest day of her life and you're trying to ruin it." The larger man approached, stopping only when he was directly in front of Jack. "You made Larissa cry. She loves you. She cares about you and you hurt her."

He never saw the fist coming. Kenny had speed and power on his side. One second there was nothing and the next a world of pain exploded in Jack's face. He heard the crunch of cartilage, but not the snap of bone. He staggered, and then went down on one knee. Probably because he hadn't eaten or slept in several days, he thought woozily. He struggled to stand, then faced his friend.

"Thanks," he said hoarsely. "Hit me again."

Kenny shook his head. "You're not trying to defend yourself. I'm not going to hit you when you're down."

"I'm not down. I'm standing."

"You're messed up. You need help."

Sam walked toward the kitchen. "You're really stupid, Jack. You know that, right?"

Jack nodded. "You're not going to hit me again?"

"No," Kenny said. "You're not worth it."

The final blow. He hadn't seen that one coming. Jack sank back onto the sofa and put his head in his hands. A big mistake when he pressed against where Kenny had hit him. His jaw was already swelling and it hurt like hell.

Good, he told himself. He would focus on the pain.

Sam returned with an ice pack, three glasses and an unopened bottle of Scotch. One of the last ones, Jack thought eyeing the bottle. He'd told himself he needed to stop drinking, but then figured it didn't matter. It wasn't as if he was driving anywhere. Staying drunk for the rest of his life might solve all his problems.

Sam poured the amber liquid into three glasses, then handed them out. He passed the ice pack to Jack.

Jack took a couple of sips. He eased the ice pack into place and hissed when it touched his bruised skin.

"You see Taryn?" he asked.

There was a moment of silence. He would guess
Sam and Kenny were exchanging glances, each urg-
ing the other to speak. Not that Jack was looking—
he had his eyes closed.

"She's pissed and hurt," Kenny said at last. "She
won't say why. We're assuming you were a dick."

"I was." The things he'd said to her. He'd been so
cruel. And for what? He loved Taryn. They'd been
there for each other for over a decade. He'd married
her and they'd nearly had a child together.

He drew in a breath. That was the worst of it. He
didn't know why he'd lashed out. But he had. He'd
hurt her and Percy and...

He couldn't even think her name, let alone say it.
Even though the sun was out, the sky was darker now,
the world colder. Without Larissa, there was nothing. And yet he'd pushed her away, too. Had forced
her to go in a way that made sure she would never
come back.

She loved him and he'd destroyed her.

He put down his glass and looked at his friends.
"Get out."

They stared at him, looked at each other, then put
down their glasses.

"Sure thing," Sam said, scooping up one of the
chiweenies.

Kenny grabbed the other. "Don't come back to
Score," he said before heading for the door. "You're
no longer welcome."

They closed the door behind them. They didn't
slam it. That would say too much. Give him too much.

Instead, they closed it quietly and Jack found himself exactly where he'd said he wanted to be. Completely and totally alone.

CHAPTER NINETEEN

"THIS ISN'T WORKING for me," Kenny said.

Larissa tried to steady her breathing. She had to get a little more control before she could speak. "Sorry," she managed, as she dug in deeper, trying to get to the scar tissue.

Kenny raised himself up on his elbows and looked at her. "You're not hurting me," he told her. "You're crying. I can feel your tears on my back."

She'd hoped he wouldn't notice. She didn't *want* to spend all her time sobbing over Jack, it was just… "This is the first massage I've given since we broke up," she admitted. "I was thinking about how much I miss him. I'm sorry."

"It's okay." Kenny glanced around, as if looking for something to distract her. "It's okay. Really. I'm fine. Go back to what you were doing."

She nodded, but didn't move. "I can't stop thinking about him. About us and how good we were together. I guess it's because I've never been in love before. This is my first real broken heart. I keep telling myself it will get better, but it doesn't feel like it will."

Kenny swore, then sat up and drew her against him. She went into his embrace, letting his strong arms comfort her. Once again, there wasn't the slightest hint of a tingle. Because Kenny was like her big brother.

"It will get better," he promised. "You'll see. Just give it time."

"I have time."

"And me. You have me."

She looked up at him and managed a smile. "Then I have all I need."

"Sure. Pile on the pressure. I can take it." He cupped her face. "You gonna be okay?"

She nodded. While she wasn't sure, she had to have faith. She had to believe, and until it was real, she had to fake it.

"These are perfect," Larissa said, looking at the furniture that had just been delivered. There were two stylized bookcases or storage units. She wasn't sure what to call them. They were open and deep, but instead of regular shelves, the openings were more square. The sizes were perfect for inexpensive baskets to hold all her supplies.

"It's all about knowing where to shop," Bailey told her. "Isabel went to the estate-sale preview and told me about these. She knows I'm looking for furniture for my new house. I want a cute bedroom set for Chloe. I can refinish it myself. If I find something before I find a house, Ford and Isabel said I can store it at their place. When I saw these, I knew they'd be right for you."

"They're perfect," Larissa said. Even better than

how functional they were going to be was the price. Together the shelving units had cost her thirty dollars. They were in great shape and didn't need much more than cleaning.

Larissa measured the openings, then checked against the list of basket sizes she'd gotten from the big craft shop outside of town.

"They'll fit perfectly," she said, showing Bailey the dimensions. "And the baskets have that cotton lining. I can wash it, so everything stays clean."

Her massage table was already on order and she had a lease on the room for the next year. Talk about taking a big step. But it felt right.

The space was perfect for her. Large, with a couple of windows. Bailey was already talking Roman shades as coverings. There was a single sink in a narrow cabinet that gave her enough counter space to heat wet packs along with river rocks if she wanted to do hot stone massage. Even with the huge massage table Kenny and Sam had picked out, she would still have room for a desk, a bench and a corner storage unit.

Bailey pulled the paint chips out of her bag. "Okay, then, onto the next thing. What color do you want? I think we should narrow it down to your favorite three or four. Then we'll go get samples and paint squares on the wall."

"You can do that?"

"Sure. The hardware store will make up little cans of paint to try at home. It's great. They're, like, three dollars each. A chip is one thing, but seeing the paint in place changes everything."

"How do you know so much about home improvement?"

Bailey shrugged. "I was raised by my grandmother. Money was tight, but that didn't stop her from being creative. She was a big believer in turning trash into treasure. I know how to make a nickel cry for mercy."

"Then you're my decorating guru." Larissa took the paint chips and flipped through them. "I need a neutral color that is calming and appealing to both men and women."

"So not pink or lavender?"

"Probably not."

They went through dozens of choices before settling on a couple of sage greens, two blues and a warm ivory.

"Perfect," Bailey said. "The next step is to get the samples. Why don't we grab some lunch and then go to the hardware store?"

Larissa wrinkled her nose. "You must have better things to do than babysit me today. What about Chloe?"

"She's with a couple of her friends. It's an all-day birthday party. She's going to be exhausted when she gets home." Bailey smiled. "Sorry, you're stuck with me."

"Not stuck. I love the company."

"Good. Let's go to Jo's. I'm dying for nachos."

Larissa couldn't remember the last time she'd felt

like eating. It would have been before things had ended with Jack. Since then she'd only picked at food. Nothing interested her and she was never hungry. But now she felt a little rumbling in her stomach.

"Nachos do sound good," she admitted. "Okay, let's go."

They left the day spa and walked along Fifth. There were plenty of tourists in town for the End of Summer festival, but they mostly kept to the main streets, leaving the rest of town for the locals. It was a good system, Larissa thought. One that allowed the dollars to flow in while keeping things livable.

"I talked to my mom a few days ago," Larissa said as they crossed the street.

"Did she try to talk you into moving back to L.A.?"

"Yes, but not very hard. I told her I liked it here, that I'd made a lot of friends and had a good life. She was sorry Jack hurt me but relieved it was over. She was very supportive." There'd been an offer of money, but with Taryn, Kenny and Sam buying her the massage table, she could swing the rest of it herself.

"I promised to go home for Thanksgiving," she continued. "So everyone can see I'm okay. By then I'm hoping to tell them my business is a success."

"It will be," Bailey said confidently. "You're good at what you do and you're going to have steady customers."

Larissa nodded. Kenny and Sam were promising to want regular massages. For a second she wondered where Jack was getting his massages. Probably in Sacramento, she thought, trying not to let the knowledge hurt her. Or maybe there was someone else in town. Not that he or she would understand how to work the scar tissue so it didn't—

Not her problem anymore, she reminded herself firmly. Jack had chosen to walk away from her. From what they could have been together. There were consequences to every action. He was going to have to deal with his.

"I should really be going on a diet," Bailey said, "and all I can think about is what kind of nachos Jo is going to have on special today. Maybe I need food counseling."

Larissa stared at her. "What are you talking about? You look great. You have curves. No one is going to think you look like a boy."

"No one thinks that about you, either," Bailey pointed out. She patted her hips. "I could lose ten pounds. Or twenty. I probably should. Maybe if I started walking or something. It's just I've never been a fan of exercise. And when I see Taryn's bony butt, I just want to eat a brownie."

"She is intimidating."

"Yeah, right. You're the same size."

Normally Larissa was a few pounds heavier, but she knew that right now she could easily fit into any of Taryn's tightest dresses. Not eating had a way of doing that to a person.

"Not all exercise requires sweat," she told her friend. "Have you tried yoga?"

"I'm not super bendy," Bailey admitted. "Or coordinated."

"Neither is necessary. All the moves can be modified to your level of flexibility and fitness. The nice part is it forces you to focus on your breathing and your body for an hour. There's no escaping that. With running or weight training, you can get lost in what you're doing. But with the emphasis on breath with movement, yoga brings you back to the present."

"That does sound nice," Bailey admitted, although she still sounded a little doubtful. "I'll see if there's a class somewhere I can try."

They walked into Jo's.

It took Larissa's eyes a second to adjust to the dimmer lighting after being out in the bright afternoon sun. When she'd blinked a couple of times she saw the familiar bar, the specials on the chalkboard—pulled pork nachos today—and the tables and booths.

Speaking of which, several of the tables had been pushed together for a large party and several of the guests were already there. She blinked again as she recognized Taryn and Isabel, along with Felicia, Patience, Dellina, Fayrene and Ana Raquel.

"You're late," Taryn said as she approached them. "We've all been drinking and it's not even one in the afternoon." She hugged Larissa. "Hey, you. How are you feeling?"

Jo carried over pitchers of margaritas. "Nachos are coming up, along with chips, salsa and guacamole." She gave Larissa a sympathetic smile. "Some men are jerks. The next one won't be."

Patience gave her a hug. "She's right. I'm so sorry about Jack. Taryn says I can't ask my husband to shoot him, but if that changes, let me know. Justice is an excellent shot."

One by one Larissa's friends welcomed her and offered words of support, threats to Jack or both. She was seated in the center of the group with everyone around her. Margaritas were poured.

She turned to Bailey. "You did this?"

"I put out the word that we'd be coming here for lunch," the redhead told her. "The rest of it just sort of happened."

Taryn grabbed her hand. "We love you. Where else would we be?"

Larissa felt a slight easing of the pain in her heart. Healing, she thought with relief. Finally there was going to be a little healing.

JACK WALKED INTO Taryn's office and put the envelope on her desk. She barely glanced at him as she typed on her computer.

"What?" she asked.

He pointed to the letter. "That's for you."

She kept her attention on her screen. "I'll deal with it later."

She was ignoring him. He got that. He even liked it. But this was different.

"That's my letter of resignation. I'm leaving the firm."

He waited for her to react. Because they'd been together a long time. He couldn't just go off on his own.

She glanced at the paper, then back to her screen. "Okay. Like I said, I'll deal with it later."

"That's it? That's all I get? I tell you I'm quitting and you'll deal with it later."

She sighed, then turned to face him. "What do you want, Jack? Should I cry? Should I beg you not to go? You're a grown man. You can make your own decisions. If you want out of Score, fine. We have plenty of clients. Bringing in new ones isn't that important. Kenny can handle that himself. So go."

He genuinely didn't understand. "Just like that? I deserve a hell of a lot more."

She rose and faced him, her desk between them. "Do you? I guess I don't agree. The Jack I used to know, the great guy who saved me from sleeping in my car when we first met, he deserves more. The man I married all those years ago, yes, I would ask him to stay. But you're not that guy anymore. You haven't been for a while. So no, I don't feel a whole lot of obligation."

Her violet eyes snapped with anger. "You're a self-indulgent bastard who's trying to ruin himself. I have no problem with that. What I object to is your attempt to take the rest of us with you. You were my friend, Jack. My best friend in the world. I trusted you more than I trusted anyone except Angel, and you betrayed me. You were deliberately cruel. But I can deal with that because there's nothing you can do to me that can compare with what I've been through before. But not Larissa."

He held himself steady as her words attacked. Each one was a cut or a body blow. Each made him a little smaller and if he stayed here long enough he would cease to exist. But he couldn't move. He deserved this. All of it.

"Her only crime is loving you," Taryn continued. "Loving all of us. She has the biggest heart of anyone I know. And you wanted that. You wanted her to be your front, so you could look like a nice guy. You wanted her causes because watching her take care of everyone around you made you feel alive. But you're not. You haven't been since Lucas died. You've been going through the motions."

She leaned toward him. "You know why Lucas got sick and died? Because he still had a heart. You never did. You fooled us all. Well, not anymore, Jack." She picked up the envelope. "You want to quit? Great. Because we want you gone."

She lowered herself to her chair and returned her attention to her computer. "Now if you'll excuse me, I have work to do."

CHAPTER TWENTY

LARISSA HELD HER brand-new certification in her hands. She had to admit, it looked really good. She had a frame waiting for it at the day spa. She was going to meet Bailey there and together they would hang it.

The past couple of weeks had been a lot of work. She'd chosen a paint color and learned what it was like to patch, sand, primer and paint. She'd ordered linens and oils, and arranged for the massage table to be delivered. She'd gone to her first estate sale with Isabel and Ford and had found a beautiful antique desk that would be perfect for any paperwork she had to do at her new location. She would officially be open for business on Monday.

She was moving forward. Painfully, slowly, but progress was made. The nights were the toughest. Not so much the evenings—she could keep those filled. But nights were long and empty and she spent them missing Jack.

Nearly everyone she knew was taking her side. Even Percy, whom she saw a few times a week, was trash-talking him. Larissa supposed she should have been gratified by the show of support. But all she could think was that he was alone in all this. Despite everything, she worried about him, wanted him, needed him. Loved him.

She accepted that maybe she was a one-man woman. That she would spend the rest of her days wanting what she could never have. And if that was the case, she was going to have to figure out how to be happy on her own.

"A problem for another day," she told herself as she hurried toward the day spa. She went inside and used her shiny new key to open the door to her room. Once there, she paused to take it all in.

The walls were a cool, restful shade of sage. The massage table—the biggest, baddest one available— stood in the center of the large open space. To the left were the two storage units, now filled with pretty baskets of fresh sheets, blankets and towels. A corner cabinet held her oils. There was a bench by the door where her clients could sit to put on shoes and socks. Hooks and hangers gave them a place to hang their clothes. Her appointment book lay open on her small desk.

She reached for the small, backless, rolling stool that she would use during massages as well as at her desk, then sat down. After picking up the phone, she hit the talk button to access her newly acquired business voice mail.

"You have seventeen messages. Press one to hear your messages."

Larissa frowned. Seventeen? Was she getting prank calls?

She pulled a pen out of her bag and a pad of paper from her single desk drawer, then pushed one.

"Larissa, it's Eddie Carberry. I want to schedule a massage. One of those hot stone ones. But I don't want any little rocks between my toes. That's too weird. Thursday afternoons work best for me." Eddie left her number and Larissa wrote it down.

The second call was from Mayor Marsha, also scheduling a massage. The next message came from Josh Golden saying he'd heard she understood about old sports injuries and he wanted to set up an appointment. And so it went. Seventeen calls with more than half of the people interested in standing appointments—either weekly or biweekly.

Larissa dutifully wrote all the information down. When she'd finished, she put the phone back on its cradle. She looked at her new license, then at the beautiful space she and her friends had created. And then she smiled.

ON DAY TWENTY-THREE without Larissa, Jack woke to the sound of rain on his windows. The house was silent otherwise. Empty. He was the only one there. He'd wanted to be by himself and now he was. He had no job, no friends, no lover, nothing. It should have been a dream come true. Instead, he found himself in hell.

He got up and crossed to the window. Low gray clouds obscured the mountains. He could have been anywhere. When he thought about it, there was nothing holding him in Fool's Gold. He could be miserable somewhere else.

But even as he thought about packing up and disappearing, he knew he couldn't go. There were things he had to see, had to know how they ended. If he was gone, he wouldn't be there when Percy took the GED test and later when he found out he'd passed. He wouldn't see Taryn get married or hear that Sam and Dellina were expecting their first child together. If he was gone, he wouldn't know if Kenny ever fell in love and if he wasn't here, he would never catch sight of Larissa again.

Because that was how he got through the day. Seeing her from across the street or by the park. He knew her routine, knew where she liked to run and who her friends were. There he was, Jack McGarry, star quarterback, Super Bowl champion, reduced to being nothing more than a pathetic stalker.

No, he couldn't leave. But he also couldn't stay like he was. Empty. Useless. Lucas would be so damned disappointed.

He pulled on his robe and went to the kitchen where he made coffee. After pouring himself a cup, he wandered into his office—a big library of a room he never used. There were books he hadn't read and a sofa he didn't sit on. Behind cabinet doors were boxes Larissa had dragged over to his place. They contained letters from families the two of them had helped. The only point of the room was the laptop on his desk that he used.

He started to walk toward it only to find himself

circling around the lower cabinets and opening one of them. He pulled out a box and carried it over to the coffee table by the sofa. After sitting down, he raised the lid and looked inside.

On the top was a threadbare stuffed giraffe. It had once been purple, but had faded through washings to a pale gray. One ear and one leg were missing. Under that were pictures of a little boy holding the giraffe.

The oldest pictures showed a small, pale boy with a weak smile. Jack would guess he was three or four. The hospital setting made him look even smaller and more helpless. His parents tried to smile at the camera, but there was no way to disguise their worry.

More pictures showed the boy—Jeffrey—in a hospital bed, celebrating a birthday, then Christmas. Then the scene changed with a big banner behind the bed proclaiming *Transplant Day!*

The next photos showed Jeffrey with the telltale scar on his chest. But he looked better, with more color. He was sitting up instead of lying in the bed and his parents, while exhausted, had genuine smiles.

He reached for the letters, the notes, the cards. Larissa documented all that they did. She'd visited Jeffrey and his family three times. She'd arranged for the rest of the family to be flown in over the holidays, and when Jeffrey was discharged and ready to start acting like the healthy little boy he now was, she'd set up a trip to Disneyland.

There was a thank-you note from Jeffrey's mother, addressed to him. She mentioned his generosity, his compassion. She said she knew about his brother and the loss the family had suffered and appreciated how he'd turned that into a blessing for them.

There were more boxes. Dozens of them, all filled with letters and pictures and mementos, like the ratty giraffe. There was a photo of him at a high-school prom because the girl they were helping was seventeen and she'd been away in hospitals for so long she didn't have any friends, let alone a boyfriend. So Larissa had talked him into taking her to the dance.

So many people helped, he thought. In such a short period of time. And these were only the humans. If he added the cats and owl and chiweenies to the mix, they were well into three figures. Hundreds of souls saved because he was a sucker for Larissa and she wanted to save the world.

He leaned back against the sofa and closed his eyes. He could imagine every part of her. How she sounded, how she moved, how she smelled. He ached for her. Not just in his bed, but in his life. He'd pushed her away because… Because…

He remembered his high-school football coach lecturing the team and the lesson that had stuck with him through his entire career was a simple one. "You are either the solution or you are the problem."

Jack had always been part of the solution. Whether it was how to break a losing streak or save a young PR associate who didn't have anywhere to live, he was front and center with the fixing. It made him feel good. It helped him belong. It kept him safe.

Taryn was right, he thought grimly. The reason Lucas had heart disease was he had a heart in the first place. Jack was all flash. He looked good on the poster, but in a crunch, the best you could count on was that he would write a check. Taryn held Score together, Larissa made him a hero by caring. But what did he bring to the table?

You're either the solution or you're the problem. Somewhere along the way, he'd become the problem.

He didn't want to risk caring. He got that. He knew why. He could list the reasons and most people would probably agree with them. They would think he was being smart. Careful. Reasonable. But the price for that was everything he had now. The price for that was nothing.

He opened the first box again and stared at the tattered giraffe. Jeffery had given it to Larissa to thank her for all she'd done. In turn, she'd given it to him because, as she put it, he made it all possible. But she was wrong. He was only along for the ride. She was the one who made everything possible. He was a sucker for Larissa. He knew that. Had always known it. Whatever she wanted, he was all in. She only had to call and he was there. She was the one person he would stop anything for.

He stood up and swore. He was in love with her. Based on his actions, he'd loved her from the first moment he'd met her. Only he'd been too stupid to realize it. Or too afraid. Larissa's mother had missed the mark by 50 percent. Larissa wasn't just in love with him. He was in love with her.

He started for the door of his office only to stop. What if it was too late? What if he'd screwed up everything to the point where it couldn't be unscrewed? What if she wouldn't forgive him?

"She has to," he said aloud. There was no other choice. He needed to be with her. He needed to show her that he was exactly who she'd always claimed he could be. She'd seen the best in him when he'd never seen it himself. Now he had to live up to what she'd always believed.

He showered and dressed, then drove out to the university. It took a little convincing but he finally got in to see President Newham, even though he didn't have an appointment.

"How can I help you, Mr. McGarry?" she asked.

"I'm here about the coaching job," he told her.

"You made it very clear you weren't interested. You said you were the last man we should pick."

"I was wrong," he told her, then wondered how many times he was going to have to say that again today.

An hour later, he parked in front of Paper Moon. While what he needed was on the bridal side, he happened to know Isabel spent most of her time in the part of the store with the regular clothes, so he started there.

The tall blonde was just finishing up with a customer when he entered. Her quick, cold glance told him word had spread all through the female community of Fool's Gold. What he didn't know was whether she was pissed at him for what he'd said to Taryn, Larissa or both.

When her customer left, she crossed to him. "What do you want?"

"I need to rent a dress."

"We don't rent dresses."

"Fine. I'll buy one. A bridesmaid gown."

Her gaze narrowed. "Why?"

"To make a point. Please. Just sell me a dress."

"The only one I have is five thousand dollars."

He handed her his credit card.

Her lips pressed together. "You're an idiot. I don't have five-thousand-dollar bridesmaids' dresses." She walked past him. "Come with me."

He followed her through the opening to the shop where Taryn had tried on wedding gowns. He ignored the wide and frilly skirts and waited until Isabel handed him a pink dress with lots of bows and ruffles.

"Will this do?" she asked.

He nodded. "It's great. How much do I owe you?"

"How long do you need it?"

"About an hour."

"Then take it. If you break it, you buy it."

Just like that. "Don't you hate me?" he asked.

"I think you're a jerk, but that's no reason for me to act like one."

Because in their hearts, most people were pretty decent, he thought. Why hadn't he realized that before?

He took the dress. His next stop was the halfway house where Percy lived these days. He hadn't seen the kid in almost a month and had no idea what his reception would be like, but this was one of the fences he needed to mend.

He gave his name to the woman who answered the door, then waited. A few minutes later, the teen appeared at the top of the stairs. His expression was wary as he approached Jack, but he held his head high and his shoulders square. He faced Jack man-to-man.

"I'm sorry," Jack said by way of greeting. "About what I said and how I let you walk away. You weren't a project. I said it because having a kid scares me. I don't want to care that much. I don't want to risk losing anyone close to me. The flaw in my plan is that I already cared. I was fooling myself, which is okay, but I hurt you and that's not."

Percy stared at him, but didn't speak. Jack didn't know what the teen was thinking, but knew he had to keep going.

"Larissa is special," he continued. "She sees how things are supposed to be. I admire that in her. I admire how you've kept it all together. You didn't get into trouble, when that would have been the easy path. You stayed strong and I admire that, too."

Percy looked away and cleared his throat. "It's okay, man."

"It's not. I miss having you around. I want to help you with your studies."

"Kenny, Sam and Taryn have that covered."

"I want you to move back," he said, looking at the teen. "I don't want this to be temporary, Percy. You're too old to be adopted, but I'd still like you to be part of my family. I'd be proud to have you as part of my family."

Percy's expression turned wary. "Why are you saying all this?"

"Because it's true. Because I've been a jerk and I want to fix it. I want to be better. But mostly because of what I said before. I miss having you around. I want to be the one you talk to about your classes and what four-year college seems like the best fit. I want to be the one you call after your first interview. I want…" Jack hesitated. "I want to matter."

"Are you for real?" Percy asked hesitantly.

"Yeah. Just as long as you know I'm going to screw up. But no matter what, I'll never stop trying to be better. I don't want to be the problem anymore, Percy. I want to be the solution."

Percy gave Jack a manly hug, more chest bump than embrace. But then Percy stepped back and wiped away tears.

"I want to come home," he admitted. "But I'm not going back to work at Score. I have a new job and I like it."

"That's fine."

"And we're getting a dog. You need a dog in that big house of yours."

"You're negotiating your return?"

Percy grinned. "I am. And I want to learn how to drive."

"A man should know how to drive."

"You have a nice car."

Jack laughed. "No, you can't borrow the Mercedes."

Percy grinned. "Good, because I need boundaries." His smile faded. "I have a shift in an hour. I'll move back after that."

Jack handed him the house key he'd brought. "I look forward to it."

"You gonna get Larissa back? Because without her, you're just sad."

"I know. I'm going to do my best."

JACK WALKED INTO the offices of Score, not sure what to expect. His pictures were still up, which surprised him. He'd thought they would be ripped down or at the very least, defaced. But nothing looked different.

He made his way back to Kenny's office first. His friend saw him and frowned.

"What?" he demanded.

"I was wrong. Sorry."

Kenny looked startled, then nodded. "Don't do it again."

"I won't."

He went by Sam's office. The other man was hanging up the phone. "Kenny just told me," Sam said. "We're good."

That made Jack chuckle. "You don't want to hug to seal the deal?"

"Get out of here."

Jack moved down the hall. He had a feeling things wouldn't go so smoothly with his third partner.

He made it to Taryn's office without being seen by

anyone else. He stepped into the empty conference room across from hers and shrugged out of his jacket.

For a second Jack hesitated. He'd never done anything like this before, but then he'd never screwed up so bad. If he won Taryn over and things went bad with Larissa, Taryn would be a formidable ally.

He took the dress off the hanger and unzipped it. Then he stepped into the god-awful ruffled pink dress and stuck his arms through the small sleeves.

It barely fit. There was no way he could have zipped it, but that wasn't the point. This wasn't a fashion show, this was a statement of intent. He opened the conference door, walked across the hall and entered Taryn's office without knocking.

She was standing by the window, looking out. Her suit was fitted and she was barefoot. He saw her ridiculously high heels by her chair.

"Taryn?"

She didn't turn, but he saw her stiffen.

"Go away."

"No. I won't do that. Not now and not ever. I'm sorry about what I said before. I'm sorry about what happened. Resigning wasn't wrong, but there were a lot better ways to handle it." He paused to draw in a breath. "I hurt you. I apologize for that. I want to promise it will never happen again, but it might. What I can promise is that I'm in this for the long haul. That you can depend on me. And if Angel ever acts this stupid, I'll hire a platoon to take him out."

Her shoulders shook, but he didn't know if she was laughing or crying.

"I brought you something."

She turned. He saw tears on her cheeks. Her gaze settled on the dress. Something brightened her eyes and her mouth twitched. "You look ridiculous."

"That's okay."

"You'd be a hideous cross-dresser. The dress doesn't suit you at all."

"I'm okay with not being the prettiest bridesmaid. As long as I can be in your wedding. If you'll still have me."

She moved with more speed than he would have thought her capable of. One second she was by the window, the next she was throwing herself at him. He wrapped his arms around her and hung on tight.

"I'm sorry," he whispered. "Please, please forgive me."

"You were a total jackass."

"I know.

She sighed. "Where did you get that dress?"

"I borrowed it from Isabel. By the way, if you destroy it, I have to pay for it."

"You can afford it." She looked up at him. "What happened?"

"The world closed in. I had Larissa and Percy, the job offer. Everywhere I turned, I was being forced to give more than I thought I was capable of. I'm only used to caring about you."

"So you lashed out?"

"With style."

She stepped back and sniffed. "You really shouldn't

be here. At Score, I mean. The coaching job is a better fit. You need that, Jack."

He smiled. "Already done. I start on Monday."

"Seriously?"

"Yeah. Which means my letter of resignation still stands, but without the drama."

She touched the front of the dress. "I wonder if they make this in a size you could wear."

"Pink isn't my color."

"Or mine," she told him. "I'd prefer you wear a tux."

He stared into her eyes. "When I attend your wedding?" he asked cautiously.

"Oh, no. You're still my man of honor. You're going to help me adjust my veil and hold my flowers and glower at Angel. You'll be busy."

He kissed her cheek. "I can't wait."

LARISSA CLIMBED THE stairs to her apartment. Her first day at her new job had gone great. She'd been booked solid with massages. The good news was after dealing with athletes all these years, taking care of regular people with ordinary muscles was a breeze.

She opened her front door only to stop when she saw Jack sitting on the sofa, Dyna draped across his lap.

He looked good, she thought wistfully. Handsome and strong. What was it about a good-looking guy with a fluffy cat on his lap? He didn't seem to mind the cat hair flying everywhere and attaching itself to his pants.

When he saw her, he picked up Dyna and moved her to the side, then stood.

"You're home," he said.

She nodded.

She hadn't seen him in twenty-three days. She'd felt the pain of every passing hour, had missed him, ached for him, cried for him and had tried to make peace with what was happening. What she hadn't done was fall out of love with him. Now as she looked at him, she felt her heart reaching toward him, straining to be closer. Nearer. Next to.

He crossed to her, then took both her hands in his. His dark eyes locked with hers.

"I'm sorry," he told her. "Sorry for what I said and how I acted. Sorry for being selfish, immature and stupid. I hurt you. I lashed out and there's no excuse for my behavior, so I won't make one. What I will say instead is I was wrong. Completely and totally wrong. I hurt everyone I care about. Worst of all, I hurt you."

He brought her hands to his chest and placed her palms flat on his shirt.

"My heart beats only because of you," he said quietly. "I breathe for you. I exist because I love you, Larissa. You are who matters and I want to spend the rest of my life proving that to you."

He seemed to melt away. It took her a second to realize she was crying. But happy tears, she thought, trying to take it all in. Joyful tears.

"I love you," he repeated, then he pulled a small box out of his pants pocket. "I know it's a lot to ask right now, but will you marry me? I want it all, but only with you. I want Percy down the hall and cats and chiweenies running around. Move in a couple of owls and snakes. Whatever makes you happy."

"I wants kids," she said, not sure where the words had come from.

"Yeah?" He grinned. "Good. Like twenty?"

She shook her head. "Three. Maybe four."

"I can do that. I can do whatever you want. Larissa, it was always you. I'm sorry I didn't see that for so long. I'm sorry I had to hurt you before I understood how lucky I am to have you in my life."

She searched his face and what she saw there healed her broken heart. "You sure?"

"Yes. Until you I didn't truly understand what love could be. I get it now."

"Then you get me," she said simply.

* * * * *